Inspector Morimoto and the Sushi Chef

Also by Timothy Hemion

Inspector Morimoto and the Two Umbrellas
Inspector Morimoto and the Diamond Pendants
Inspector Morimoto and the Famous Potter

INSPECTOR MORIMOTO AND THE SUSHI CHEF

A Detective Story set in Japan

Timothy Hemion

iUniverse, Inc.
New York Lincoln Shanghai

Inspector Morimoto and the Sushi Chef

A Detective Story set in Japan

Copyright © 2005 by Timothy Hemion

All rights reserved. No part of this book may be used or reproduced by any means, graphic, electronic, or mechanical, including photocopying, recording, taping or by any information storage retrieval system without the written permission of the publisher except in the case of brief quotations embodied in critical articles and reviews.

iUniverse books may be ordered through booksellers or by contacting:

iUniverse
2021 Pine Lake Road, Suite 100
Lincoln, NE 68512
www.iuniverse.com
1-800-Authors (1-800-288-4677)

ISBN: 0-595-34950-1 (pbk)
ISBN: 0-595-67173-X (cloth)

Printed in the United States of America

Okayama - Kagawa Region

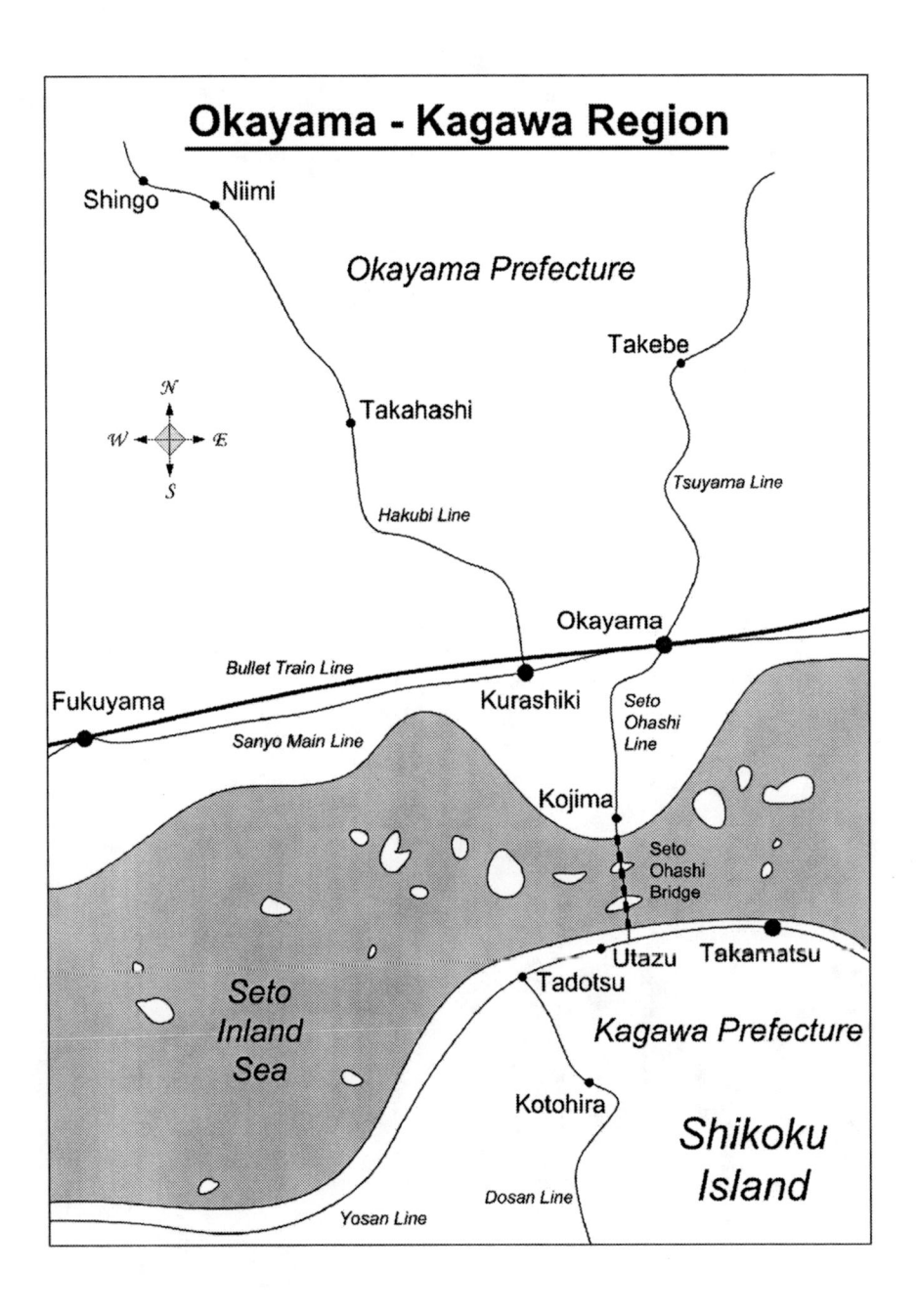

Okayama City Map

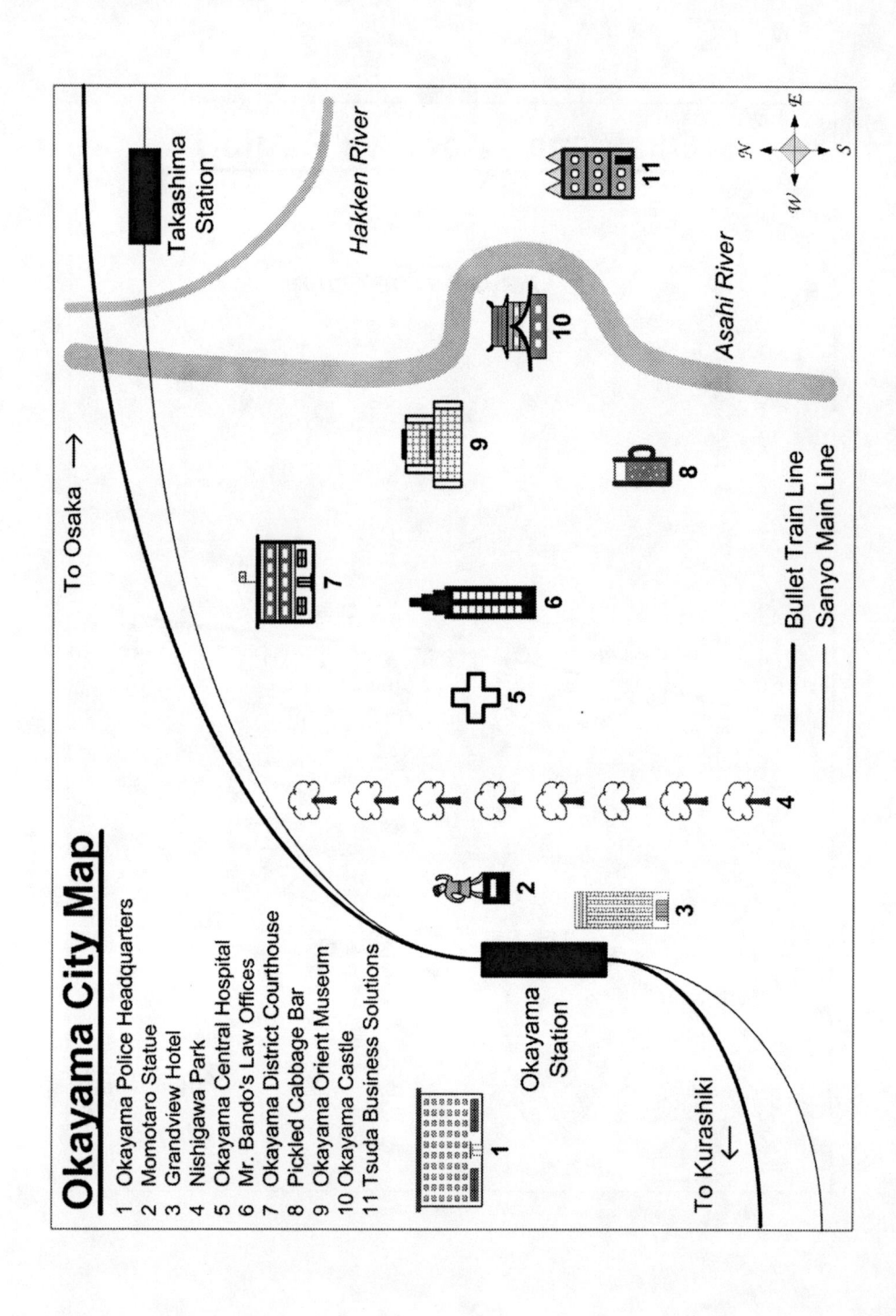

1. Okayama Police Headquarters
2. Momotaro Statue
3. Grandview Hotel
4. Nishigawa Park
5. Okayama Central Hospital
6. Mr. Bando's Law Offices
7. Okayama District Courthouse
8. Pickled Cabbage Bar
9. Okayama Orient Museum
10. Okayama Castle
11. Tsuda Business Solutions

To Osaka →

← To Kurashiki

Takashima Station

Okayama Station

Hakken River

Asahi River

— Bullet Train Line
— Sanyo Main Line

Chapter 1

Mr. Yosano picked up the bottle of lukewarm rice wine from the table in front of him and poured the last few drops into his empty cup. When the bottle had been served to him some twenty minutes earlier, it had been so hot that he had only been able to pick it up by gingerly pinching the narrow neck between his fingers. But during the time that it had taken him to consume its contents, the bottle had cooled down to a very manageable warmth.

It was his third bottle of the night, and he clumsily slammed it down on the wooden tabletop before reaching for the small round cup. He himself was slightly startled by the noise that the empty bottle made when it hit the table, but the incident went otherwise unnoticed among the clamor and bustle of the bar, and the young waitress smiled at him as she whisked the empty bottle away a moment later.

Mr. Yosano sat with his cup cradled between his hands for a few minutes in a contemplative trancelike state, before eventually downing the rice wine in one mouthful. This time he made a point of replacing the cup on the tabletop very carefully, and then he rose to his feet and struggled into his coat, placing his hand on the edge of the table to steady himself. The waitress called out to bid him farewell as he slowly threaded his way between the tables and chairs that were packed into the small room, and when he reached the door he turned to offer her a hurried bow before stepping out into the crisp night air.

It was a cloudless night, and a mass of tiny stars were distinctly visible in the dark sky high above Mr. Yosano, but he was completely oblivious to their presence as he headed down the quiet deserted street with a determined yet nevertheless decidedly unsteady gait. His path was adequately lit by the electric street lights and the neon signs outside the other bars that he passed, and after making a left turn he crossed over a river where the still night air amplified the sounds made by the shallow water as it flowed over the rocky bed.

With the river behind him, he passed by a small park on his left where a tall wooden lookout tower with an ornate roof was silhouetted against the night sky. The tower stood on a solid stone base, whose gracefully curved contours bore testimony to the superlative craftsmanship that had been employed in its construction over a hundred years before. A set of stone steps led up to a door at the top of the base that provided access to the wooden tower, although its warning beacon had been rendered redundant by modern technology many years previously.

As Mr. Yosano walked on he approached the railway station, whose one-story white building and red tile roof were brightly lit up. However, there was no evidence of anybody else being around that late at night as he trudged across the open plaza in front of the station. Two rows of decorative stone lanterns, that in a way each resembled miniature versions of the ancient lookout tower that he had just passed by, formed a path towards the station entrance, and there were two stone statues of lion-like creatures standing on plinths at the ends of the rows of lanterns. After passing between the statues, Mr. Yosano turned right directly in front of the station building and headed along a street that led away from the station, running parallel to the railway lines.

The street became darker as Mr. Yosano thrust his hands deep inside his coat pockets and headed towards the outskirts of the small town, leaving the station further and further behind him. As he walked along he was surrounded by an almost absolute silence, which was only broken by the sound of his own footsteps on the hard concrete pavement that resonated unnaturally loudly through the night air, and which was mixed with the sound of his own rhythmic breathing. He pressed on resolutely with his head down, staring steadfastly at the pavement in front of him, although he did look up once as a black taxi with a white oval-shaped light on top drove up the road towards him. The taxi momentarily lit up the street with its headlights as it passed him by, heading back towards the railway station and the town center.

About fifteen minutes after he had left the bar, Mr. Yosano turned into a side street on his left that crossed over the railway lines, and he came to an abrupt halt. He swayed slowly from side to side as he stared in front of him with a confused look on his face, while his brain frantically endeavored to make some sense of what his eyes were seeing. The cash machine outside the Metropolitan Trust Bank that he had walked past hundreds of times before on his way home had a significantly different look to it this night, which was because its front panel had been completely smashed in.

Mr. Yosano himself would be the first to admit that after three bottles of hot rice wine his mind was not at its very sharpest, but the gaping hole in the front of the machine and the debris littered around the ground in front of it provided sufficient information for his brain to be quite sure that something was not the way it should be. This contention was compounded when Mr. Yosano's attention shifted to the man standing beside the cash machine, who was holding a blue crowbar in one hand while he stuffed bank notes into his backpack with his other hand. This was very definitely not something that Mr. Yosano had ever encountered before on the very numerous times that he had returned home late at night from one of the town's convivial bars, where he was accustomed to consuming a generous quantity of the beverages that were on offer.

The man with the crowbar did not notice Mr. Yosano until he had emptied almost all of the cash out of the machine. However, he abruptly stopped what he was doing when he did detect Mr. Yosano's presence, and the two men stood and stared at each other in silence for a few moments, one of them tilting gently from side to side, and the other one frozen in alarm. The man with the crowbar had a good look at Mr. Yosano's face with its astonished expression, but in return, Mr. Yosano could tell nothing about the expression on the other man's face because his whole head was covered in a woolen mask, in which the only openings were two small slits where his eyes peered out.

Mr. Yoshino raised his hands and rubbed both of his eyes, and then without either of them having uttered any sound, the man in the mask carefully zipped up his backpack and securely fastened it onto his back with both of his arms through the straps. He then turned and ran off down the street and across the railway lines in the direction that Mr. Yosano had been heading. Mr. Yosano stood and stared after him until he was completely out of sight, and then he walked over to the vandalized cash machine and blinked at the pile of bank notes that was still sitting there. After scratching his bald head and rubbing his eyes once again, Mr. Yosano reached into his coat pocket, took out his phone, and began to dial a number.

Chapter 2

▼

It was a dull overcast Monday morning in the middle of April when Inspector Morimoto was sitting next to his young assistant, Police Officer Suzuki, in the crowded main auditorium on the first floor of the Police Headquarters in Okayama city. Morimoto and Suzuki had been working together for about two years, ever since Suzuki had graduated with a mathematics degree from the prestigious Tokyo University, and they had forged a successful partnership together that blended Suzuki's youth and energy with Morimoto's experience, judgment, and inimitable style.

The key to the success of their partnership was the intellectual curiosity that they both shared for solving puzzles and for making sense out of ostensibly nonsensical sets of events. While most of the other members of the Okayama city detective force may have tried to distinguish themselves by rushing around in a hectic manner once they had been assigned to a new case, Morimoto was much happier sitting in his office with his feet up on the corner of his desk, employing his brainpower to test out various hypothetical theories for what might have happened. And when the solution of a case came down to a matter of mental ability, Suzuki's mathematical skills and her precise logical reasonings meant that she was a perfect match for Morimoto, and the synergistic combination of their talents had already proved itself during several complex investigations in which they had triumphantly prevailed.

Morimoto was at his happiest when he had a baffling set of events to mull over in his mind, and since on this Monday morning he was not involved in any case of noteworthy interest, his only solace was to reflect on the astounding case of the famous Bizen potter that they had just concluded shortly beforehand. And as he sat unenthusiastically in the auditorium that morning, his spirits were further dampened by the fact that a general meeting of the Police Headquarters staff, which from time to time the Chief of Police obliged everybody to attend, was very low down on his list of the ways that he would have liked to spend that Monday morning.

When the Chief finally entered the auditorium and walked over to the podium that had been set up with a microphone on the stage at the front of the room, the low level of chatter gradually died down as the assembled ranks of detectives, policemen and policewomen, together with the general staff members, all fixed their eyes on the middle-aged lady dressed in an expensive business suit who had accompanied the Chief up onto the stage.

The Chief tapped the microphone and grinned good-naturedly at the police force arrayed in front of him of which he was so proud.

"Good morning, everybody!"

The Chief paused to grin again at those eager occupants of the front rows who had responded to his greeting.

"I know how busy you all must be fighting crime and keeping our lovely city so safe and peaceful, so you can all be assured that I won't be taking up too much of your time this morning."

Morimoto was not convinced that it was going to be a quick meeting, and he slid a little lower down into his seat.

"However, I decided that it would be a good idea to call this meeting so that I could introduce you all to Ms. Tsuda."

The Chief turned and beamed at the lady who was standing beside him on the stage.

"Some of you may already know her. She's the president of her own management consulting company here in Okayama—Tsuda Business Solutions. I'm extremely pleased to be able to report to you all this morning that I've hired her to undertake a very thorough analysis of our work here in the Police Department. And I'm just delighted that we've managed to obtain such an outstanding company to help us in this task."

Ms. Tsuda bent over in a low bow, which she held for several seconds before straightening up again.

"Ms. Tsuda's company has advised some of this city's preeminent businesses," the Chief continued enthusiastically, "and her company has earned a truly excellent reputation. They're at the very top of their profession. However, I hope that Ms. Tsuda won't mind me mentioning to you the fact that I was able to negotiate a slight reduction in her usual rates since we are a public service institution!"

The Chief chuckled amiably, and he turned to look at Ms. Tsuda again who smiled back at him. At the same time, the occupants of the front rows erupted into displays of ostentatious laughter, hoping that the Chief would notice and remember what reliable team players they were.

"And I believe that our collaboration with Tsuda Business Solutions has the potential to herald in a new age for the way in which we conduct police work in this city. I myself have learned so much from the fascinating discussions that I've had with Ms. Tsuda so far, and I believe that we have a fantastic opportunity here to improve our performance and productivity. And it's my intention that this Police Department will grasp that opportunity!"

"You see, Ms. Tsuda has taught me that the fundamental key issue in revolutionizing our day-to-day work is that we need to start thinking of the Police Department as if it were just like any other business. That's right…we're really just a business! And the good citizens of Okayama with whom we interact…well, they're our customers! Do you see what I mean?"

"Once we start to think of things in those terms, then it opens up a whole range of new possibilities, and we're able to more properly calculate and assess the relative values of each of the vast array of tasks that we perform on a daily basis. And the bottom line is that we need to start thinking more critically about how we should go about providing our products to our customers in the most cost-effective and economical manner."

Just as he had expected, Morimoto was now well aware that this meeting was not going to be the highlight of his day, and as the Chief expounded on how certain he was that the latest fads from the management consulting industry had the capability to transform police work, Morimoto's mind drifted off to other matters. In particular, he contemplated once again the puzzles that the recent case involving the nationally renowned Nagasawa family of Bizen potters had provided.

Oblivious to the complete lack of interest felt by a substantial portion of the audience, notably those members in the rear of the auditorium near to where Morimoto and Suzuki were seated, the Chief continued to describe the benefits that he expected would arise from the new venture that he was launching.

"And I hope that you'll all realize that a successful overhaul of our *modus operandi* with the help of Tsuda Business Solutions will be a tremendous boost to our reputation among the police authorities in Tokyo. It could really give us an edge over the other police forces in this country. As you all know, we were all very much in the national spotlight last month with the Nagasawa family affair…an episode during which I'm proud to say that we handled ourselves very creditably indeed!"

Several heads turned to look at Morimoto and Suzuki.

"And I'm sure that the police powers in Tokyo must have sat up and noticed how well our small Police Department dealt with a crisis of that scale. And so now the time is ripe to build on that success and to seize the initiative and to show Tokyo just how capable we are of aligning ourselves with the very latest management techniques. We mustn't let this golden opportunity slip away from us. My hope is that we'll build on our past successes, and that very soon we'll shine out as the most modern Police Department in the country today! And each one of you sitting here this morning has a vital role to play in this transformation."

Morimoto's concentration drifted again, and he began to wonder when another challenging case would arise to offer some puzzles that he could set his mind to work on, and that he could carefully dissect with Suzuki's valuable assistance. He had enjoyed collaborating with her during the two years that they had been working together, and he had developed a considerable respect for her mathematical brain and the excellent aptitude that she had already demonstrated for detective work.

"Now, one thing that I've learned from my initial discussions with Ms. Tsuda," the Chief continued, "is that the essential first step towards improving our operations here is the collection of some data. The key to our improvement is data collection. We need to construct a database that will allow us to find out just how well we're doing at the moment. In order to see how much we improve, we need to know how well we're doing at the moment. It makes sense, doesn't it?"

"And we need to develop some ways in which we can measure our productivity. So in that regard, I'm glad to be able to announce to you this morning that in the upcoming weeks you'll each be personally contacted by a member of Ms. Tsuda's team, who will make arrangements to sit down with you for a lengthy interview exploring the manner in which you carry out your work and the ways in which you spend your time. Once we've collected some data on how everybody goes about their work, we'll be in a much better position to be able to judge what changes need to be made."

Upon hearing this announcement, the eager occupants of the front few rows nodded vigorously as they tried to catch the Chief's eye in the hope that he would notice their approval of such an evidently wise course of action and their enthusiastic support for it. However, the majority of the members of the Police Department groaned inwardly, while at the same time endeavoring, with mixed degrees of success, not to betray any of their unease on their facial expressions.

"And you should all know that I won't be making any exception for myself! Oh, no, I won't! I'm sure that you all know that I treat myself as though I'm out in the frontline just like you all are…as though I'm out walking the beat alongside you all. Whatever's good enough for you is good enough for me…that's the rule I live by. So I won't be taking any special privileges at all during this process. As a matter of fact, I shall be working with Ms. Tsuda herself, who'll be personally evaluating my own performance, and who I hope will be giving me some valuable tips on how I can organize my own workday more efficiently."

The Chief grinned self-consciously as he searched through the documents that he had brought with him, and he selected a sheet of paper that he held up for everybody to see.

"Now take a look at this form here…you're all going to become very familiar with it during the next few weeks. It's something that I've developed with Ms. Tsuda's help, based on her ideas and suggestions regarding data collection. It's a Police Performance Score Sheet! Do you like that name? Rather catchy, isn't it? As a matter of fact, I came up with the name myself. If you like, you can refer to it as a PPSS, or perhaps as a Double-PS!"

The Chief chuckled again, and his laughter was inevitably reciprocated along the front row.

"Anyway, we're going to be using these sheets whenever any of us has any kind of interaction with the general public…or should I say with our customers! Ha, ha!"

This time the Chief turned and grinned at Ms. Tsuda.

"In basic terms, whenever we do a job for our customers, we'll be giving them a Double-PS so that they'll be able to record their level of satisfaction with how well we did our job. They'll be able to grade our performance on a scale from 1 to 5, and there's a space for them to include some comments as well if they want to. So, as you can see, these sheets provide our customers with the opportunity to let us know just how well we've met their needs. You know what I mean, don't you? Whether we responded promptly and efficiently to their requests…how completely we solved their problems for them…those kinds of things. And using the feedback that we get from these sheets that I've developed, we'll be able to build up a database with information about all kinds of aspects of the service that we're providing for our customers. I'm sure that you've all got the general idea of what I'm talking about, haven't you?"

As the Chief elaborated on his plans, increasingly more effort was required by the majority of the audience to maintain expressions of polite interest on their faces.

"Oh, and by the way...I shouldn't forget to mention that we'll also be using these sheets ourselves to evaluate our own internal activities. So at the end of any of our own committee meetings, for example, you'll each have the opportunity to fill out a Double-PS to record how useful and productive you feel that your time was spent. And you'll be able to suggest any improvements that you think we should make. Isn't that a great idea? At the end of each meeting we'll schedule five minutes for the Double-PS! We're going to be able to collect a wealth of information on all of our activities. It's tremendously exciting, isn't it? I myself can't wait to see what we find out!"

Chapter 3

▼

Later that same morning, Inspector Morimoto and Police Officer Suzuki were sitting together in their corner office on the fourth floor of the Police Headquarters. Morimoto's chair was tilted back, his feet were up on the corner of his desk, and his hands were locked behind his neck as he stared out of the window. His desktop was completely bare except for a telephone, an unused notepad, and several pens and pencils that were arranged in a tidy row.

"You know, Suzuki, I hope that another interesting case comes along before we're interviewed by Ms. Tsuda's team of hotshot management consultants, because otherwise they might think that all we ever do is sit up here and stare out of the window all day. It might be difficult for them to fully comprehend just how truly vital our role is in maintaining the peace and tranquility of this lovely city."

Suzuki laughed as she typed away at her laptop computer. Her desk was one of the three desks that were arranged together in the middle of the office, and about half of it was covered with neatly stacked directories and reference materials that she liked to have close at hand. On the desk beside her was a tray that contained what she and Morimoto both judged to be among the most important objects in their office—an electric water heater, a teapot, several small round teacups, a tin containing an assortment of teabags, and a packet of chocolate biscuits.

"Well, sir," Suzuki replied, "the Chief made it quite clear that Tsuda Business Solutions is very enthusiastic about collecting a plethora of evaluations on how well we're all doing. The question that occurs to me, though, is whether at the end of the day we're all going to be given the chance to fill out an evaluation sheet on just how useful we think our overhaul by Tsuda Business Solutions has really been, and whether it's managed to accomplish anything towards improving our chances of catching criminals?"

"That's a very good point, Suzuki. In fact, if it had occurred to me earlier, I'd have stuck up my hand and put that very question to the Chief during the meeting."

At that moment there was a sharp knock on the door, and Sergeant Yamada bounded into the room in a cheerful mood. As the captain of the Police Judo Team for Okayama prefecture, he was always a useful person to have around whenever anybody needed handcuffs placing on them.

"Good morning, sir, and how are you doing today, Officer Suzuki?"

"Oh, hello, Sergeant," Morimoto replied. "We're hard at work keeping our customers satisfied."

"And trying to come up with some new ideas that will help improve the efficiency with which we deliver our products to them," Suzuki added.

"I'm sure that the Chief will be very pleased to hear that," Sergeant Yamada said with a wide grin.

"How useful do you think our evaluation by Tsuda Business Solutions will be, Sergeant?" Morimoto asked.

Sergeant Yamada shrugged.

"Well, it would be nice if they made a recommendation to the Chief that he buys a new minibus for the Judo Team. He promised that he'd buy us one last year, but nothing ever came of it."

"Hmmm…well we must try to remember to bring up the pressing issue of the Judo Team's minibus when we have our own personal interview with Tsuda Business Solutions!"

Sergeant Yamada laughed.

"That would be very kind of you, sir. Anyway, talking about our customers, there's one of them down in a second floor interview room right now who wants to talk to somebody. He says that he's got some important information for us. Would you be interested in handling that, sir?"

"Some important information, did you say, Sergeant? Well, that might be interesting, I suppose. And I don't have much else on my schedule at the moment, so in the interests of maximizing my efficiency according to the best tenets of management consultancy, I think that I will go down and see what he wants to tell us. Are you interested in coming along, Suzuki?"

"Very well, sir. As they say, the customer is always right, so if he says that he's got some important information to tell us, then we'd better take him at his word."

"Quite right, Suzuki. Well, we'd better go down at once then…after all, we shouldn't keep our customers waiting, should we?"

A policewoman in a dark blue uniform, a white blouse, and a blue tie was standing outside one of the interview rooms when Morimoto and Suzuki stepped out of the elevator on the second floor, and she bowed and opened the door for them as they approached her. The nicely tailored jacket that she was wearing was done up with three brass buttons, and a gold badge was pinned on its left side that displayed a five-sided cherry blossom motif that was the symbol of the Japanese police force. A white plastic tag with her name printed on it was fastened underneath the gold badge.

As Morimoto and Suzuki entering the brightly lit carpeted interview room, a young man jumped to his feet and bowed energetically to them several times.

"Good morning. I'm Inspector Morimoto and this is Officer Suzuki. How exactly can we help you? We were told that you had some information that you wanted to pass on to us."

Morimoto studied the man as they sat down opposite each other in the comfortable chairs that were set around the polished wooden table. Suzuki sat down next to Morimoto, and she also had a good look at the man who appeared to be in his mid-twenties. His height was about average, but his build was more muscular than was typical. He was wearing an ordinary dark business suit, and the only thing that distinguished him from the masses of young businessmen in Okayama that Suzuki encountered in her daily commute to and from the Police Headquarters was that his blue necktie was arranged with an overly large knot that would have been considered unnecessarily flashy in most of Okayama's more conservative business establishments.

The man looked slightly nervous, and he hesitated for a moment before answering Morimoto's question.

"Well…err…I hope that you won't think that I'm wasting your time, but yes…err…there is something that I'd like to tell you. Well, to be more exact, there's something that I think that I ought to tell you. Not that I'm the kind of person who wants to get involved in police matters, but I feel that I have some kind of a duty to report the incident to you. That's why I've taken some time off from my job this morning. I think that I may have some information about the cash machine robberies, you see."

Morimoto nodded.

"Oh, really? Well, we'd be very grateful for any information that you might be able to offer us," he said reassuringly.

"Thank you. I'm afraid that it may turn out to be nothing, but to get straight to the point, the fact is that somebody was boasting to me last night about having carried out the robberies. It sounds remarkable, I know, but that's exactly what he told me…in a sort of confidential way, I guess. However, I should mention that he'd had rather a lot to drink by the time he told me."

Morimoto's expression remained unchanged.

"I see. Do you know this person?"

"Oh, no—he's not somebody that I know. I just happened to meet him by chance in a bar last night. And we started up a conversation, and had some drinks together. We got on very well actually, and we must have talked for a couple of hours at least. And we chatted about all kinds of things, but then quite late in the evening he whispered to me that he'd carried out the robberies of the cash machines. That's all there is to it, really. That's all that I wanted to report. Perhaps he was just joking, of course. Perhaps I'm wasting your time."

"Did this person tell you his name?"

"Yes he did—Masuhiro Hattori. That's what he told me, anyway. And he also told me the name of the apartment complex where he lives. He said that he had an apartment at the Rising Sun complex, which he seemed to indicate was somewhere close to where we were drinking. We were in one of the bars near the castle."

Morimoto leaned back in his chair and stared at the man who was volunteering such potentially critical information about the series of cash machine robberies that had been troubling the Okayama police for almost a year.

"Well, this could certainly be very important information that you've brought to our attention, and I'd like to thank you for taking the trouble to come in here this morning. You've certainly done the right thing in reporting the incident, and we're very grateful for that. Before we proceed any further, perhaps you won't mind providing us with a little information about yourself. What's your name?"

"Oh, my name is Noritoshi Tokuda."

"And do you live in Okayama?"

"Yes, I've lived here all of my life."

"And where do you work?"

"I work for a computer company. It's quite a small company, so you probably won't have heard of it. We provide training and support services for businesses that need help setting up new software on their computers—that kind of thing. And sometimes we take care of small jobs for them—things that we can handle on our own computers."

"I see. And what's the name of this bar near to the castle where you were drinking with Mr. Hattori last night?"

Mr. Tokuda frowned.

"Umm...the Pickled Cabbage, I think...or something like that. I can show you where it is if you like."

"Was last night the first time that you'd been there?"

"No, I've been there several times before...on the odd occasion, that is. But it's not somewhere that I go often."

"And what time did you arrive there last night?"

"Oh, let me think. It must have been just before eight o'clock, I should imagine."

"And was Mr. Hattori already at the bar when you arrived?"

"Yes, he was. He was sitting up at the counter, and that's where I went to sit as well. And before long we'd struck up a conversation. And then, after we'd been chatting for quite a while, we moved to one of the tables closer to the back of the bar."

"What did you talk about?"

Mr. Tokuda shrugged.

"Oh, lots of things...all kinds of things, really. We talked about baseball, our jobs, music groups, cartoon magazines, and many other topics as well. I can't remember everything that we talked about at the moment."

"What did Mr. Hattori tell you about his job?"

Suzuki was staring intently at Mr. Tokuda's face as he answered Morimoto's questions.

"Umm...he said that he worked in one of the car factories over by Kurashiki."

"I see. And you said that Mr. Hattori had quite a lot to drink last night, didn't you?"

"Oh, yes, he drank a great deal."

"What was he drinking?"

"Beer...he stuck to beer the whole evening."

"And what about you, Mr. Tokuda? Did you have much to drink yourself last night?"

Mr. Tokuda looked a little sheepish.

"Yes, I did have a fair amount to drink myself, I have to say. But I didn't drink nearly as much as Mr. Hattori did. I wasn't keeping pace with him at all."

Chapter 4

Police Officer Suzuki scribbled some notes in her notebook as Inspector Morimoto continued with his questioning of Mr. Tokuda.

"Was last night the first time that you'd met Mr. Hattori?"

"Yes, it was…last night was the first time that we'd ever met. It was just a coincidence that I met him, as I explained."

Mr. Tokuda looked completely relaxed, and he answered Morimoto's questions quickly and easily.

"And was it while you were sitting together at the table that Mr. Hattori whispered to you about the cash machine robberies?"

"Yes, that's right."

"How exactly did the subject come up? Do you remember? Did Mr. Hattori just suddenly raise the matter himself?"

Mr. Tokuda frowned again.

"Umm…let me see. We were talking about banks, if I remember correctly. That's right. I'd been complaining to him about the way in which my bank had treated me. My balance had fallen below some minimum allowable level that they'd set, and it was only below the required level for three days, but they slapped all sorts of fees and penalties on me. I was telling Mr. Hattori how angry I was about the way they'd acted, and he told me how much he sympathized with me. In fact, I remember that he said that he'd often had the same kind of trouble with his own bank. And that's when he told me that he was the person who'd carried out the cash machine robberies."

"I see. And what exactly did he say about the robberies? Did he give you any details about how he'd done them? Did he describe them in any way?"

"Well, first of all he asked me whether I'd heard about them, and of course I told him that I had. Then he leaned over towards me and whispered that he was the person who'd done them. And he gave me a wink, and he told me that he didn't feel so badly about the bank fees that he'd been charged because he'd stolen a lot of the bank's money anyway. But that's all that he said. He didn't elaborate any further."

Morimoto nodded slowly, and he rubbed his chin as he gazed at Mr. Tokuda and pondered the implications of the information that he was providing.

"Did Mr. Hattori change in any way after he'd told you that he'd robbed the cash machines? Did he perhaps seem to regret having told you?"

"Oh, no…he didn't seem to regret it at all. On the contrary, he seemed very proud of the fact, and he looked like he was very happy that he'd managed to get some sort of revenge on the banks. At least, that's how it seemed to me."

"Did Mr. Hattori ask you not to tell anybody else about what he'd told you?"

Mr. Tokuda shook his head.

"No, he never said anything like that. He just changed the subject and started talking about some other topic, and he acted as though he hadn't told me anything that was particularly important."

"I see. Well, what about you, Mr. Tokuda? What was your reaction when Mr. Hattori told you that he'd robbed the cash machines?"

Mr. Tokuda shrugged.

"I have to say that it took a while for the full significance of it to really sink in, I guess. It took me a while before I was able to completely come to terms with what Mr. Hattori had confided in me. At first, as I was sitting there at the table drinking with him, I really didn't know just what to make of it. I thought for a while that he might simply have been joking, but then the more I thought about it, the more it seemed to me that he wasn't making it up. At least, he never told me that he'd just been kidding about the matter. Anyway, I got up and left the bar shortly after he told me about the robberies."

"So you were the first one to leave, were you?"

"Yes, that's right. I left at about ten thirty, I guess, and went straight home."

"And when did you decide to come in here and tell us about what happened yesterday evening?"

"Well, I did think about the matter last night after I'd left the bar, but it was late when I got home and I wanted to go to sleep. But I was still bothered about the matter when I woke up this morning, and I began to feel that I ought to do something about it. I had to get to my office on time, though, but I was able to arrange things so that I could take some time off to come over here and talk to you. As I said before, I really do hope that you don't think that I've been wasting your time."

Mr. Tokuda laughed nervously.

"No, not at all, Mr. Tokuda. As I indicated before, you've done exactly the right thing coming over here this morning, and we're very grateful that you did. We'll certainly be following up on what you've reported to us, and we'll definitely be checking into this Mr. Hattori who lives at the Rising Sun apartment complex. It may turn out that you've provided us with a very valuable lead."

Mr. Tokuda looked pleased.

"Well, I just wanted to do my duty, you know. I felt that I ought to at least tell you what happened, even if it turns out to be nothing important."

"You acted quite properly. Oh, there is one other point before you go, Mr. Tokuda. What do you yourself know about the cash machine robberies?"

Mr. Tokuda looked surprised.

"Me? What do I know about them? Well, I only know what everybody else knows, I guess. The television news programs and the newspapers have covered them very extensively, haven't they? That's how I learned about them. There have been three robberies, haven't there? And as far as I can remember, they occurred in a different place each time. They all took place in small towns around here, didn't they? That's all that I know, really."

"Well, let me thank you one last time for coming in here this morning, Mr. Tokuda. I'll ask the policewoman who's waiting outside to show you out of the building, and I'll also ask her to get some contact information from you in case we ever need to get in touch with you again, if that's all right?"

"Oh, yes—that'll be no problem at all."

Morimoto stood up and walked towards the door. Mr. Tokuda stood up as well, but Suzuki noticed that he seemed to want to linger in the room for a moment longer.

"Err...I was wondering...there is one other little thing," Mr. Tokuda said awkwardly.

"Yes?" Morimoto replied.

"Well, the fact is that I do remember from the television and newspaper reports that some kind of a reward is being offered. And actually, come to think of it, there's a notice about it on the wall of my bank as well. Isn't there a reward for any kind of information relating to the cash machine robberies? I don't suppose...err...I was just wondering...is it at all possible that I might in some way be eligible for that reward if the information that I've provided you with turns out to be useful?"

"Ah, yes—a reward. I believe that you may be right about that, Mr. Tokuda. There has been a reward offered in conjunction with the cash machine robberies, hasn't there, Officer Suzuki?"

Suzuki nodded.

"Yes, sir, there has. The Metropolitan Trust Bank has offered a reward for any information that leads to the arrest of the culprit or culprits."

Morimoto smiled.

"Well, Mr. Tokuda, I'm glad that you've raised the matter of the reward because that could be very good news for you. If this Mr. Hattori's boast last night was genuine, then you could well be in line for that reward. And come to think of it, that's all the more reason to make sure that you leave us your address and phone number!"

Mr. Tokuda laughed.

"Yes, you're certainly right about that!"

As the policewoman led Mr. Tokuda down the corridor on their way out of the building, she handed him a sheet of paper.

"Before you leave, perhaps you'd be willing to take a moment to fill out this Police Performance Score Sheet? It shouldn't take you more than a minute, and there's a box in the lobby where you can put it when you've finished filling it out. You can do it anonymously if you want to, but I recommend that you fill out your name and address, because everybody who fills out one of these score sheets and who participates in our survey automatically has their name entered into a drawing that we'll be having later on in the summer. There are some great prizes that you could win. In fact, the first prize is two free tickets to the end of year concert given by the Police Department Choral Ensemble! They're tremendously popular, did you know?"

Chapter 5

It was a bright sunny Thursday morning in the middle of May when Inspector Morimoto and Police Officer Suzuki entered the nondescript three-story white tile building that was the Okayama District Courthouse. The only thing that distinguished the courthouse from the other office buildings in the vicinity was the national flag that hung limply on its rooftop, and the occasional police cars that drove around the back of the building to deliver and collect those participants of the legal proceedings who were required to be kept in police custody.

Morimoto and Suzuki asked about the location of the trial that they were interested in at the reception desk in the lobby, and they were directed up the stairs to Courtroom 3, where they selected two vacant seats in the back row of the visitors gallery. Courtroom 3 was a small rectangular shaped room with a tall ceiling and plain white wallpaper, and the strong fluorescent lighting was complemented by the sunshine that streamed in through the three large windows on the left wall, as viewed from where Morimoto and Suzuki were sitting. Each window had two long curtains on either side that were tied together with ribbons halfway up, and Suzuki felt that they added a rather pleasant touch to the meticulously clean and tidy room.

The visitors gallery was at one of the narrow ends of the room, and at the opposite end there was a raised dais that contained three high-backed black leather chairs for the judge and the two judicial assistants. The dais provided its occupants with a significant height advantage over everybody else in the room, thereby enabling the judge to look down on the proceedings that unfolded in the courtroom with an air of authority and superiority. In front of the judge's dais and below it was a lower level rostrum where two court reporters were sitting in front of their computers, ready to transcribe the court proceedings.

The space between the judge's dais and the visitors gallery was the main floor of the courtroom. A waist-high wooden barrier served as a separation between this area and the front row of the visitors gallery, which was filled with reporters from the Okayama Tribune and many other newspapers and news organizations. The defendant was sitting with his back against the middle of this barrier, directly facing the empty judge's chair, and he was flanked on either side by two uniformed policemen who were sitting stiffly with blank expressions on their faces. There was nothing unusual about their blue caps and uniforms, their white shirts, their blue neckties, and their white socks, but the fact that one of the policemen was wearing white running shoes while the other one was wearing black running shoes provided an indication that it would be unwise for the defendant to attempt a sudden dart for freedom.

A thermostat on the wall indicated that the temperature of the room was being maintained at the comfortable twenty-two degrees centigrade that was specified in the court regulations, and although Morimoto would in many ways have preferred to have been somewhere else that morning where he could have obtained more pleasure from the summer sunshine, he was nevertheless more than a little interested to see how the trial was going to turn out. Glancing up at the clock on the wall at the back of the visitors gallery, he noticed that it showed exactly ten o'clock, and at that precise moment the door at the back of the judge's dais opened, and the judge stepped into the deathly silent courtroom accompanied by her two advisors.

The judge was an elderly lady draped in a long black robe with a white neck-scarf tied in a bow at the front, and the streaks of gray in her neatly coiffured hair added a touch of dignity and gravity to her appearance. She seated herself in the middle of the three chairs, and her two middle-aged male advisors, who were similarly dressed in long black robes, took their seats on either side of her.

The judge looked at the clock on the wall and then adjusted the microphone that was positioned on the table in front of her.

"Good morning. I am Judge Ayako Noda and this court is now in session. The defendant, Mr. Masuhiro Hattori, is charged with having committed robberies at three cash machines belonging to the Metropolitan Trust Bank. The first incident is reported to have occurred in August of last year in the town of Shingo in Okayama prefecture, the second incident is reported to have occurred in November of last year in the town of Takebe in Okayama prefecture, and the final incident is reported to have occurred in February of this year in the town of Kotohira in Kagawa prefecture."

Judge Noda peered down at the courtroom on her right-hand side where the Public Prosecutor, Mr. Genda, was sitting at his desk behind a substantial collection of reference books, each of which had a bright purple ribbon sticking out at the page where it had last been consulted.

"Would the Public Prosecutor please begin his case now," Judge Noda said as she settled back into her comfortable black leather chair.

Mr. Genda rose from his desk and walked out across the shiny floor into the middle of the courtroom. He was wearing a light brown suit with a white shirt and a brown tie, and he maintained a full head of bushy jet black hair even though his fiftieth birthday had passed several years before. He looked confidently back up at the judge.

"Good morning, your honor. I'd like to start my case by calling my first witness, Sergeant Yamada of the Okayama Police Department."

The door opened at the side of the courtroom, and Sergeant Yamada was ushered inside by the court attendant. As he sat down in the solitary chair that was in the middle of the courtroom behind a small table with a microphone on it, facing the judge and with his back to the defendant, Suzuki noted approvingly that he had taken some care to ensure that his uniform was in pristine condition that morning, and that his black shoes were as finely polished as the floor.

Sergeant Yamada was handed a sheet of paper by the attendant, and in a clear voice he read out the words that attested to the veracity of the evidence that he was about to present. When this swearing in procedure had been completed, the attendant took back the sheet of paper and retreated to his position at the side of the room, while Mr. Genda walked over and stood beside Sergeant Yamada.

"Could you please state your name for the court records?"

"Shinichi Yamada."

"And you hold the rank of Sergeant in the Okayama Police Department, do you not?"

"Yes, I do."

"Thank you. Last month you were in charge of a search that was conducted at the apartment belonging to the defendant, Mr. Masuhiro Hattori, at the Rising Sun apartment complex, weren't you, Sergeant?"

"Yes, I was."

"And that search was authorized by a warrant issued by the Office of the Public Prosecutor, wasn't it?"

"Yes, it was."

Mr. Genda turned to look up at the judge again.

"You'll find a copy of that warrant in the set of documents that we've supplied you with, your honor."

Judge Noda nodded, and Mr. Genda turned back to face Sergeant Yamada.

"How many other members of the police force did you take with you when you conducted your search, Sergeant?"

"The search was conducted by myself together with two other policemen and one policewoman."

"And the apartment was empty when you entered it, was it?"

"Yes, it was."

Mr. Genda turned to the judge once more.

"I'd like to call for Exhibit 1 now, if I may, your honor."

Judge Noda signaled her acquiescence, and the court attendant walked over to Mr. Genda and handed him a clear plastic bag containing a heavy metal crowbar that was painted bright blue. Mr. Genda took the bag from the attendant and showed it to Sergeant Yamada.

"Did you find this crowbar when you searched Mr. Hattori's apartment, Sergeant?"

"Yes, we did."

"And could you please tell us exactly whereabouts inside the apartment you found it?"

"It was in a cupboard in the kitchen, hidden inside a container of rice."

"Thank you. When you say a container of rice, you're referring to a typical plastic container that you might find in any kitchen, used for the purpose of storing food, aren't you?"

"Yes, that's right."

"And the container in Mr. Hattori's kitchen was large enough to contain this crowbar, was it?"

"Yes, it was."

"Would you say that the container was full of rice, Sergeant?"

"Yes, it was almost completely full."

"And the crowbar was at the very bottom of the container, completely covered by the rice, wasn't it?"

"Yes, it was."

"So you would certainly describe the crowbar as having been hidden, wouldn't you, Sergeant?"

"Yes, I would."

Mr. Genda paused for a moment to emphasize his point, and he glanced up at the judge.

"Thank you, Sergeant," he said eventually. "I'd now like to introduce Exhibit 2 to the courtroom, your honor."

This time the attendant brought a plastic bag to Mr. Genda that contained a thick wad of bank notes.

"Did you find anything else hidden inside the rice container in Mr. Hattori's kitchen, Sergeant?"

"Yes, we did. There were some bank notes wrapped up in newspaper."

"And what did you do with those bank notes, Sergeant?"

"Well, we put them inside one of the bags that we'd taken along with us to store evidence of that kind for forensic analysis, and we took them back to the Police Headquarters together with the crowbar."

"Thank you, Sergeant."

Mr. Genda walked back towards his desk, and he held up the bag of bank notes for the judge to see.

"Your honor, I should like to point out that Exhibit 2 contains the bank notes that Sergeant Yamada logged in at the Police Headquarters after returning from his search of Mr. Hattori's apartment. And, in addition, I would like to remind you that the full report that Sergeant Yamada filed concerning his search of Mr. Hattori's apartment has been included in the set of documents that we've supplied you with. I have no further questions for this witness at this time, your honor."

"Thank you, Mr. Genda," Judge Noda said.

Mr. Genda walked behind his desk and sat down.

Judge Noda turned towards her left and looked down at Mr. Bando who was sitting behind a desk on the opposite side of the courtroom from Mr. Genda.

"Does the defense wish to put any questions to the witness?" she asked.

Mr. Bando stood up slowly, and the heavy gold watch chain that was hanging out of the waistcoat of his expensively tailored dark pinstripe suit sparkled in the bright courtroom lighting. His heavy build was quite similar to that of the judo champion Sergeant Yamada who remained seated in the witness chair in front of him, although he was significantly taller, and after he had drawn himself up to his full height he returned Judge Noda's gaze with a strong confident look of his own.

"No, thank you, your honor. The defense does not have any questions for this witness."

Judge Noda nodded, and turned back to face Sergeant Yamada.

"Well then, Sergeant, thank you for your assistance. That will be all."

As Sergeant Yamada was being shown out of the courtroom by the attendant, Morimoto turned and whispered to Suzuki.

"Well, he seems to have remembered his lines all right."

"It was a flawless performance, sir."

"And he wasn't even subjected to the slightest bit of a grilling from our good friend, Mr. Bando."

Mr. Bando was an enthusiastic admirer of Bizen pottery who had been involved in Morimoto and Suzuki's previous case.

"I expect that Mr. Bando is saving his ammunition for later, sir."

"Yes, and he may also have a very healthy respect for the high standard of police work in this city."

"I expect so, sir."

"By the way, Suzuki, do you think that Sergeant Yamada is supposed to offer the judge a Double-PS?"

Chapter 6

From where they were sitting in the visitors gallery, Inspector Morimoto and Police Officer Suzuki could only see the back of the defendant's head, so unlike the judge they were not able to tell whether he had registered any visible reaction to Sergeant Yamada's testimony. They had been quite familiar with the details of Sergeant Yamada's evidence, which he had delivered to the courtroom quite efficiently and without any surprises, but Morimoto was secretly looking forward to seeing how the Public Prosecutor managed his next witness, who Morimoto expected would not be quite so adapt at remembering his lines.

Judge Noda conferred briefly with each of her two advisors before addressing Mr. Genda again.

"The prosecution may continue with its case now."

"Thank you, your honor. I'd like to call my next witness—Dr. Jimbo from the Police Department Forensic Laboratory."

Dr. Jimbo was led into the courtroom looking remarkably uncomfortable in an ill-fitting suit, and with one look at him it was readily apparent to everybody present that he would much rather have been back in his state of the art laboratory, wearing his white laboratory coat and searching through the precariously stacked piles of scientific research articles and journals that covered every available space in his office. The new Forensic Laboratory was the pride and joy of the Chief, who had worked tirelessly to secure its funding, and Dr. Jimbo and his team of scientists had already distinguished themselves in several important cases. But Morimoto and Suzuki were both well aware that outside of his laboratory, Dr. Jimbo was just like a fish out of water.

Dr. Jimbo was a short bald man with a thick mustache, and while Suzuki was familiar with the manner in which his thick glasses were perched on his nose with one side noticeably much higher than the other, she was alarmed to notice just how crooked his tie was. Taking the seat that Sergeant Yamada had just vacated, Dr. Jimbo peered up at Judge Noda through his glasses as the attendant handed him the sheet for his swearing in. When that had been completed, Mr. Genda walked over towards him and established his identity and occupation as head of the Forensic Laboratory for the court records, before beginning his questions in earnest.

"Now, Dr. Jimbo, can you confirm that your laboratory has carried out an examination of the three cash machines that were broken into?"

Dr. Jimbo nodded.

"Yes."

"And where did you carry out your examination?"

"In our laboratory."

"So the three cash machines in question were brought from the towns of Shingo, Takebe, and Kotohira to the Police Department Forensic Laboratory here in Okayama, were they?"

Dr. Jimbo nodded again.

"Yes."

"Together with all of the debris that was created when they were broken into?"

"Yes."

"Thank you, Dr. Jimbo."

Mr. Genda walked over to his desk and picked up a large envelope.

"With your permission, your honor, I'd like to distribute a set of photographs to the court."

Judge Noda nodded.

"Very well, Mr. Genda."

Mr. Genda opened up the envelope and took out several sets of photographs that the court attendant came and took from him. Dr. Jimbo sat with a bored expression on his face as the attendant distributed the photographs to Judge Noda and to each of her two advisors. The attendant also handed a copy to Mr. Bando, before giving a final set to Dr. Jimbo.

"Now, Dr. Jimbo," Mr. Genda continued, "these photographs show the three cash machines that you examined, don't they?"

Dr. Jimbo flicked through the photographs that he had been given.

"Yes."

"And what can you tell us about the condition of these cash machines?"

"They've all been smashed up."

Mr. Genda waited for a moment, hoping that his witness would elucidate further and provide some of the details of the damage that his laboratory had analyzed, but he soon realized that Dr. Jimbo was going to need some severe prodding if he were ever to divulge the information that Mr. Genda wanted the judge to hear.

"So in each of the three cases, the complete front panel of the machine has been ripped open, hasn't it, Dr. Jimbo?"

"Yes."

"And we can see from the photos that the sections containing the bank notes have been broken into so that the money could be removed, can't we, Dr. Jimbo?"

"Yes."

Dr. Jimbo pulled out a scruffy handkerchief from his jacket pocket that made Suzuki wince, and he wiped his forehead with it before screwing it up into a ball again and shoving it back inside his pocket.

"Thank you," Mr. Genda said as he turned to look up at the judge. "May I ask that Exhibit 1 be shown to the witness, your honor?"

Judge Noda nodded, and the court assistant brought the plastic bag containing the blue crowbar over to Dr. Jimbo and held it out in front of him.

"You've performed an analysis of this crowbar in your laboratory, haven't you, Dr. Jimbo?" Mr. Genda asked.

"Yes."

"Thank you. The exhibit can be removed now."

The court assistant took the crowbar away and replaced it on his trolley along with the other exhibits.

"Now, Dr. Jimbo, based on the results of your laboratory's analysis and your own expert opinion, what can you tell the court about the relationship between the crowbar that was just shown to you and the three cash machines?"

Mr. Genda held his breath, hoping that his witness was not going to fluff the key part of his testimony, but the confused expression on Dr. Jimbo's face did not bode well.

"Err…relationship? What exactly do you mean?"

Mr. Genda took a deep breath.

"That crowbar could have been used to cause the damage to the cash machines that we saw in the photos, couldn't it, Dr. Jimbo?" he said as patiently as he could, trying very hard not to let his exasperation show in his voice.

Dr. Jimbo nodded.

"Yes."

"Or to put it in different words, Dr. Jimbo, the damage that was caused to those three cash machines, which can be clearly seen in the photos that we have in front of us, is consistent with the supposition that it was caused by that crowbar, isn't it?"

"Yes."

"And you conducted an experiment in your laboratory to confirm that supposition, didn't you, Dr. Jimbo?"

"Oh…yes, we did."

Mr. Genda paced up and down in front of his desk for a few moments as he desperately tried to steel himself for the remainder of the questions that he needed to put to the witness.

"Could you please describe that experiment to the court, Dr. Jimbo?"

Dr. Jimbo smiled.

"We smashed up a cash machine with a crowbar."

This answer was about as much as Mr. Genda had been hoping for this time, and he was ready to fill in the details of the experiment himself.

"So you obtained a brand new cash machine from the company that manufactured the three cash machines that were broken into, didn't you? You obtained a brand new cash machine of exactly the same type and model as the three damaged machines—isn't that right, Dr. Jimbo?"

"Yes."

"And then you purchased a crowbar identical to the one that you were just shown, didn't you?"

"Yes."

"And can you describe to the court exactly how you carried out your experiment, Dr. Jimbo?"

"We smashed up the new cash machine with the crowbar."

"That's right, Dr. Jimbo. You conducted a carefully planned and conceived scientific experiment to demonstrate that a crowbar of that size and weight could be used to break open a cash machine of that type in order to gain access to the bank notes inside it, didn't you?"

"Yes."

Morimoto wondered whether Mr. Bando was going to jump up and object to his adversary's leading of the witness, but Mr. Bando sat quite still behind his desk on his side of the courtroom and allowed Mr. Genda to continue uninterrupted with his painful questioning of Dr. Jimbo.

"And so you observed from your scientific experiment, Dr. Jimbo, that the resulting damage to the new cash machine was of a similar nature and severity as the damage that was caused to the three cash machines in question, as evidenced from the photos in front of us, didn't you?"

"Yes."

"Thank you very much, Dr. Jimbo."

Chapter 7

▼

Mr. Genda was having as much difficulty with Dr. Jimbo's testimony as Inspector Morimoto had anticipated that he might, and as Police Officer Suzuki monitored the events that were unfolding in the courtroom, she desperately hoped that Dr. Jimbo would leave his scruffy handkerchief in his pocket for the remainder of his testimony.

After having completed the first part of his questioning, Mr. Genda took a few moments to pace back and forth in front of his desk again with a satisfied look on his face for the judge's benefit, although the truth was that he was miserably contemplating just how much more information he still needed to extract from his witness, and just how excruciatingly difficult that was likely to be.

Having marshaled his inner strength to the best of his ability, Mr. Genda approached his witness once again.

"Now, Dr. Jimbo, that crowbar that we looked at a moment ago was blue, wasn't it?"

"Yes."

"That is to say, it had been painted blue, hadn't it?"

"Yes."

"And at either end of the crowbar some of the gray metal could be seen showing through the paintwork, couldn't it?"

"Yes."

"And that's because some of the blue paint had been chipped off at the ends when the crowbar had been used—am I right, Dr. Jimbo?"

"Yes."

Mr. Genda stepped closer to Dr. Jimbo and looked straight at him.

"And what can you tell this court," he said slowly and deliberately, "about the implications of some of the blue paint having been chipped off that crowbar that we looked at, with specific regard to the three cash machines that were broken into and which you analyzed in your laboratory?"

There was complete silence in the courtroom as Dr. Jimbo looked up at Mr. Genda with a quizzical look on his face.

"Err...err...are you referring to the traces of blue paint that we discovered on the three cash machines?" he said hopefully.

"That's exactly the point that I'm interested in, Dr. Jimbo."

This time Mr. Genda was not able to conceal the evident relief in his voice.

"Well, why didn't you say so?" Dr. Jimbo complained.

"Ha...ha," Mr. Genda laughed jovially, being careful not to look anywhere near the direction of the judge. "So you did find some traces of blue paint on the three cash machines, did you, Dr. Jimbo?"

"Yes, that's what I said."

"And how did you find them?"

"Oh, well it's one of the many tests that we do in this kind of circumstance. It's standard procedure that any decent laboratory would follow. We examined each cash machine and all of the pieces of debris very carefully for any evidence of paint residues or similar evidence of that nature. The paint particles were clearly evident in several places when we scanned the parts of the cash machines with some of our high magnification equipment. You wouldn't notice them with your naked eye, of course, but they were there, nevertheless. Does that answer your question?"

To Mr. Genda's ill-concealed delight, Dr. Jimbo seemed to have suddenly come to life.

"Thank you, Dr. Jimbo. And did you run any tests on the paint particles that you discovered on the cash machines?"

"Yes, of course we did. Once we'd detected the particles we photographed them and took representative samples from each of the three cash machines. And the other thing that we did was to take a paint sample from that crowbar that you just showed me, and then we performed a standard chemical decomposition of all of the samples to see what kind of a match they were. It's a trivial procedure really, the sort of thing that we carry out all of the time."

"And what kind of a match did you find, Dr. Jimbo?"

"Oh, they matched, all right. There's no doubt about it—it's the same kind of paint."

"So you're telling this court, are you, Dr. Jimbo, that based on your expert knowledge of forensic science, together with the state of the art tests that you ran in your laboratory, that you are quite certain that there is a complete match between the paint particles on each of the three cash machines that were broken into, and the paint on the blue crowbar that was exhibited to you a moment ago?"

"Yes."

"Thank you, Dr. Jimbo."

Mr. Genda took a deep breath, attempted to straighten his bushy hair, and made a silent prayer that the sudden jump in the level of Dr. Jimbo's cooperation would be maintained throughout the remainder of his questioning.

"And I'd like to raise one final point with you on this issue, Dr. Jimbo. If the crowbar that we looked at had been used to break open the cash machines, is it your expert opinion that it would have left residues of paint particles on the machines similar to the ones that you observed?"

"Oh, yes, there's no doubt about that. I've looked at similar pieces of evidence hundreds of times before, and it's just what I'd have expected. If you told me that the crowbar had been used to pry open anything like the cash machines, then I'd be fairly certain that I'd be able to find some paint particles remaining on the object if I looked carefully enough with the right equipment."

Mr. Genda felt a mixture of relief and delight as he stepped away from his witness and headed back towards his desk. However, these emotions received a sudden jolt when he realized that Dr. Jimbo had not completely finished his answer.

"You see, forensic science has made some remarkable advances in the recent past. If you look through the research journals, you'll find numerous articles relating to the issue of paint residues."

"Well, thank you very…"

"Of course, I'm familiar with all of the latest research in this area, and I have made some contributions myself. The topic of paint particles is a fascinating one because…"

"Yes, thank you very much, Dr. Jimbo," Mr. Genda said firmly.

"Oh…alright. I was just trying to be helpful."

Mr. Genda took a few deep breaths, and hazarded a glance up at Judge Noda whose deadpan expression revealed absolutely nothing about her feelings. After taking a few more moments to compose himself as best as he could, Mr. Genda bravely stepped back towards his witness.

"Now, Dr. Jimbo, there's one final matter that I'd like to deal with, and it's to do with the crowbar that we looked at. Can you tell the court what you found on the crowbar when you examined it?"

Dr. Jimbo slowly raised his head and looked up at Mr. Genda through his thick spectacles that were just as askew as when he had walked into the courtroom. Suzuki's heart skipped a beat as he appeared to reach towards the pocket that contained his scruffy handkerchief, but instead he raised his hand and scratched his bald head.

"You're talking about the fingerprints now, aren't you?"

"Yes, Dr. Jimbo."

"I thought that you were."

"Did you find any fingerprints on the crowbar, Dr. Jimbo?"

"Yes."

"And who did they belong to?"

"The fellow who's on trial—Mr. Hattori."

"So you were able to obtain a match between the fingerprints that you found on the crowbar and the fingerprints that were taken from Mr. Hattori."

"Yes."

"And you're quite certain of that, are you?"

Dr. Jimbo looked insulted.

"Yes, of course I am. It's really not that complicated, you know?"

"Thank you, Dr. Jimbo. And were there any other fingerprints on the crowbar besides those belonging to Mr. Hattori?"

"No."

Mr. Genda walked back to his desk and looked up at the judge.

"That's all of the questions that I have for this witness, your honor," he said, and the relief in his voice reverberated clearly throughout the courtroom.

Judge Noda nodded at Mr. Genda, and she exchanged a few whispered words with each of her advisors before she peered down at Mr. Bando on the other side of the courtroom.

"Would the defense like to put any questions to this witness?"

Mr. Genda sank gratefully into the chair behind his desk as Mr. Bando stood up and strode purposefully out into the courtroom.

"Thank you very much, your honor. I just have a couple of quick questions that I'd like to put to the witness."

Mr. Bando stayed close to the front of his desk, keeping quite a distance between himself and Dr. Jimbo.

"I'd like to consider the question of whether the crowbar that was introduced as evidence in this courtroom was really the instrument that was used to break into the three cash machines, Dr. Jimbo."

Mr. Bando spoke in a cultured manner with crisply enunciated words, and although he did not give the appearance of raising his voice, each word resonated strongly and clearly throughout the courtroom.

"Your analysis of the type and severity of the damage suffered by the cash machines verified that the crowbar that you examined could have been the instrument that was used to extract the bank notes from the cash machines. But am I not correct in pointing out to the court, Dr. Jimbo, that there are in fact many other types and shapes of instruments available to the general public, which are also capable of inflicting that kind of damage on the cash machines?"

Dr. Jimbo shrugged.

"Yes, of course there are. I never said that I'd proved that a crowbar was used to open up the machines. All I said was that…"

"Thank you, Dr. Jimbo."

Mr. Bando's no-nonsense tone cut Dr. Jimbo off in midstream, as it had many other witnesses during his long and eminent legal career.

"And also," Mr. Bando continued, "with regard to the paint particles that you found on the three cash machines. Am I not correct in clarifying for the court that you matched the type of paint on the cash machines with the type of paint on the crowbar, but that it's quite possible that the paint particles could have been deposited on the three cash machines by any other object covered with that particular paint type, and that the paint particles may not have come from that specific crowbar?"

Dr. Jimbo shrugged again.

"Yes, that's correct. If you'd listened to me carefully, you'd know that I never said that we'd proved that the paint particles on the cash machines came from that specific crowbar with one hundred percent certainty. But we did obtain a match of the paint particles, so they could have come from the crowbar that was found in that fellow's rice box."

Mr. Bando turned to face the judge.

"Thank you, your honor. That's all of the questions that I have for this witness."

Chapter 8

After Dr. Jimbo's testimony, Judge Noda called a short recess in the morning's proceedings, and Inspector Morimoto and Police Officer Suzuki took advantage of the break to step outside the courthouse so that they could soak up some of the warming sunshine. While they enjoyed the fresh air, they discussed the implications of what Mr. Genda had been able to establish with his first two witnesses.

"Well, Suzuki, how do you think the trial's going so far?"

"Hmmm…it looks like Mr. Genda's off to a good start, sir, just as we'd expected. From Sergeant Yamada's testimony, he's managed to establish that the crowbar and the bank notes were in Mr. Hattori's apartment, and furthermore, it was made crystal clear to the court that significant efforts had been made to hide them."

"Yes, that's right. It might not be that unusual for somebody to hide their savings at the bottom of a rice container in their kitchen, but it's a very peculiar place to keep a crowbar."

"Exactly, sir. And with a little effort, Mr. Genda was able to establish from Dr. Jimbo's testimony that a crowbar of that size and weight would be the ideal instrument to open up a cash machine in a hurry. And since the paint particles on the vandalized machines match the paint on the crowbar, everything points to the contention that the crowbar hidden in Mr. Hattori's kitchen was the actual implement used for the crimes."

"Yes, although when his turn came, Mr. Bando was quick to point out that the crowbar that was hidden in Mr. Hattori's kitchen is actually only one of possibly many implements that could have been used to carry out the attacks on the cash machines."

"That's true, sir. Perhaps Mr. Bando has plans to introduce some evidence of his own later on relating to exactly how many crowbars with that kind of paint there are in this region?"

"Knowing Mr. Bando's reputation, I'm sure that he's got some clever tricks up his sleeve."

A group of newspaper reporters standing around the doorway to the courthouse were busily chatting away into their phones as they conveyed their impressions of the morning's events to their offices.

"But what about the fingerprints?" Morimoto asked. "Dr. Jimbo told the court that Mr. Hattori's fingerprints were all over the crowbar. Consequently, if that crowbar was the implement that was used to break open the cash machines, then Mr. Hattori's going to have some explaining to do, don't you think?"

"He most certainly has, sir. Of course, if it is Mr. Hattori's own crowbar, then it would naturally have his fingerprints on it. But if Mr. Bando's strategy is to deny that the crowbar that was found in Mr. Hattori's apartment was used to vandalize the cash machines, he's still going to have to come up with an explanation for why it was hidden in the rice container."

"You're right, Suzuki. Who knows? Perhaps Mr. Hattori is going to tell the court that his young niece and nephew came around to his apartment and amused themselves by playing a game of hunt the crowbar?"

Suzuki laughed.

"I wonder how Judge Noda would react to that, sir? Presumably, Mr. Hattori will tell her that the children were interrupted in the middle of their game, and consequently they were never able to retrieve the crowbar from its hiding place. And I wonder whether he'll also explain to the judge that his niece and nephew always wear gloves when they visit his apartment? We shouldn't forget that Mr. Hattori's fingerprints were the only fingerprints that Dr. Jimbo found on the crowbar."

"Hmmm…that's a good point, Suzuki."

At that moment a brand new police car turned off the road and drove into the parking area outside the courthouse, and Morimoto and Suzuki watched as it came to a gradual halt just near to where they were standing. The bottom half of the car was black, while the top half was a shiny white, and there was a strip of red lights on the top of the roof. The words 'Okayama Police' were printed in black letters on the doors, and a gold cherry blossom insignia was fastened in the middle of the grill at the front of the car between two more red warning lights.

One of the back doors burst open, and the Chief stepped out into the morning sunshine.

"Ah, good morning, Morimoto," he called. "Good morning, Officer Suzuki. I had a bit of spare time in my schedule this morning, so I thought that I'd drop by to see how the trial's progressing. Those people at Tsuda Business Solutions have helped me to completely rethink the way in which I arrange my time, and I've found that I can fit in a lot more things now. Have you been incorporating the latest time management policies into your scheduling procedures, Morimoto?"

"Err...actually, sir...err...we've been so busy that we haven't had time to do that yet."

"Oh, that's a shame. Anyway, what's been happening in the trial so far? Has it been going well?"

"Going well, sir? Do you mean well for the prosecution or well for the defendant?"

"Oh, for the prosecution of course, Morimoto. I don't think that there can be much doubt about this case, can there? I've read all of the reports. It was absolutely splendid work by Sergeant Yamada and his team to find that hidden crowbar. That's very incriminating evidence, that is. What a strange place to hide it! At least that's what I thought. But do you know what? When I told my wife about it she didn't seem to be particularly surprised. She told me that it was an obvious place for a wife to hide something from her husband. Actually, come to think of it, I seem to recall that there was a policewoman on Sergeant Yamada's team. Perhaps she made a beeline for the kitchen and checked the rice container first thing? What do you think, Officer Suzuki?"

"Hmmm...come to think of it, sir, I believe that rice containers might have been a traditional hiding place for money and valuables before banks became widespread—just like people have a tendency to hide a front door key in the ledge over the door or under a nearby plant pot."

"Well, it can't have improved the taste of the rice...I can tell you that! Anyway, didn't our new Forensic Laboratory do another outstanding job! I hope that the judge was suitably impressed by Dr. Jimbo's testimony."

Morimoto and Suzuki maintained a diplomatic silence.

"Mind you," the Chief continued, "I was a little bit concerned when I found out that they spent all of that money on a brand new cash machine, just so that they could demolish it with a crowbar. Do you really think that was absolutely necessary? They're not cheap those machines, you know. Surely they could have found a cheaper way to conduct their experiment? But on the other hand, if we do manage to get a conviction in this trial, then it will be a tremendous credit to the Police Department. And in that case, I suppose that it will all have been worthwhile. Do you agree, Morimoto?"

Morimoto knew that the prevailing opinion among most people at the Police Headquarters was that the scientists' delight in being able to demolish a brand new cash machine had more than likely overridden any sober consideration of the scientific merit behind their experiment, but he was sure that it was unnecessary to bring this to the Chief's attention.

"Anyhow," the Chief continued, "let's not forget the information that was volunteered by that fine citizen who overheard Mr. Hattori bragging about his crimes after he'd had too much to drink in a bar. What an absolutely splendid chap that informant is! Our police work would be much easier if everybody else in Okayama remembered their public duty and assisted us in maintaining peace and order in a similar way. Well, shall we go inside now? I have to keep to my schedule or I might be reprimanded by Ms. Tsuda!"

After Judge Noda had called the court proceedings back into session, Mr. Genda introduced his third witness who was duly sworn in.

"Could you please state your name for the court records?"

"Kenji Izumi."

"And where are you employed, Mr. Izumi?"

"I work for the Metropolitan Trust Bank."

"And you work at the Okayama main office, I believe?"

"Yes, that's correct. I used to be the manager of the Takashima branch of the bank, but at the beginning of last month I was transferred to the main office."

"Thank you. And the cash machines in Shingo, Takebe, and Kotohira that are the focus of these proceedings were each operated by the Metropolitan Trust Bank, were they not?"

"Yes, they were."

"And isn't it true, Mr. Izumi, that a very considerable amount of money was stolen from each of those cash machines?"

"Yes."

"In fact, your bank knows exactly how much money was stolen from each machine, doesn't it?"

"Yes, we know exactly how much money was taken."

"And how is it that you're able to know that, Mr. Izumi?"

"Well, we do of course have exact records of the amounts of cash with which we stocked the three machines in question before they were broken into. Furthermore, we were able to retrieve the computer chips from each of the vandalized machines, and from those chips we were able to obtain records of all of the transactions that had occurred on the machines between when we last serviced them and when they were broken into. Consequently, it's a simple mathematical exercise to calculate how much cash was in the machines at the times when they were robbed, and therefore we have enough information to calculate how much money was stolen."

"Thank you, Mr. Izumi. You mentioned that when you stock the cash machines you obviously keep a record of how much money you deposit in them, but you also keep track of which particular bank notes you use to stock the machines, don't you?"

"Yes, that's correct. We keep detailed records of the serial numbers of all of the bank notes that we place inside our cash machines."

"Thank you very much, Mr. Izumi."

Mr. Genda turned and looked up at Judge Noda.

"If your honor has no objection, I'd like to have Exhibit 2 brought out and shown to the witness."

Judge Noda nodded her acquiescence curtly, and the court assistant brought out the plastic bag containing the wad of bank notes that had been found buried inside Mr. Hattori's rice container. He held it out in front of Mr. Izumi.

"Did your bank conduct an examination of these bank notes at the request of the Public Prosecutor's Office, Mr. Izumi?"

"Yes, we did."

"And were you in charge of that examination?"

"Yes, I was."

"And what did you find from your examination, Mr. Izumi?"

"These bank notes were stolen from our cash machine in Kotohira. We examined the serial numbers on these notes, and our records show that we placed them in the Kotohira cash machine the morning before it was broken into."

There were some murmurs from the reporters in the front row of the visitors gallery as they furiously scribbled down their notes, which attracted an equally furious glare from Judge Noda.

"You're absolutely certain of that, are you, Mr. Izumi?" Mr. Genda continued.

"Yes."

"And did you provide us with copies of your bank's records which establish that fact?"

"Yes, I did."

Mr. Genda walked away from the witness, making a silent wish that all of his witness examinations in the future might proceed just as smoothly as this one had.

"I have no further questions for this witness, your honor, and I would like to remind you that in the set of documents that we've provided you with, you'll find a copy of the records that we were given by the Metropolitan Trust Bank that link the bank notes in Exhibit 2 with the Kotohira cash machine."

"Thank you, Mr. Genda," the judge said as she turned to look down at Mr. Bando. "Does the defense have any questions for this witness?"

Mr. Bando stood up.

"No questions, your honor."

"Very well, then. The witness may step down."

As Mr. Izumi was being led out of the courtroom, the Chief turned and grinned at Morimoto and Suzuki in their seats at the back of the visitors gallery.

"What a splendid performance by Mr. Izumi!" he whispered. "Don't you think so? A very professional job! I've always said that it's a very reliable bank, the Metropolitan Trust Bank…it has a very solid reputation. Anyhow, the defendant's going to find it rather difficult to wriggle out of all of this trouble that he's in, don't you think? I thought that Mr. Izumi's evidence was very significant, and I bet that the judge did too!"

Chapter 9

Mr. Genda's fourth witness that morning was Mr. Tokuda, who appeared in the courtroom with a tie that was just as flashy as when he had visited Inspector Morimoto and Police Officer Suzuki at the Police Headquarters the previous month. There were no surprises for Morimoto and Suzuki in his testimony, as Mr. Genda led him through a description of his visit to the Pickled Cabbage bar and his chance encounter with Mr. Hattori. Mr. Tokuda responded smoothly and clearly to Mr. Genda's questions, and before long the Public Prosecutor turned his witness over to be cross-examined by the defense.

As Mr. Genda sat down behind his desk, Mr. Bando strode confidently across the shiny floor out into the middle of the courtroom, and he walked right up to Mr. Tokuda, towering over him.

"Mr. Tokuda, this court has heard you give evidence this morning that you happened to meet Mr. Hattori in the Pickled Cabbage bar one evening just by chance. Why did you decide to go to a bar on the evening in question?"

Mr. Tokuda looked surprised, and he smiled amicably.

"There wasn't any particular reason. I often go out for a drink on a Sunday evening. It wasn't unusual."

"And why did you specifically decide to go to the Pickled Cabbage bar?"

This time Mr. Tokuda shrugged.

"Again, there wasn't any particular reason why I chose that bar. It was sort of a random choice, I guess."

"Have you ever been to the Pickled Cabbage bar before the night in question?"

The confident tone of Mr. Bando's voice provided him with an aura of superiority and certainty as it reverberated around the courtroom.

"Oh, yes—I've been there quite a few times. I rather enjoy the atmosphere there."

"When have you been there before?"

Mr. Tokuda smiled again, and he adjusted the flamboyantly large knot of his bright blue tie.

"Well...err...I don't think that I can remember the dates exactly. But I could try to find out for you if you like. I went there at least one other time this year before the night when I met Mr. Hattori, I think, and I must have gone there several times last year as well."

"And you gave evidence that you entered the bar on the night in question slightly before eight o'clock—is that correct?"

"Yes, that's right."

"And was the bar crowded when you arrived?"

"Oh, no—it was still early. There weren't many people around at that time. The bar was still rather empty."

"About how many other people were there in the bar when you arrived?"

"Oh...well, I'm not really sure...maybe about five or six people, perhaps?"

"So there weren't any more than at most six people already in the bar when you walked in there just before eight o' clock that evening?"

"Yes, that sounds about right."

"So there must have been a lot of empty chairs in the bar when you walked in, weren't there?"

"Yes, there were."

"About how many empty chairs do you think there were?"

Mr. Tokuda burst into laughter, but not a single muscle on Mr. Bando's face altered an iota as he continued to stare straight at the witness.

"Well, really...I don't know...I didn't count them all! I mean, I have to confess that I'm not in the habit of walking into bars and counting the number of empty chairs! Is that a crime? Is it really important how many empty chairs there were?"

After Mr. Tokuda had finished his reply, there was a dead silence throughout the courtroom as Mr. Bando paused before asking his next question.

"Would you say that there were at least thirty empty chairs in the bar when you entered?"

Mr. Tokuda shrugged.

"Well…let me see…thirty? Yes, I guess so…that sounds about right. It's quite possible that there were about thirty empty seats."

"And whereabouts did you decide to sit, Mr. Tokuda?"

"Oh, I went to sit up at the counter. That's where I usually sit when I go to bars. I prefer that to sitting at one of the tables by myself. It's more interesting up at the counter."

"So you walked into the bar, and you sat down at one of the empty seats at the counter, did you?"

"Yes, I did."

"And did you sit down next to anybody?"

There was a slight pause before Mr. Tokuda answered.

"Yes, I sat down next to Mr. Hattori."

"Right next to Mr. Hattori?"

"Err…yes."

"So to summarize what you're telling this court, Mr. Tokuda, you walked into the Pickled Cabbage bar just before eight o'clock when there were very few people there, and with a substantial choice of empty seats available, you specifically chose to sit down right next to Mr. Hattori—am I correct?"

There was another pause before Mr. Tokuda answered.

"Yes, that's right."

"You could have selected a seat that wasn't next to anybody, couldn't you?"

Mr. Tokuda shrugged.

"Yes, if I'd wanted to."

"But instead, you specifically chose to sit down right next to Mr. Hattori, a person who you'd never met before. You specifically decided to sit down next to a complete stranger, didn't you?"

Mr. Bando made sure that the incredulous tone of his question was obvious to everybody in the courtroom, and when he had finished asking it he stared straight at Mr. Tokuda with a look of complete astonishment written all over his face.

Mr. Tokuda began to appear annoyed.

"Well, why not?" he replied irritably. "It's nice to have somebody to chat with, isn't it? I felt like talking to somebody that evening. There's nothing wrong with that, is there? I like to talk to people when I go out to a bar in the evening."

As Mr. Bando and Mr. Tokuda were engaged in their verbal tussle, Judge Noda was watching the witness very carefully with an expression that she had carefully crafted over her many years in the legal profession. It showed the requisite authority and intelligence that was expected of a judge, while at the same time it did not reveal any hints about her own individual feelings and emotions.

"Earlier this morning," Mr. Bando continued, "you gave evidence to this court that you'd been talking to Mr. Hattori for about two hours before you claim that he made some remarks about the robberies of the cash machines, didn't you?"

"Yes," Mr. Tokuda replied sullenly, trying to regain some of his composure.

"And you yourself had been drinking throughout those two hours, hadn't you?"

"Yes."

"So by the time that you claim that Mr. Hattori said something to you about the cash machine robberies, you'd had a substantial amount to drink, hadn't you, Mr. Tokuda?"

"Well, it depends on what you mean by a substantial amount, doesn't it? I've said that I did have some drinks, but I wasn't drinking nearly as much as Mr. Hattori was. He had much more to drink than I did."

"My question concerns you, Mr. Tokuda, not Mr. Hattori. I'm asking you about how much you drank that evening. Is it not your testimony that you yourself had been drinking for at least two hours before you claim that Mr. Hattori brought up the subject of the cash machines?"

There was another pause before Mr. Tokuda answered.

"Yes."

"And by the time that you claim that Mr. Hattori spoke to you about the cash machine robberies, you'd both already moved from the counter to a table, hadn't you?"

"Yes."

"And by that time of the evening, were there more people in the bar compared with when you'd arrived at just before eight o'clock?"

"Yes."

"In fact, isn't it the case that by ten o'clock the bar could have been described as being very crowded?"

Mr. Tokuda shrugged again.

"Yes, I guess that you could say that."

"And the Pickled Cabbage bar had become very noisy, hadn't it, Mr. Tokuda?"

"Well, yes…it was noisy. At least it was noisier than earlier on in the evening."

"Does the Pickled Cabbage bar have a karaoke machine?"

Mr. Tokuda thought for a moment and then nodded.

"Yes, it does."

"How do you know that, Mr. Tokuda?"

"Well, I've heard people using it while I've been there."

"So when you're sitting in the bar, you can hear people singing on the karaoke machine, can you?"

"Yes, of course."

"And once the bar had filled up on the night in question, did any of the customers use the karaoke machine?"

"Well, I don't remember exactly."

"You don't remember?"

Mr. Tokuda frowned.

"Well, I guess there were some people singing songs, yes."

"In fact, Mr. Tokuda, wasn't there a line of people waiting for a turn at the karaoke machine?"

"Err…well, yes. That sounds quite possible."

"And you'd have been able to hear the music and the singing throughout the bar, wouldn't you?"

"Yes."

"And against the background chatter of the crowded bar, and against the noisy background music and singing from the karaoke machine, what exactly do you claim that Mr. Hattori told you about the robberies of the three cash machines, Mr. Tokuda?"

"He said that he'd carried out the robberies himself."

"What were his exact words?"

Mr. Tokuda laughed again.

"Well, I don't remember his words exactly! I mean, it was more than a month ago when it happened. You can't expect me to be able to repeat his exact words."

"Could you please try to paraphrase for the court exactly what you claim you thought you heard Mr. Hattori say to you?"

"All right…I'll do my best. Mr. Hattori leaned across the table towards me and he whispered something like 'You know those three cash machine robberies—I carried them out myself'. As I indicated, I don't remember his exact words after all of this time, but I'm quite certain that he did say something like that."

"So Mr. Hattori whispered to you, did he?"

Mr. Tokuda suddenly blushed.

"Well, when I say whispered, what I mean is that he lowered his voice a bit. Or at least he seemed to lower his voice a bit. I guess that it was the tone of his voice that changed more than anything else. He altered the tone of his voice and he began to speak in a sort of confidential manner."

"I see, Mr. Tokuda, because if Mr. Hattori had actually whispered to you, then in such a noisy environment you wouldn't have been able to hear him clearly, would you?"

"No, I guess not."

"You wouldn't have been able to hear Mr. Hattori clearly with all of that background noise in the crowded bar from all of the customers talking and drinking, and with the loud music coming from the karaoke machine, would you?"

"No. I meant that Mr. Hattori lowered his voice a bit and changed his tone when he boasted about the robberies that he told me that he'd committed."

"And you didn't mishear what Mr. Hattori said, did you, Mr. Tokuda?"

"No."

"How do you know that you didn't mishear what Mr. Hattori said to you?"

Mr. Tokuda looked confused, and he fidgeted with his flamboyant tie.

"Well, that's not a fair question! I mean…I heard what I heard, didn't I? I've told you what I heard Mr. Hattori say to me. I know that's what he told me."

The witness was fixed in Judge Noda's steady gaze.

"But after several hours of heavy drinking, and in such a noisy and boisterous environment, isn't it correct, Mr. Tokuda, that what you thought you heard may not be what Mr. Hattori actually said to you?"

Mr. Tokuda looked exasperated.

"Well…I don't think that you're right. I'm certain that I heard him tell me about the cash machine robberies, and I'm certain that he said 'I carried them out myself'. That's all that I can tell you."

"Is it possible that Mr. Hattori actually said 'I wish I'd carried them out myself'?"

Mr. Tokuda shook his head.

"No, he didn't say that."

"How can you be sure that he didn't say that?"

"That's not what I heard him say."

"But you gave evidence, did you not, Mr. Tokuda, that you and Mr. Hattori had been discussing how angry you both were with the banks for imposing penalties and fees on your accounts, and you gave evidence that Mr. Hattori seemed to feel that the cash machines robberies were some kind of revenge that he'd obtained?"

"Yes, I did. That's because I remember that Mr. Hattori told me that he didn't feel so bad about the banking fees that had been imposed on him because he'd managed to get his revenge by robbing the cash machines."

"Can you be absolutely certain, Mr. Tokuda, that Mr. Hattori wasn't simply saying to you, in this confidential manner that you've described, that because of his personal dissatisfaction with the manner in which he'd been treated by the banks, he wished that he'd carried out the cash machine robberies himself?"

"Well, that's not what I heard!" Mr. Tokuda cried out in frustration. "I heard Mr. Hattori tell me that he'd carried out the robberies himself!"

Chapter 10

▼

Along with everybody else who was present in the courtroom that morning, the Chief was captivated by the verbal wrestling match that was enfolding in front of him, and as he sat in the back row of the visitors gallery next to Inspector Morimoto and Police Officer Suzuki, he carefully followed every lunge of Mr. Bando's cross-examination and every parry that Mr. Tokuda defended himself with. And as Mr. Tokuda firmly stuck to his account of what he had heard Mr. Hattori tell him in the Pickled Cabbage bar that Sunday evening in April, Morimoto did not need the occasional nudge in his ribs and the approving wink from the Chief to know which side his boss was rooting for.

Mr. Bando waited thoughtfully in front of his desk for a few moments before approaching the witness once again.

"In your evidence, Mr. Tokuda, you stated that you left the Pickled Cabbage bar shortly after you thought that you'd heard Mr. Hattori admit to being the cash machine robber—am I correct?"

"Yes, that's right. I'd become a little tired by then, and I was ready to go home. It was quite late, anyhow."

"At the time when you left the bar, did you consider the possibility that Mr. Hattori might be the cash machine robber to be at all important information?"

"Well...yes. Of course the identity of the robber would be important information. The police have been searching for him for a long time, haven't they?"

"In that case, why didn't you contact the police as soon as you'd left the bar?"

"It wasn't that simple. I wasn't exactly sure what to do. I needed some time to think it over."

"You thought that you'd just heard somebody confess to having carried out three bank robberies, and you weren't sure what to do about it?"

"Well…I mean…it wasn't that straightforward…at least, at the time it didn't seem so straightforward. I was kind of shocked, I guess. I thought that I'd better sleep on the matter. But when I woke up the next day and thought about it again, I realized immediately that I ought to tell the police what I'd heard. And that's exactly what I did."

"So as you left the Pickled Cabbage bar that evening, you felt a sense of shock at what you thought Mr. Hattori had told you, did you?"

"Err…yes…in a way."

"And after leaving the Pickled Cabbage bar, you went directly home and went to bed, did you?"

"Yes, that's right."

"So the shock that you felt about what you thought that you'd heard in the bar didn't prevent you from going straight to sleep?"

"Well…no…not really. I must have thought about it a bit when I got home, I guess. But like I just told you, I was tired that evening and I didn't make up my mind what to do about it until the next morning."

Mr. Bando was staring at Mr. Tokuda sternly as he put his questions to him.

"Why did you decide to report the matter to the police?"

"Well, I thought that I ought to. Isn't that what anybody would do? I thought that it might be important information for the police to have. I guess that I must have come to the conclusion that it was my civic duty."

"So you went to the police out of a sense of civic duty, did you, Mr. Tokuda?"

"Yes, that's right. I did."

"And is that the only reason why you reported the matter to the police?"

Mr. Tokuda shrugged.

"Yes."

Mr. Bando waited for a short while before putting his next question.

"Are you aware that the Metropolitan Trust Bank has offered a reward to anybody who provides information that plays a significant role in leading to the conviction of the person or persons responsible for the cash machine robberies?"

Mr. Tokuda looked slightly embarrassed.

"Yes, everybody knows about that."

"And how do you know about the reward, Mr. Tokuda?"

"Well, there are signs all over the place announcing the reward. I've seen them in my bank, for example…and in the post office too, I think. And the reward's been mentioned in the newspapers and on the television as well."

"When did you first become aware that a reward was being offered in conjunction with these robberies?"

"Oh, I don't know. It was some time ago. I can't remember exactly when it was that I heard about the reward for the first time. It was probably some time in the early part of this year. Isn't that when the Metropolitan Trust Bank announced the reward? I think it was."

"So when you woke up on the morning after you'd been drinking in the Pickled Cabbage bar with Mr. Hattori, and as you began to recollect what you thought you'd heard him say to you, you were already well aware at that time that there was a very substantial reward being offered for any information that related to the cash machine robberies, were you not, Mr. Tokuda?"

Mr. Tokuda shrugged and laughed awkwardly.

"Yes, I knew about the reward at that time."

Mr. Bando raised the level of his voice very slightly.

"So, isn't it the case, Mr. Tokuda, that the thought of the large sum of money being offered by the Metropolitan Trust Bank had a very real influence on your interpretation of what you thought Mr. Hattori might have said to you in that noisy bar the previous evening after you'd been drinking there for several hours?"

Mr. Tokuda shifted around in his chair and shook his head.

"No…no…that's not true! I told you that I felt that I had an obligation to tell the police what I'd heard. I'm sure that anybody else would have felt the same way. We're all supposed to help the police fight crime, aren't we? I think that anybody in my position would have felt that the police should be told what Mr. Hattori had boasted about."

"Isn't it the case, Mr. Tokuda, that your account of what Mr. Hattori said to you in that bar that evening is a complete fabrication that you invented for the sole purpose of trying to get your hands on the reward money?"

Mr. Genda sprang to his feet.

"Objection, your honor! The defense is treating the witness in an inappropriately intimidating manner."

Judge Noda conferred briefly with her two advisors.

"The objection is sustained. Mr. Bando, would you please withdraw the question."

Mr. Bando had been fully aware that his last question would be challenged by the Public Prosecutor, and that the judge would in all likelihood uphold the challenge, but he also knew, along with everybody else in the courtroom, that he had managed to make his point to the judge that pecuniary motives may have had a very real effect on Mr. Tokuda's interpretation and account of what he had heard Mr. Hattori tell him in the bar.

Mr. Bando walked away from the witness back towards his desk.

"I do apologize, your honor. I withdraw my question, and I have no additional questions for this witness."

Judge Noda nodded.

"Very well. Thank you, Mr. Bando. This court will now be in recess until tomorrow morning."

The judge and her two advisors stood up and walked out through the door behind them, and the defendant was escorted away by the two policemen who had been sitting next to him throughout the proceedings. Mr. Genda spread out a large square cloth on his desktop and placed all of his papers and documents in the center of it. Then, after folding the corners of the cloth inwards and tying them together, he picked up his bundle, nodded an acknowledgement to Mr. Bando, and walked out of the courtroom as well.

The Chief lingered in the corridor outside the courtroom chatting with Morimoto and Suzuki for a while.

"Well, how about that?" he said excitedly. "That was an extremely good cross-examination from Mr. Bando, don't you think? It was very professional…very clever. I've come across Mr. Bando before on more than one occasion, and I can tell you that he's a very fine lawyer with an impeccable reputation…oh, yes, he is. There's absolutely no doubt about that. And he certainly demonstrated his talents this morning, didn't he? Mr. Hattori couldn't have found anybody better to defend him."

Morimoto and Suzuki nodded their agreement.

"But did you see the way that our chap stuck to his guns? He didn't budge one little bit, did he? It was fantastic! It was wonderful to see how he fended off those questions that Mr. Bando was firing at him from right, left and center. And I'm sure that the judge got the correct message, don't you think so? I'm sure that she can see that Mr. Tokuda is just an ordinary citizen who's trying to do his own small part to help us fight crime. Didn't it just make your heart melt when he explained that all he wanted to do was to help the police? Wasn't it just fantastic when he said that all he was trying to do was to simply perform his civic duty? It was wonderful stuff!"

The Chief did not seem to notice that neither Morimoto nor Suzuki were nodding any more.

"Our work would be a lot easier if everybody in Okayama were as solid a citizen as that young fellow is. Well anyhow, I'm off now. I've got to keep to my schedule and get back to Headquarters on time. I've another meeting arranged with Ms. Tsuda…she's going to give me a preliminary report on how our performance evaluations have been turning out. I can't wait to find out how things are going. What else do you have scheduled today, Morimoto?"

"Me, sir? Oh…err…numerous things. There's an overabundance of matters that need our attention."

"Jolly good! I'm glad to hear that you're keeping so busy. Well, good-bye then!"

After the Chief had hurried away, Morimoto and Suzuki headed off down the corridor themselves at a much more leisurely pace, and as they reached the top of the stairs, Mr. Bando came up behind them. Just like Mr. Genda, he was also carrying his papers tied up in a cloth, and he greeted Morimoto and Suzuki with a big smile. They all bowed and shook hands with each other.

"Hello, Inspector Morimoto! Hello, Officer Suzuki! What a pleasure it is to meet you both again so soon after you so successfully wrapped up that pottery case that we were all involved in."

"How are you, Mr. Bando?" Morimoto replied. "I trust that all's going well over at the Bizen Ceramic Art Museum? Are you and the other directors keeping busy?"

Mr. Bando laughed.

"Everything's been going very well recently, thank you. Things are definitely looking up for Bizen pottery. In fact, we have some wonderful special exhibitions lined up for this summer."

"Oh, really? I'm glad to hear that, Mr. Bando."

"I hope that you'll both have time to visit them."

"We most certainly will."

Mr. Bando lowered his voice.

"By the way, Inspector, I'm glad that I've managed to catch up with you because I was hoping to have a brief word with you. I noticed that you were present at the proceedings this morning, and I had a word with my client during the recess. And with his assent, I'm wondering whether I might impose upon you to attend a short meeting with Mr. Hattori—with myself present, of course. There are some very puzzling aspects to this case which I've a feeling that you and Officer Suzuki might find rather intriguing."

Chapter 11

After having made some arrangements with Mr. Bando to visit his client at the City Jail that afternoon, Inspector Morimoto and Police Officer Suzuki left the courthouse and walked off down the street in the midday sunshine. They headed westwards, and after several blocks they reached Nishigawa Park where they turned left so that they were walking southwards towards Okayama station.

"I hope that the Chief won't mind if we rearrange our carefully planned schedule so that we can enjoy a stroll in the park before lunch, Suzuki?"

"Hmmm…before Mr. Bando invited us to meet Mr. Hattori this afternoon, I wasn't aware that we did have anything else scheduled for today, sir."

"Ah…well that's one of the secrets of being a good detective, Suzuki. You have to give yourself plenty of time to think!"

"That's very wise, sir."

The Nishigawa River had served as a center of the Okayama community from very early times, and about four hundred years previously it had been fashioned into an irrigation canal that had provided drinking water to the city's inhabitants, as well as being a pleasant place for fishing and swimming. It had also served as a valuable source of water for some businesses, notably the cloth dyeing industry.

However, the canal's development into an oasis of greenery in the middle of modern day Okayama city had not been without some difficulties. Morimoto was well aware that the park owed its existence to the strength and foresight of one of the city's former mayors, who had needed to fight off strong pressure in order to prevent the canal from being paved over with concrete. Fortunately, the mayor's wisdom and vision had prevailed, and the canal had been turned into a spacious park that stretched almost two and a half kilometers through the city in a north-south direction.

After its construction, the park was soon recognized as an irreplaceable part of Okayama's green environment and it quickly became popular among all sectors of the community, serving as a play area for children and as a green haven for office workers whenever they were able to take a break from their work. Along with the city's other residents, Morimoto was justly proud of the park, and he knew that it was one of the many reasons why Okayama had received international recognition as one of the world's most livable cities.

As Morimoto and Suzuki strolled down the footpath on the eastern side of the canal, they admired the flower beds of bright yellow, red, and white tulips, and the boxes of decorative plants that resembled small purple and yellow cabbages. Along the way they passed a group of schoolchildren who were busily attending to some of the flower beds under the supervision of their teachers, as well as excitedly peering into the canal to watch the fat orange and white carp as they slowly swam upstream against the gentle current of the clear water. The trees that stood along the banks of the canal provided a canopy of shade for the children as their branches spread out over the water from either side and touched together in the middle.

Large black crows called out noisily from the trees, and several pigeons scurried along the path in front of Morimoto and Suzuki before flying off to settle on the pretty stone bridges that allowed access from one side of the canal to the other. Many members of the city's workforce had escaped from their offices for a lunch break, and they munched on their sandwiches and rice balls as they sat on the benches that were set out between the statues and monuments along the footpath, enjoying the quiet and making the most of the sunshine.

After an enjoyable twenty minute saunter through the park, Morimoto and Suzuki turned left next to a group of willow trees and crossed over a road to a small Italian restaurant that had an appealing lunch menu on offer. They were able to find an empty table in the corner, covered with a red and white checkered tablecloth that Suzuki found particularly attractive, and before long Morimoto was enjoying his spaghetti covered with a meat and tomato sauce, while Suzuki was making fast work of her own spaghetti that was mixed with olive oil, garlic, and a mass of small white chirimen fishes that were each no longer than the end of her fork.

The restaurant's clientele that lunchtime was comprised mainly of well-dressed young ladies in their twenties who worked as receptionists and helpers in the nearby offices, and as she ate, Suzuki kept her ears open for the snippets of conversation that drifted her way concerning their diets, their designer handbags, and their recent trips to Hawaii and Europe.

However, Morimoto's concentration was fully focused on his plate of spaghetti, and when he was about halfway through it he asked Suzuki about her impression of Mr. Tokuda's testimony. Suzuki pulled her mind back to the trial.

"Well, sir, overall I imagine that the judge will consider Mr. Tokuda to have been a generally credible and reliable witness. Mr. Bando did his very best to put some doubts into her mind about the authenticity of what Mr. Tokuda claims to have heard Mr. Hattori tell him, but I suspect that the judge will give more than a little weight to Mr. Tokuda's testimony."

"Yes, I believe that you're right, Suzuki. But if Mr. Tokuda is telling the truth, then isn't it just amazing what you can hear in a bar? Perhaps we should arrange to have some of our own police officers spend their evenings drinking in bars in order to see what they might overhear?"

"I imagine that's the way that a lot of them already spend their evenings, sir."

"Yes, that's a good point, Suzuki! And come to think of it, we shouldn't forget Mrs. Tanaka at the Sour Plum bar. She's just around the corner from the Pickled Cabbage bar, and she's particularly good at eavesdropping."

The former beauty queen, Mrs. Tanaka, owned the Sour Plum bar that was often frequented by elements of Okayama's criminal community, and she had provided Morimoto with some very useful information about their conversations on more than one occasion in the past.

"Anyway, Suzuki, Mr. Hattori is certainly going to deny ever having told Mr. Tokuda that he had anything to do with the cash machine robberies, and consequently, that part of the evidence will presumably end up simply being a case of one person's word against another. And with that in mind, Mr. Bando made sure that he didn't miss the opportunity to raise the possibility that Mr. Tokuda may have genuinely misheard what Mr. Hattori said to him."

Suzuki twiddled some spaghetti around the end of her fork.

"That's true, sir. And moreover, Mr. Bando also managed to raise the suggestion that Mr. Tokuda's role in all of this may be influenced by the reward money."

"And that's not too hard to believe, actually, considering the sum that the Metropolitan Trust Bank has offered. A sense of civic duty and having done one's job as a citizen are all very nice, but the reward money will pay the bills quite a long way into the future!"

"It certainly will, sir. Nevertheless, I'm sure that the judge will realize that even if Mr. Tokuda's decision to come forward with his information was motivated purely by a desire to get the reward money, that doesn't in any way invalidate his testimony. She may still assess Mr. Tokuda's account of what Mr. Hattori told him to be credible."

"You're quite correct, Suzuki. And in that case, it would seem as though Mr. Hattori has got some explaining to do if he's going to get himself out of this mess. And furthermore, it looks like Mr. Tokuda really is in line to receive that reward money after all."

"Yes, it certainly does, sir."

Chapter 12

Early that afternoon, Inspector Morimoto and Police Officer Suzuki arrived at the City Jail accompanied by Mr. Bando, and after they had all completed the signing in process at the reception desk, they were shown into a Spartan meeting room where they sat down and waited for Mr. Hattori to be brought in to them.

"Perhaps I should tell you a little bit about my client," Mr. Bando offered. "He's twenty-five years old, unmarried, and he lives all by himself. For the past five years he's been employed at a car assembly plant near Kurashiki, where he has an exemplary work record. I've been able to obtain some very complementary references from his boss and from some of his colleagues there—apparently he's a very competent and popular member of the workforce."

Morimoto nodded.

"I see."

"And he's never been in trouble with the law before—he has a completely clean record in that respect. I will, of course, be making it clear to the judge that his profile is quite unlike that of a typical bank robber."

At that moment there was a knock on the door, and a tall uniformed guard showed Mr. Hattori into the room. He was dressed casually in an open necked shirt, slacks, and comfortable athletic shoes, and he sat down at the table beside Mr. Bando. The guard informed Mr. Bando that he would be waiting outside the room, and he closed the door behind him as he left.

During the trial that morning, Morimoto and Suzuki had only been able to see the back of Mr. Hattori's head as he sat in front of the visitors gallery facing the judge, but now they were able to take a good look at him. He had an athletic physique with a slightly more muscular build than most men of his age, but he was of an average height. He had a full beard that stretched around both sides of his chin and up to his ears, and his face was tanned, although not surprisingly considering the circumstances, it revealed that he was very distraught.

"Ah, good afternoon, Mr. Hattori," Mr. Bando said cheerfully. "I'm sure that it must have been extremely difficult for you sitting there in court all morning. But don't worry—we'll have our turn as well before the trial is over."

"That Mr. Tokuda is a shameless liar!" Mr. Hattori muttered in disgust. "Isn't it obvious to everybody that he's setting me up just so that he can get his dirty hands on that reward money? What he said in court this morning was just ridiculous! The truth is that I never told him that I'd carried out the cash machine robberies, and in fact, we never talked about the robberies at all. He's making the whole thing up—what he said is a pack of lies. Can't everybody see that? I didn't carry out the robberies—I'm completely innocent."

"And that's what we're going to convince Judge Noda," Mr. Bando said in a reassuring tone. "Don't worry—we'll have our chance to tell the judge what really happened, and we're going to find a way to persuade her that you're innocent. Now, to help us do that, I'm pleased to tell you that I've invited along the two finest brains in the Okayama Police Department to meet you, Mr. Hattori—just as I said that I would when we talked in court this morning. This is Inspector Morimoto and this is Officer Suzuki. I think that it would be helpful if you let them ask you a few questions."

Mr. Hattori looked at Morimoto and Suzuki and managed a wan smile.

"Well, thank you for coming to meet me. I'll be more than happy to answer all of your questions. I don't have anything to hide—nothing at all. And it would be nice to be able to put forward my side of the story and to correct all of those lies that we heard in the courtroom this morning."

Morimoto leaned back in his chair and slowly rubbed his chin as he gazed back at Mr. Hattori.

"Well, good afternoon, Mr. Hattori. It's nice to meet you, and I'd be very interested to hear your version of the events that were covered in court this morning. So, where shall we start? Perhaps we should begin by going back to that evening in April when Mr. Tokuda says that he met you in the Pickled Cabbage bar?"

Mr. Hattori nodded.

"All right, Inspector."

"That was a Sunday evening, wasn't it?"

"Yes, it was."

"And you did go to the Pickled Cabbage bar that evening?"

"Oh, yes, I did. I'm not denying that."

"And you did talk with Mr. Tokuda?"

"Yes, I did, although I wish now that I'd never met that despicable character!"

"Do you often go out drinking on a Sunday evening, Mr. Hattori?"

"Well, yes, I go out to a bar almost every Sunday evening that I'm in Okayama. And I go out most Saturday evenings as well."

"Do you always go out alone?"

"Not always, no. I often arrange to meet my friends somewhere. It's more fun to go out with my friends from work."

"Had you arranged to meet anybody on the evening when you met Mr. Tokuda?"

"No, I hadn't. My friends were all busy that night with some other things that they had to do so I went out alone."

"I see. And do you often go to the Pickled Cabbage bar?"

"Oh, yes…that's one of my favorite bars. I go there a lot. I like the atmosphere they have, and the waitresses are nice too."

Suzuki was watching Mr. Hattori's face closely as he responded to Morimoto's questions.

"In Mr. Tokuda's testimony this morning," Morimoto continued, "he said that you were already in the bar when he arrived—is that true?"

"Yes, that part of what he said was true."

"So how long had you been there by yourself before Mr. Tokuda walked in?"

"Oh, I hadn't been there very long. I'd only been there for a short time before he arrived—maybe a couple of minutes, that's all."

"And as Mr. Bando established in his cross-examination this morning, Mr. Tokuda came and sat down right next to you at the counter, did he?"

"Yes, that's right. I was sitting up at the counter and he specifically came and sat down right next to me, and then he started talking to me. I have to admit that I was glad to have somebody to chat with, actually. And then he ordered a drink for himself and he bought me one too. And we ended up talking together the whole evening. We got on very well, to be honest with you. I have to say that at the time I rather liked him. He was good company. Of course, I didn't know then what I know now about him."

Morimoto stroked his chin.

"You hadn't met Mr. Tokuda before that evening then?"

"Oh, no—that was the first time that I ever met him. At least, I don't remember ever having met him before."

"I see. And you did move over to a table at one point in the evening, did you?"

"Yes, after about half an hour or so. Mr. Tokuda suggested that we'd be more comfortable at a table because the counter had become crowded."

"And is it true that Mr. Tokuda left the bar and went home first?"

"Yes, it is. He said that he was tired, and he left at about ten thirty. That part of what he said in his testimony was true."

"And you stayed in the bar by yourself after he left, did you?"

"Yes."

"How much longer did you stay?"

"Oh, well...let me see. Probably for about twenty or thirty minutes, I expect."

"So you must have left shortly before eleven o'clock?"

Mr. Hattori shrugged.

"That sounds about right, yes."

"And did you go straight home when you left the bar?"

"Yes, I did."

"You went straight back to your apartment at the Rising Sun complex?"

"Yes."

"I see."

Morimoto nodded slowly, and Mr. Bando smiled encouragingly at his client.

"Well then, Mr. Hattori," Morimoto continued, "while you were chatting in the bar with Mr. Tokuda, did you tell him your name at any point?"

"Oh, yes, I did. And I told him exactly where I lived and where I worked as well. Perhaps it was silly of me, but it just came out naturally in the conversation. I didn't think anything about it at the time. As far as I knew, I was just having a friendly chat with somebody over a drink. I probably told him about some of the problems that I was having with my landlord, and that's when I must have mentioned where I lived. And we chatted about the new car models that we're introducing at our factory, so that's how he'd have known where I worked."

"And did Mr. Tokuda tell you anything about himself?"

Mr. Hattori thought for a moment as he gently tugged on his beard.

"Yes, I think that he must have done. At least, I didn't get the impression that he was trying to hide anything from me. He told me his name anyway, and I remember that he talked about his work. It's something to do with computers, isn't it? That's what he said in court this morning, anyway. And he may have told me where he lived as well, but I'm not completely sure now."

Morimoto nodded again.

"I understand. Anyhow, the essential point, Mr. Hattori, is whether you discussed the cash machine robberies at all."

"No, we didn't!" Mr. Hattori replied adamantly. "We didn't discuss them at all! That's what Mr. Tokuda's lying about. In fact, that topic didn't come up in our conversation at all, and I certainly didn't say that I'd carried out the robberies. That's a ridiculous idea! I'm not the kind of person who goes around with a crowbar breaking into cash machines."

"Well, if you didn't discuss the cash machine robberies with Mr. Tokuda, did you perhaps discuss banks at all? Did the Metropolitan Trust Bank come up in your conversation at all?"

"No, I don't think that it did. I don't remember talking about banks with Mr. Tokuda at all. I'm pretty sure that what he said this morning about our having had a discussion about bank fees is just plain false. I'm almost certain that we didn't talk about that. I'm not particularly annoyed about my bank charges, anyhow. I might have had a few in the past, but I usually manage to avoid them by keeping my balance high enough."

Morimoto rubbed his chin.

"Hmmm...that's very interesting, Mr. Hattori. By the way, did you have much to drink while you were talking to Mr. Tokuda?"

Mr. Hattori frowned.

"Yes, I did. I have to admit that I did drink quite a lot. I was having a good time. But I didn't drink any more than I usually do—nothing very excessive, really. And Mr. Tokuda was drinking as well, although again, I have to admit that it's true that he wasn't drinking nearly as much as I was."

Chapter 13

▼

Inspector Morimoto and Police Officer Suzuki had been looking forward to hearing Mr. Hattori's version of what had happened in the Pickled Cabbage bar on the evening of his chance encounter with Mr. Tokuda, although, as it turned out, they were not at all surprised by his account of the events. And even though Mr. Bando was very familiar with what Mr. Hattori had to say, he still followed the discussion very carefully, ready to intervene and cut it off if the conversation ever appeared to be heading in a direction that might turn out to be disadvantageous for his client.

"Well, Mr. Hattori," Morimoto continued, "we've covered the incident in the Pickled Cabbage bar. The other evidence this morning related to the apparently incriminating items that were found buried inside the rice container in your kitchen. What can you tell us about the blue crowbar and the bank notes that were taken from the cash machine in Kotohira?"

"Somebody went into my apartment and put them there," Mr. Hattori replied angrily. "That's the only explanation. I didn't put them there."

"You do have a rice container in your kitchen, do you?"

"Oh, yes, I have a rice container all right. Doesn't everybody have one? But I've never ever hidden anything in it."

"Had you ever seen the crowbar and the bank notes before they were discovered in your rice container, Mr. Hattori?"

"Well, that's the thing, you see. I'd seen the crowbar before—they set me up with the crowbar—that was very clever of them. That's how they managed to get my fingerprints all over it. I fell for that, all right. But that's not my money, and I've never seen it before. Anyway, I wouldn't keep that amount of money lying around my apartment. Other than what's in my wallet, I don't keep any cash at home."

"I see. So how was it that you came across the crowbar before it was found in your kitchen?"

"Well, it was the same evening that I met Mr. Tokuda. It happened when I was on my way out of my apartment to go to the Pickled Cabbage bar. I opened up the door, and I found a package lying on the doormat outside in the walkway with my name written on it. So, naturally, I picked it up and took it back inside my apartment, and I opened it up. Surely, that's what anybody would do? And to my bewilderment, I found the blue crowbar inside. And as you can see, that's how my fingerprints got all over it. They tricked me, didn't they?"

Morimoto stroked his chin slowly.

"That's very interesting, Mr. Hattori. What kind of a package was it? Was the crowbar in a box?"

Mr. Hattori shook his head.

"No, it wasn't in a box. It was just wrapped up in brown paper and tape."

"And was there an address label or anything like that?"

"No, my name had just been written on the paper with a thick marker pen. They must have hand-delivered the package. There wasn't an address, and it didn't have any stamps on it or anything like that. It was just a plain brown paper parcel with my name written on the outside."

Morimoto nodded.

"You must have been quite surprised, I imagine?"

"Oh, yes I was! I didn't know what to make of it at all. If I knew then what I know now, I'd have called the police immediately. But other than being surprised that the package had suddenly turned up out of nowhere, at the time I wasn't really worried about it. So I just left the crowbar in my apartment and went off for a drink as I'd been planning to do. I thought that one of my friends from work might have left it for me, although I was quite puzzled by it."

"Whereabouts did you leave the crowbar in your apartment?"

"I left it on the table in my living room."

"And what about the brown paper that it had been wrapped in?"

"I left that on the table as well."

"I see. Do you happen to own a crowbar of your own, Mr. Hattori?"

"No, I don't have one. I wouldn't have any need for a crowbar at home."

Morimoto thought for a few moments, and there was a lull in the conversation. Just as before, Suzuki had been keeping a close eye on Mr. Hattori, but other than appearing to be angry and frustrated with the whole situation, he had not show any signs of having the slightest difficulty in answering Morimoto's questions.

"Well, that's very remarkable, isn't it?" Morimoto said eventually. "What do you make of that crowbar suddenly turning up on Mr. Hattori's doorstep, Suzuki?"

"Hmmm...it's quite fascinating, sir. But the bottom line is that Mr. Hattori's fingerprints were left all over the crowbar, as Dr. Jimbo pointed out in court this morning."

Mr. Hattori nodded.

"That's exactly right. I was tricked! If I ever find any strange parcels outside my door again, I'll be sure to put some gloves on before I open them up!"

Mr. Hattori made a rather unsuccessful effort to chuckle at his own humor, but Mr. Bando burst into hearty laughter, trying to raise his client's spirits.

"Ha, ha, ha! That's very funny! Maybe we should all remember that advice? But it certainly looks as though somebody went to some rather remarkable lengths to frame my client, wouldn't you say, Inspector?"

"Well, that's certainly a possible explanation for what's been going on here."

"That's the only explanation as far as I'm concerned," Mr. Hattori added.

Morimoto nodded.

"Yes, I quite understand. By the way, Mr. Hattori, how did you get from your apartment to the Pickled Cabbage bar that evening?"

"Oh, I walked. It only took me about fifteen minutes. And all the way I was puzzling over why somebody would have wanted to leave me the crowbar, and why they didn't knock on my door to give it to me personally. As I said, the only reasonable explanation that I was able to come up with was that it might have been put there by somebody that I work with who'd needed to leave in a hurry. That's why I was planning to ask my friends about it at the factory the next day."

"Did you mention the crowbar to Mr. Tokuda in the bar that evening?"

Mr. Hattori thought for a moment.

"No, I don't think that I did. I'm pretty sure that I didn't say anything to him about it. I'd have felt rather silly letting somebody know that I have crowbars turning up mysteriously on my doorstep."

"Yes, I see. And when you left the bar that evening at about eleven o'clock, how did you get back to your apartment?"

"Oh, I walked again—so I'd have been home by about eleven fifteen, I guess."

"And the crowbar and the wrapping paper were still on your living room table when you returned home, were they?"

Mr. Hattori shook his head and smiled sadly.

"No, they weren't! As I said, I left the crowbar and the brown paper in the middle of the table when I went off to the bar, but they were both gone when I returned home. That's why I can tell that somebody must have been in my apartment while I was at the Pickled Cabbage bar. And I think that must have been when they hid the crowbar in my rice container along with those bank notes."

"Well, in that case, why didn't you call the police immediately if you felt that somebody had been in your apartment?" Morimoto asked as he glanced at Mr. Bando.

"That's the other thing, you see. I probably would have called the police if I'd remembered about the crowbar, but the problem was that I'd forgotten all about it while I was out drinking. By the time that I left the bar, the crowbar had gone completely out of my mind, and I didn't even notice that it was missing when I got home."

Mr. Hattori looked despairingly at Mr. Bando.

"It may sound strange, I know," he continued, "but when I returned home from the bar and walked into my living room, everything looked quite normal to me. I'd forgotten about the package that I'd opened and left on the table. So I went straight to bed. I mean, it's not like I was used to seeing the crowbar on my table, is it? I only put it there just before I left to go off to the bar."

"And the next morning when I woke up and left for work, I still didn't remember anything about it. I only remembered about the package when I was at the factory that day. And then I became confused, because at first I was sure that I'd left it on my living room table, but I knew that it hadn't been there in the morning when I'd had my breakfast. So then I thought that I must have left it somewhere else. Anyway, when I went home that evening the police were already searching my apartment, and that's when all of this trouble started."

There was a long moment of silence as Morimoto and Suzuki digested this explanation from Mr. Hattori. Eventually, Mr. Bando spoke up.

"Don't worry, Mr. Hattori, you're going to have your chance to explain to Judge Noda everything that you've told us. You'll be able to tell her exactly how the crowbar was sent to you wrapped up in brown paper, and how it subsequently disappeared from your living room table."

Mr. Hattori frowned again.

"Well, to tell you the truth, I'm not sure that she's going to believe me," he replied miserably. "I know that it all sounds so ridiculous, but that's really what did happen."

"Well, you can be quite assured, Mr. Hattori, that we're not going to stop working on this until we've found a way to convince the judge of the truth, and to prove to her that you're innocent."

Mr. Bando patted his client on the back.

"Is there anything else that you'd like to ask Mr. Hattori, Inspector?"

Morimoto stroked his chin and nodded slowly.

"Yes, there is another very important matter that I'm rather curious about at this point. Do you wish to tell us where you were on the nights that the three cash machines were robbed, Mr. Hattori?"

Mr. Hattori glanced at Mr. Bando nervously, and he began to shift around in his chair uncomfortably.

"Well, that's rather awkward," he said quietly. "That's another problem, I'm afraid. I have to tell you that I was staying in Shingo, Takebe, and Kotohira on the exact nights when the robberies occurred there. I like to play golf, you see."

Chapter 14

The next morning, Friday, Inspector Morimoto and Police Officer Suzuki were sitting together in their office at the Police Headquarters discussing the previous day's court proceedings and their meeting with Mr. Hattori at the City Jail. A copy of the Okayama Tribune newspaper lay on the table in the middle of the office, and there was a column on the front page that had a report on the first day of the trial under the headline *'Prosecution Makes Strong Start in Cash Machine Trial'*.

Morimoto had already adopted his favorite thinking position, with his feet up on the corner of his desk and with his hands locked behind his neck.

"Well, Suzuki, what do you make of the trial up to this point? And how do you think Judge Noda will have read yesterday's events?"

Suzuki folded her arms and crossed her legs, and she too leaned back in her chair as she looked back at Morimoto.

"That's a very good question, sir. The newspaper reporter seems to think that Mr. Genda made a strong start to his case yesterday, and all things considered, I imagine that the judge feels exactly the same way as well."

"Yes, I agree with you."

"Mr. Genda has laid out several pieces of evidence, which taken together suggest that it may well be the case that Mr. Hattori really is guilty of having carried out the robberies. Mr. Genda is hoping to convince the judge that Mr. Hattori kept the crowbar that he'd used for the robberies hidden away in his kitchen, together with part of the stolen cash from the third robbery. In addition, he wants the judge to believe that Mr. Hattori became overly exuberant after drinking too much one night, and that he really did boast to Mr. Tokuda about what he'd done."

"Yes, and the case that Mr. Genda has been building is quite a reasonable one—everything seems to fit together nicely. Other than Mr. Hattori's own insistence of his innocence, there hasn't been anything so far to suggest that things didn't happen just the way that the prosecution is suggesting."

"That's right, sir. Mr. Bando tried to point out to us that his client's profile doesn't match that of a typical bank robber, but that in itself doesn't amount to much of a defense. And if you look at the historical records that we have for these kinds of crimes, it's apparent that all types of people have decided to have a go at robberies of one kind or another."

"That's true, Suzuki."

"Incidentally, sir, I did have a quick look into the details of Mr. Hattori's bank account, and he has had some typical fees and charges assessed, just like most people have. But of course, most people wouldn't consider that to be a sufficient reason for opening up three cash machines with a crowbar."

"No, they wouldn't, but I'm glad that you checked into that because Mr. Tokuda's testimony would have sounded remarkably odd if it had turned out that Mr. Hattori hadn't ever had any bank charges."

"That's what I thought, sir."

"So all things considered, there's no reason to doubt the possibility that Mr. Hattori is guilty as charged."

"Exactly, sir. But on the other side of the equation, we have to consider the possibility that Mr. Hattori is innocent, and that the tale he told us yesterday afternoon about having found a package containing the crowbar on his doorstep really is true. We'd then have to accept his claim that he forgot all about the crowbar when he returned home from his visit to the Pickled Cabbage bar, and that he didn't notice that it was missing from his living room table. Similarly, we'd also have to accept that fact that he didn't remember about it the next morning until he was busily working at his factory."

"Yes. It's not a totally implausible scenario for what might have happened, but I rather feel that Mr. Genda will be able to make it sound quite ridiculous when he gets the opportunity in court."

"Of course, sir, if Mr. Hattori really is guilty, then he'll have realized that he needed to come up with some kind of an explanation for why the crowbar and the bank notes were found in his kitchen, and what he told us yesterday may have been the best set of lies that he was able to cook up. After all, how many other ways are there to invent a plausible explanation for why the crowbar and the money were hidden in his kitchen, and the fact that his fingerprints were all over the crowbar?"

"Yes, Suzuki, that does require some rather imaginative thinking. But while it's certainly true that Mr. Hattori did look somewhat nervous and uncomfortable when he gave us that explanation yesterday afternoon, that may have been simply because he knew just how silly his explanation sounded. And after all, most people are pretty uncomfortable when they've being confined to the City Jail. But the essential point is that Mr. Hattori's account of what happened might be true, even though it sounds so bizarre."

"That's right, sir."

"Anyhow, a pertinent point here is that if Mr. Hattori really did carry out the three cash machine robberies, is it likely that he'd still have had possession of the crowbar?"

"Well, it would have been safer from his perspective to throw it away, I suppose. But maybe he was planning another robbery? Why stop at three? Perhaps he was keeping the crowbar for his next attempt? In any case, he may not have realized the full extent to which it linked him to the crimes, because he may not have been aware of the traces of blue paint that it was leaving on the cash machines."

"Yes, that's true—although it looks like he did go to some lengths to keep it hidden. In any case, if Mr. Hattori is the culprit and if he really is guilty as charged, then I doubt that even Mr. Bando with his considerable talents is going to be able to avoid a conviction in the trial."

"I agree with you, sir."

"But on the other hand, if Mr. Hattori is innocent, then the question remains as to whether Mr. Bando is going to be able to put forward sufficient evidence of his own to tilt the judge's opinion in his client's favor."

There was a moment of silence as Morimoto stared out of the window at the distant lines of clouds in the blue morning sky. Okayama was renowned for its clear sunny weather throughout much of the year, because even when the rest of the country was suffering from rain and heavy cloud cover, the mountains of Shikoku island to the south of Okayama and the air currents and air pressures that were consequently generated in the Okayama region often sheltered it from the bad weather.

"Anyway, Suzuki, from an unbiased and purely academic perspective, the possibility that Mr. Hattori is innocent is considerably more interesting than the possibility that he's guilty, don't you think?"

Suzuki nodded.

"Very definitely, sir, although I expect that the Chief may not agree because he's apparently very eager for a conviction in the trial."

"Yes, he made that quite clear yesterday."

"Nevertheless, regardless of the implications for the Police Department's reputation, there's no escaping the fact that the possibility of Mr. Hattori's innocence does raise some rather intriguing puzzles."

"It certainly does. And if Mr. Hattori is innocent, then I believe that we can assume that his account of a crowbar wrapped up in brown paper suddenly appearing on his doorstep out of the blue is quite accurate. If he's innocent, then there'd be no reason for him to have made up such a ridiculous story, as far as I can see. So what do you make of the crowbar's mysterious appearance on his doorstep, Suzuki?"

"The obvious implication, sir, is that somebody is out to frame Mr. Hattori, just as he kept claiming yesterday. The crowbar would have been left on Mr. Hattori's doorstep so that he'd handle it and leave his fingerprints all over it. And again, just as Mr. Hattori said yesterday, it seems that somebody really must have broken into his apartment before he returned from the Pickled Cabbage bar that evening and removed the crowbar from the living room table. It's entirely plausible that the intruder brought the bank notes along as well so that they could be hidden in Mr. Hattori's rice container along with the crowbar. And presumably, the intruder must have also taken the brown paper packaging away when he or she left the apartment."

"Exactly, Suzuki. And that would imply that the crowbar and the money were already hidden in Mr. Hattori's kitchen when he returned from the Pickled Cabbage bar on Sunday evening."

"Yes, it does, sir. Moreover, we can also deduce that whoever it was who broke into Mr. Hattori's apartment to do all of those things must have been connected in some way with the actual robberies, because otherwise, how would they have been able to obtain some of the money that was stolen during the third robbery in Kotohira?"

"That's a very important point."

"And on top of all that, if Mr. Hattori really is innocent, then we need to ask ourselves what exactly Mr. Tokuda's role is in all of this? If Mr. Hattori didn't carry out the cash machine robberies, then he surely wouldn't have boasted about having committed the crimes. And that implies that Mr. Tokuda's account of what he heard Mr. Hattori tell him in the bar is mistaken. And I suppose that there are two possible explanations that could account for that. One explanation, as Mr. Bando tried to suggest in his cross-examination of Mr. Tokuda yesterday, is that after several hours of drinking and with the noisy background of the crowded bar, Mr. Tokuda genuinely misheard what Mr. Hattori said to him."

"Yes, that's not altogether impossible, I suppose. But Mr. Hattori was quite adamant that they didn't talk about the cash machine robberies at all, so if we're to believe that it was a genuine mistake on Mr. Tokuda's part, then we have to conclude that he has some serious hearing problems. And furthermore, it would be a remarkable coincidence if a stranger in a bar mistakenly thought that he heard Mr. Hattori talk about the cash machine robberies, and thought that he heard Mr. Hattori admit to having carried them out, on the exact same evening that an intruder was hiding some bank notes from one of those robberies inside Mr. Hattori's rice container."

"That would indeed be a very peculiar coincidence, sir. And so, that leads us to the only other explanation, which is that Mr. Tokuda is purposely lying about what he claims to have been told by Mr. Hattori."

"Quite right, Suzuki. And why might he have decided to do that?"

"Presumably, so that we'd send somebody over to search Mr. Hattori's apartment—which is exactly what happened. Mr. Tokuda must have been expecting that we'd find the hidden crowbar and bank notes."

"Precisely. And consequently, we can deduce that Mr. Tokuda must have known that they were hidden there."

"That's absolutely correct, sir. And that in turn implies that Mr. Tokuda must be connected in some way with whoever broke into Mr. Hattori's apartment to hide the crowbar and the money, which also implies that Mr. Tokuda must be connected in some way with whoever really did carry out the three cash machine robberies."

"I agree, Suzuki."

There was another break in the discussion as Morimoto and Suzuki both reflected on the extraordinary idea that the witness whom Mr. Genda had presented in court the previous day might in fact be more closely connected to the crimes than the defendant himself.

"Well, Suzuki, there are a lot of questions that still remain to be resolved in this case, and paramount among them is the issue of why the true criminal or criminals suddenly decided to try to frame Mr. Hattori for their crimes, if Mr. Hattori is indeed innocent."

"Hmmm...that's a very fascinating question, sir."

Morimoto looked at his watch.

"Anyway, we ought to get a move on and hurry over to the courthouse right away. We'd better save our favorite seats before the visitors gallery fills up. I believe that this morning's session is going to be particularly interesting, because I'm sure that Mr. Genda's going to want to tell Judge Noda and the court all about Mr. Hattori's insatiable appetite for golf."

Chapter 15

The courtroom looked very similar to the previous day when Inspector Morimoto and Police Officer Suzuki took their seats in the back row of the visitors gallery slightly before ten o'clock. Just as on the first day of the trial, Mr. Hattori was sitting with his back to them chaperoned by two uniformed policemen, and over on the right Mr. Bando sat confidently behind his desk, dressed in another of his elegant suits that had been personally tailored from the highest quality cloth.

At the precise moment when the long hand on the clock behind Morimoto and Suzuki reached the vertical position, Judge Noda entered the courtroom with her two advisors, and without any delay she reopened the proceedings and invited the Public Prosecutor to continue with his case.

Mr. Genda stepped out from behind his desk carrying a pile of papers.

"If it pleases your honor, I'd like to distribute these documents to the court."

Judge Noda nodded her assent, and the court assistant hurried over to Mr. Genda to collect the documents, which he then distributed throughout the courtroom.

"Thank you very much," Mr. Genda continued. "Now if you'll look at the first page, your honor, you'll see a copy that I've had made of the logbook at the Resort Club Golf Course in the town of Shingo. I'd like to draw your attention to the date, your honor, which is the Saturday in August of last year when the cash machine robbery occurred in that town. And in addition, your honor, please notice that the defendant, Masuhiro Hattori, has signed the logbook at 11:20."

Mr. Genda paused to let the judge study the document for a few seconds before he continued.

"And on the next page, your honor, you'll find a copy of a hotel registration card from the Green Forest Hotel and Spa in Shingo, which confirms that the defendant stayed at that hotel on the same Saturday night in August of last year. The registration card clearly shows the defendant's name and his signature."

Judge Noda turned to the next page and studied the information that Mr. Genda had referred to.

"And furthermore, your honor," Mr. Genda continued, "the next two documents that I've provided you with show that the defendant played golf at the Takebe Green Golf Course and lodged at the Takebe Hot Springs Hotel on the Sunday in November of last year when the cash machine in the town of Takebe was broken into."

After he had allowed the judge enough time to look through these pages, Mr. Genda concluded his description of the documents.

"And finally, your honor, I've provided you with a copy from the logbook of the Rolling Hills Golf Club in Kotohira, and a copy of a hotel registration card from the Kotohira Hot Bath Inn. These documents demonstrate that the defendant played golf and stayed in Kotohira on the exact Saturday night in February of this year when the cash machine was broken into in that town."

Mr. Genda walked back to his desk and put down his papers, and there was a murmur from some of the members of the press corps seated in the front row of the visitors gallery, which Judge Noda quickly silenced with a stern stare.

"So in summary, your honor, these documents establish that the defendant was lodging in each of the three towns where the robberies occurred on the nights when the robberies occurred."

Mr. Genda reached down and sorted through some of the other papers on his desk.

"In addition, your honor, I would like to draw you attention to the statement that the defendant gave to the police, in which he indicated that he was in the habit of playing golf once a month with his friends. And at the end of the documents that I have just handed out to you, you'll find a list of the golf courses where the defendant has played going back to the beginning of last year. You'll see, your honor, that there's one golf course listed for each month of last year, together with the golf courses where the defendant played between January and April of this year. I've also indicated the dates that the defendant played golf at each of those locations."

Mr. Genda paused again while Judge Noda looked through the list of golf courses that she had been given.

"Of course, your honor, the golf courses listed for the months of August and November of last year, and the golf course listed for February of this year, are the ones to which I referred earlier, and for which I've provided you with copies of the logbook entries made by the defendant when he signed in at the course. Those are the courses in Shingo, Takebe, and Kotohira in which we will be particularly interested. I would also like to let you know that I also have copies of the defendant's registrations at all of the other golf courses that are shown on your list, and I'd be happy to provide your honor with those copies should your honor wish to see them."

Judge Noda nodded as she finished looking through the final page of the documents and settled back in her chair.

Mr. Genda walked back out into the center of the courtroom again.

"And now, your honor, I'd like to introduce my next witness."

The court attendant led a man in his early sixties into the courtroom, who sat down in the witness chair behind the small table in the middle of the room. He was wearing a light gray suit with a dark brown tie, and he calmly looked up at the dais where the judge and her two advisors were sitting. When he had been sworn in, Mr. Genda turned to address him.

"Could you please state your name for the court records?"

"Ah, yes…I'm Professor Kazuo Shirane," the witness replied with a smile.

"Thank you, professor. And where are you employed?"

"Err…I'm on the faculty at the Osaka Science University."

"And how long have you been employed there, professor?"

"Oh…let me see…it's been more than thirty years now," Professor Shirane replied and smiled again.

"And what specific academic fields do you specialize in at the university, professor?"

"I'm a mathematician, and I'm particularly interested in the area of probability theory."

"Thank you. And do you teach classes as part of your work at the university?"

"Yes, that's right. I teach classes in introductory probability theory, and I also teach several classes in advanced level probability."

"And you teach both undergraduate and graduate students, do you, professor?"

"Yes, that's correct."

"And you also conduct research into mathematics and probability, do you not?"

"Yes, I do."

Professor Shirane smiled again.

"Could you briefly describe your research activities for the court, please, professor?"

"Well, I study probability theory, and I identify unsolved problems, and I try to work out solutions to those problems. And when I've developed some news ideas and have produced some new results—when I've constructed some new theorems, for example—I write them up into research papers and I publish them in our mathematical research journals. And as part of my research activities I also attend conferences and give lectures on my work, and I discuss my new research ideas with my colleagues and I learn about their work as well."

"So I believe that it should be quite apparent to this court, Professor Shirane, that you can be described as being a participant in the frontiers of new research in the area of probability theory."

"Yes, I am," Professor Shirane replied with another rather immodest smile.

"And you yourself are actually the editor of one of those research journals that you referred to, are you not, professor?"

"Yes, I am."

"And what does that work entail, professor?"

"Well, other mathematicians from other universities and research institutions around the world send me the research papers that they've written, and I'm in charge of the evaluation process which determines whether the papers are accurate and substantive, and whether they are worthy of publication in the journal."

"Thank you very much. And you have spent several years as the head of your department at the Osaka Science University, haven't you, professor?"

"Yes, that's right. I served a spell as head of the mathematics department for five years."

"Thank you."

Mr. Genda looked up at the judge.

"Based on the very impressive academic record of Professor Shirane, your honor, I present him to the court as somebody who can provide expert testimony in the area of probability theory."

Chapter 16

As Mr. Genda introduced his expert witness on probability theory to the courtroom, Inspector Morimoto turned and whispered to Police Officer Suzuki in the back row of the visitors gallery.

"Well, Suzuki, this testimony ought to be right up your street. Mind you, I hope that the professor realizes that he's got a mathematics graduate from Tokyo University sitting behind him who'll be scrutinizing his every word. You'd better listen carefully, Suzuki, and make sure that he's done all of his sums properly."

Suzuki nodded.

"Absolutely, sir."

"I hope that you took a class in probability theory?"

"Oh, I did, sir—it was great fun."

Having established the credentials of his witness, Mr. Genda embarked on the main part of the testimony that he wanted Judge Noda to hear.

"Now, Professor Shirane, I've asked you here today to explain to the court what the theory of probability can tell us about the locations of the defendant's golf games with regards to the three cash machine robberies. And I do need to stress to you, professor, that I for one am nowhere near as clever as your students at the Osaka Science University when it comes to mathematics and probability!"

Mr. Genda laughed modestly.

"And so I hope, professor, that you'll endeavor to explain the concepts very slowly and simply for us all in layman's terms, so that we'll all be able to follow along and understand exactly what it is that you wish to tell us."

"Yes, of course I will," Professor Shirane replied with a patronizing grin.

"Thank you very much, professor. So could you please explain to the court what your analysis of the defendant's golf games has revealed?"

"Yes, I'd be very happy to do that. And please be sure to interrupt me if I start going too fast for everybody. The first step in my investigation was to look through the list of golf courses that Mr. Hattori has visited. He's played at a different course every month, and I was given a list of the courses where he's played. The list covered every month of last year and the first four months of this year. And when I examined it, I noticed that the golf courses were either in Okayama prefecture or in Kagawa prefecture, just over on the other side of the Seto Inland Sea."

Mr. Genda nodded as he stood and listened attentively to the explanation that his witness was giving the court, although he himself was perfectly familiar with Professor Shirane's testimony since the two of them had rehearsed it together several times the previous afternoon.

"Now it turns out," Professor Shirane continued, "that in the whole of Okayama prefecture there are 55 golf courses, and in addition there are 22 golf courses in Kagawa prefecture, so that when you combine those two sets together you get a grand total of 77 golf courses in these two prefectures all together, and I then asked myself the question…"

"Err…just a moment…excuse me, professor," Mr. Genda interrupted. "If you don't mind, I'd like to stop you there for just a moment and ask you to tell the court how you found out the number of golf courses in Okayama prefecture and Kagawa prefecture that you used for your calculation."

"Oh, yes…of course. What I did is, I simply contacted the Japanese National Golf Association and they told me."

"Thank you, professor. And those 77 golf courses that you mentioned are all eighteen hole courses that are open to any member of the National Golf Association, aren't they?"

"Yes, they are."

"So that means that any member of the National Golf Association, such as the defendant, would be able to play at any one of those 77 courses—is that right?"

"Yes, that's exactly right."

"Thank you, professor. I'm sorry to have interrupted you. Please continue with the explanation that you were giving us of your analysis."

"Oh, that's quite all right. Well, as I was saying, I began to think about how Mr. Hattori might have decided where he was going to play golf each month, and I decided that the simplest model to explain that with would be to assume that each month he chose a golf course at random from the list of those courses where he hadn't already played."

Mr. Genda jumped in again.

"Err...I heard you use the word 'model' there, professor. Perhaps not all of us are quite familiar with what you mean by that word?"

"Oh, yes. Well, when I say model, I'm actually referring to a mathematical model...err...or in other words, to a set of rules. Let's just think of it as a set of rules...err...perhaps that would be the easiest thing."

Professor Shirane smiled at Mr. Genda.

"Thank you, professor—I think that I've got it now," Mr. Genda said.

However, since the whole courtroom was perfectly well aware that Mr. Genda obviously had a very good understanding of the testimony that he was allowing his witness to present, everybody knew perfectly well that Mr. Genda was really hoping that Judge Noda was following what his witness was saying.

"So you decided to establish a set of mathematical rules that you could then use to understand how Mr. Hattori had decided on the venues of his golf games, did you, professor?"

"Yes, that's the basic idea. And what I'm saying is that a simple set of rules for explaining how Mr. Hattori might have selected a new golf course each month would be to say that it was randomly selected from a list of courses where he hadn't played recently. And based on that simple set of rules, I performed an analysis that showed how unlikely it would be for Mr. Hattori to have been playing golf in the three towns where the robberies occurred at the exact same time that the robberies occurred there."

"Yes, and that's the crucial point of your testimony, isn't it, professor? You're going to show us just how extremely unlikely it is that the defendant's golf locations could have matched each of the cash machine robbery locations if that coincidence had arisen purely by chance."

"Yes, that's precisely what my analysis has shown."

Morimoto could only see the back of Mr. Hattori's head so he was not able to judge his reaction to Professor Shirane's testimony, but he could see that Mr. Bando was staring at the witness with a completely blank expression.

"Well, professor," Mr. Genda continued, "please could you explain to the court how you performed your calculation."

"Yes, I'd be happy to do that. Let's start off with the month of August of last year when the robbery occurred in Shingo. There's one golf course in Shingo, so what's the probability that Mr. Hattori played at the Shingo golf course in August of last year? Well, it's 1 out of 77. There are 77 possible golf courses that he could have chosen, and if we assume that he chose a course at random with each of those courses being equally likely, then it's clear that there's a probability of 1 out of 77 that he happened to be playing in Shingo in August, which is when the robbery occurred there."

Mr. Genda glanced at the judge.

"Yes, I think that we can all see that," he said. "You're simply saying, are you not, professor, that there are 77 golf courses where the defendant could have been playing in August of last year, and so the chance that he happened to be playing in Shingo, which is where the cash machine robbery occurred, is just 1 chance out of 77?"

"That's precisely correct. It's very elementary probability theory."

"Thank you, professor. Please continue with the explanation of your analysis."

"All right. The next thing that I did was to take the month of November of last year, which is when the robbery occurred in Takebe. And exactly one of the 77 golf courses is in Takebe, so I asked myself what would be the chance that Mr. Hattori happened to be playing in Takebe in November just by chance? And the answer is 1 out of 76."

"Ah...you said 1 out of 76 there, professor, and not 1 out of 77 like you had in August. Why is that?"

"Oh, it's quite simple, really. Our model says that...err...that is to say that our set of rules stipulates that Mr. Hattori wouldn't choose to play at the same course twice...at least not at two time points...err, months...that are reasonably close together. So since Mr. Hattori played at the Shingo course in August, we assume that he didn't want to play at the Shingo course again in November, which left him with a choice of 76 courses where he could play in November. And consequently, the chance that he actually selected the Takebe course is 1 out of 76."

"Yes, so that's the chance that Mr. Hattori would have played at the Takebe golf course in November if he'd selected the venue of his golf game completely at random."

"That's correct, yes."

"So, what you've told us so far, professor, is that there's a 1 in 77 chance that the defendant would have played golf in Shingo in August, and in addition, there's a 1 in 76 chance that he'd have played golf in Takebe in November. But isn't it important to know what would be the chance of both of those events having occurred together?"

"Yes, it is. And we can calculate that probability by multiplying the two individual probabilities together. Now, when 77 is multiplied by 76 the number

5,852 is obtained, and therefore the probability that Mr. Hattori would have played golf at Shingo in August and at Takebe in November just by chance is 1 out of 5,852."

"Ah...I see, professor. And you multiplied those two individual probabilities together to get the final answer because that's the correct way to carry out the probability theory, is it?"

"Yes, that's right. Again, it's an application of very basic and elementary probability theory."

"Thank you, professor. And did you extend your analysis to include the defendant's golf trip to Kotohira in February of this year which is when the cash machine robbery occurred there?"

"Yes, I did. In dealing with Kotohira I used a probability of 1 out of 75, since Mr. Hattori had 75 possible choices for his golf course in February if the Shingo and Takebe courses are discounted, and only one of those courses is in Kotohira. That's how you get a probability of 1 out of 75. And just as before, if you want to calculate the probability of all of the three events having happened together, that individual probability needs to be multiplied by the previous probabilities. The final answer that you get is 1 out of 77 multiplied by 1 out of 76 multiplied by 1 out of 75, which is a probability of 1 out of 438,900."

"All right, professor. Let's stop there for a moment."

Mr. Genda had been keeping a close eye on the judge as Professor Shirane presented his probability calculations, and he decided that it would be a good time to summarize his witness's testimony and the favorable implications that it had for the case that he was attempting to build against Mr. Hattori.

"Am I correct in saying, professor, that what you're telling this court is that if the defendant's golf trips had been arranged completely at random, then the probability that he'd have played golf in Shingo, Takebe, and Kotohira during the exact same months that the cash machine robberies occurred in those three towns is only 1 chance out of 438,900 chances?"

"Yes, that's exactly what this part of my analysis has shown."

"And 1 chance out of 438,900 chances is a very small probability, wouldn't you say, professor?"

"Yes, it is."

Chapter 17

Inspector Morimoto and Police Officer Suzuki had both been paying very close attention to the testimony of Mr. Genda's expert witness on probability theory, and as far as Morimoto could tell, Judge Noda appeared to be completely unfazed by the mathematical derivations that were being presented in her courtroom. Furthermore, if Mr. Bando felt a growing sense of alarm at the potentially damaging implications of the testimony for his client, then he was managing to conceal it very well as he sat at his desk with an attitude that suggested that he did not have a single care in the whole world.

Mr. Genda waited for a few moments before continuing with his questions, so as to allow Judge Noda to digest the full force of Professor Shirane's testimony up to that point, and during the pause Professor Shirane sat back in his chair and straightened his thin wispy hair.

"Well, professor, your testimony so far this morning has addressed the issue of where the defendant played golf in the key months of August and November of last year, and February of this year. But in addition to that, you've also performed an analysis of the actual days within those months when the golf games took place, haven't you?"

"Yes, I have."

"Could you describe that analysis to the court now, please?"

"Yes, I'd be happy to do that. I looked again at the records that I'd been given of Mr. Hattori's golf games, and I noticed that they all took place on either a Saturday or a Sunday. In about half of the months Mr. Hattori played golf on a Saturday, while in the other half of the months he played on a Sunday. So what I said to myself is this. For simplicity's sake, let's say that there are four weekends in a typical month, which gives us 8 days that are either a Saturday or a Sunday. Actually, some months may have more than 8 weekend days, but for our purposes it's sufficient to consider that there are just 8 days. And I then applied the model…or the set of rules, as we're saying…that Mr. Hattori would have randomly chosen any one of those 8 days for his golf game. That implies that each of those weekend days has a chance of 1 in 8 of being the day on which Mr. Hattori played golf."

"Okay, professor, so just to make sure that I understand what you're doing now—that would be the same idea that we used before when we said that there'd be 1 chance out of 77 of playing on a particular golf course if there were 77 golf courses to choose from. Now we have 8 weekend days to choose from, so each of those days has 1 chance out of 8."

"Yes, that's exactly right."

"Thank you. Please proceed, professor."

"Well, if we start off by taking August of last year, we can say that there's a probability of 1 out of 8 that Mr. Hattori played golf on the exact same day of the month that the robbery occurred. And similarly, the same is true for November of last year and February of this year—in each month there's a probability of 1 out of 8 that Mr. Hattori's golf game took place on the exact same day as the robbery."

"I see, professor. So now you're not concerned with the locations of the defendant's golf games, you're only concerned with the timing of the golf games within the months, am I right?"

"Yes, that's right."

"Well, when we were talking about the locations of the golf courses earlier in your testimony, you combined the three individual probabilities into one overall probability by multiplying them all together. Can we do a similar thing here with respect to these probabilities concerning the timing of the golf games?"

"Yes, we certainly can. And since 8 multiplied by 8 multiplied by 8 is equal to 512, we get an answer of 1 chance out of 512."

"Thank you, professor. So are you saying that if the defendant scheduled his golf games at random among the weekend days within the three months of interest, then there is only 1 chance out of 512 chances that he'd have played golf on the three days when the cash machine robberies occurred?"

"Yes, that's quite right. That's exactly what I'm saying."

"So when we look at the locations of the defendant's golf games, we arrive at a probability of 1 chance out of 438,900 chances for the match with the robberies, and in addition, when we look at the timing of the defendant's golf games, we arrive at a probability of 1 chance out of 512 chances for the match with the robberies, don't we?"

"Yes, we do."

"Now, professor, what if we're interested in both the location and the timing? Can we combine those two probabilities?"

"Yes, we can. As I explained before, we have to multiply the two probabilities together."

"And what do you get when you perform that calculation, professor?"

"Well, if you multiply 438,900 by 512 you get 224,716,800. And consequently, the final answer is a probability of 1 chance out of 224,716,800."

"I understand, professor. And for all practical purposes we could round that up to a chance of 1 out of 225 million, couldn't we?"

"Yes, that would be sensible."

"Thank you."

Mr. Genda paced in front of his desk for a moment and passed his hand through his bushy hair as he considered how best to summarize the testimony for the judge's benefit.

"So, professor, after your detailed analysis based on your expert knowledge of probability theory, are you telling the court that if the defendant had randomly selected the times and the places of his golf games, then the probability that he would have played in the three towns of interest on the exact same days as the cash machine robberies is only 1 chance out of 225 million?"

"Yes, that's my testimony to this court."

"And I don't think that we need to be clever enough to be on the faculty of a leading university like yourself, professor, to be able to understand that 1 chance out of 225 million is an extremely unlikely event, isn't it?"

Professor Shirane laughed.

"It's a very small chance."

"Thank you, professor."

Mr. Genda walked over to his desk and picked up a book.

"This is a detective story that I happen to be reading at the moment," he said with a smile. "I'm rather fond of them, actually. Anyway, as you can see it's a typically sized paperback with about 200 pages. Good stories like this one have at least 60 thousand words, which is an average of about 300 words per page. If that's the case, professor, how many copies of this book would I need to pile up in order to have a total of 225 million words?"

"Well, you can get that answer if you divide 225 million by 60 thousand, which turns out to be 3,750."

"So if I somehow managed to stack 3,750 copies of this book in this courtroom, then there'd be about 225 million words in the books all together, would there?"

"Yes, there would."

"So we could get a good feeling for how small the probability of 1 chance out of 225 million is by thinking about the chance of selecting one word out of a pile of 3,750 copies of this book, could we, professor?"

"Yes, that would be a very good way to think of it. For example, suppose that I chose one word from one of the books without telling you which one it was. Would you be able to guess which word I'd chosen? You'd have to be unbelievably lucky. First of all, you'd have to be lucky enough to correctly guess which of the 3,750 books I'd used to select my word. Then, in addition, you'd have to correctly guess which of the 200 pages my word was on. And on top of all that, you'd then have to correctly guess which of the 300 words on the page I'd chosen. I don't think that any of us would fancy those odds!"

"And those are the odds that the defendant's golf games would have coincided with the cash machine robberies just by chance, aren't they?"

"Yes, they are."

"If the defendant's golf games had been scheduled at random without any connection to the robberies, then those are the odds that they would have provided the exact match that they did?"

"Yes, that's right."

"So, as an expert in probability theory, do you therefore conclude, professor, that the contention that the exact match between the defendant's golf games and the robberies arose purely by chance, is a contention that is just so completely unlikely that it cannot reasonably be believed?"

"Yes, that's precisely what I would conclude."

"Thank you very much, professor."

Mr. Genda turned triumphantly towards the judge.

"I have no further questions for this witness, your honor."

Judge Noda conferred with her two advisors for several moments before peering down in Mr. Bando's direction.

"Do you have any questions for this witness, Mr. Bando?"

Mr. Bando stood up and walked out across the shiny floor into the center of the courtroom.

"Yes, I do, your honor."

Judge Noda conferred with her two advisors again.

"Well, I think that this court has had all of the mathematics that it can digest for one day, so we'll be in recess until Monday morning. Your cross-examination of this witness can take place first thing on Monday, Mr. Bando."

Chapter 18

▼

Early that afternoon, Inspector Morimoto and Police Officer Suzuki were back in their office at the Police Headquarters discussing the events that had unfolded that morning in Mr. Hattori's trial. Suzuki walked over and handed Morimoto a cup of hot green tea, and as he cradled it between his hands he lifted his feet up onto the corner of his desk.

"Well, Suzuki, Mr. Hattori seems to be in somewhat of a sticky position based on this morning's evidence, wouldn't you say? I'm pretty sure that those odds of 225 million to 1 must have made quite an impression on Judge Noda. And I'm sure that Mr. Genda has managed to plant in her mind the idea that Mr. Hattori was using his golf trips as some sort of a camouflage for his robberies."

"Yes, I believe that you're correct, sir," Suzuki replied as she sat down at her desk with her own cup of tea.

"So let's take a look at those golf trips of Mr. Hattori a little more carefully. The first robbery occurred in Shingo, didn't it? That's up in the mountains in the northern part of Okayama prefecture."

"Yes, that's right—it's a small town nestled in the Chugoku Mountains. You can get there by train on the Hakubi Line, for example. From Okayama you first go to Kurashiki, and then you head north past Takahashi and Niimi. And also, it's just next to one of the highways if you want to drive there."

"And the robbery was last August, so I imagine that the town must have been packed with holidaymakers enjoying the summer weather up there at that time."

"I would expect so, sir. I looked Shingo up on my computer to find out some information about the town. Its basic population is only several thousand, so it's quite a small place, but it's a popular holiday destination so its population must swell quite considerably in the summer. It has a golf course, as we know, and it's well located for all of the usual mountain activities like hiking and sightseeing. It's also well provided with hotels and other lodging facilities, and there are a couple of campgrounds in the vicinity as well."

"And it has some hot springs, hasn't it?"

"Yes, sir, which must add to its popularity. Mr. Hattori stayed at the Green Forest Hotel and Spa, so he presumably enjoyed the hot baths there."

"Hmmm...it sounds nice, doesn't it?"

"It does indeed, sir. And incidentally, Shingo is a popular winter sports destination as well—there are several ski slopes in that area that attract a lot of visitors during the winter months."

"I see."

Morimoto sipped his tea.

"Well, Suzuki, what a lovely setting to carry out a robbery. What did the police report say?"

"I have a copy of it here on my desk, sir, but they didn't really come up with anything particularly interesting."

Suzuki looked through the report.

"It says that the damage to the cash machine wasn't discovered until after dawn on the Sunday morning, and so the robbery could have occurred at any time during the night. The cash machine was fairly close to the center of the town, which apparently would have been pretty much deserted at nighttime. The hotels and campgrounds are mostly situated around the edge of the town. Anyway, the bottom line is that the local police weren't able to come up with any clues or any other information about what happened."

"No, I'm not surprised. Still, I suppose that Mr. Genda's going to try to convince the judge that Mr. Hattori could have slipped out of his hotel room in the middle of the night with a crowbar, extracted the money from the cash machine, and then returned to his hotel room without anybody in the sleepy little town being any the wiser."

"I'm sure that's what he has in mind, sir."

"Yes, undoubtedly so. Well, what about the second robbery, Suzuki?"

"That was in Takebe, sir. It's much closer to Okayama, and you can get there by train on the Tsuyama Line that runs along the side of the Asahi River, or again you can easily reach it by highway if you're driving. It's another town that's popular with tourists, but it's in a river valley this time. Its website highlights the fishing opportunities and its display of cherry blossoms in the spring. There are some pottery workshops around there as well, and just like Shingo it also has some hot springs."

"Does it really? This cash machine robber certainly chose his locations well, didn't he? I'm starting to feel like a soak in a hot spring myself. How large a place is Takebe?"

"It's just a small town, sir, but it's a little bit larger than Shingo. Apart from the golf course, there are some museums and several other tourist attractions, and it's a good place for hiking as well. And just like Shingo, there's a good selection of hotels and restaurants for the tourists. The robbery was in November, though, which I expect is not during its peak season, but I imagine that there still must have been quite a few visitors enjoying the hot springs."

"Yes, I would think so. And did the police report of the Takebe robbery come up with anything interesting?"

"Nothing at all, sir. This time the robbery occurred on a Sunday night, but again it wasn't discovered until dawn of the next day. In fact, the only noticeable thing about the crime is its remarkable similarity to the robbery in Shingo earlier that year."

"Yes, there's an obvious pattern—small quiet tourist towns in the countryside, and isolated cash machines in the middle of the night. In each case the person responsible for the robbery must have known that there'd be very little likelihood of anybody witnessing the crime. And of course, the similarity of the two crimes suggests that the same person or organization was responsible for both of them, although a copycat robbery is not out of the question."

"No, it's not, sir. The Shingo robbery might have given somebody else the idea for the Takebe robbery."

"Exactly. Anyway, the pattern of those two robberies was continued in the third robbery in Kotohira, wasn't it?"

"Yes, it was, sir. Kotohira is in Kagawa prefecture on the island of Shikoku, of course, but apart from that the robbery was similar to the two previous robberies in Shingo and Takebe in many respects. Again, Kotohira is easily accessible by train and road, and it's a major tourist attraction because of the famous Kompira shrine."

"Yes, that's right. So in addition to the seasonal tourists, the town must be full of people on pilgrimages all year round, I imagine."

"That's exactly right, sir. Kompira is one of the most revered shrines in Shikoku, and so Kotohira is fairly crowded at any time of the year. The shrine is renowned for housing the deities that protect sailors. Anyway, Kotohira is another reasonably small town close to the mountains with all of the usual tourist facilities, like the golf course where Mr. Hattori played, and it's also another hot spring location."

"I see. But this time the local police were able to come up with much more from their investigation, weren't they?"

"That's right, sir. This time there was a witness."

Suzuki picked up another of the files from her desk and flicked through it.

"I have the Kotohira police report here as well, sir. This robbery occurred on a Saturday night in February, and that evening a Mr. Yosano reported seeing a masked man with a crowbar taking the money out of the cash machine. It was just after one o'clock in the morning when the police were contacted, and they reached the scene within a few minutes. The robber got clean away, though. Mr. Yosano works as a sushi chef in one of the hotels in Kotohira, and according to his statement he was on his way home when he came across the robber."

"Yes, I remember. And isn't it true that the masked robber didn't have time to remove all of the money from the cash machine because he was interrupted by the sushi chef?"

"That's correct, sir. There was still some cash remaining in the machine when the police arrived."

Chapter 19

Inspector Morimoto got up from his desk and inspected the teapot on the tray in the middle of the office. Finding that it was still half full, he took it over to Police Officer Suzuki's desk and topped up her teacup, and after replenishing his own teacup as well, he returned the teapot to its tray and sat down again, lifting his legs up onto the corner of his desk.

"Well, Suzuki, you'd better give me your opinion of Professor Shirane's probability lecture this morning. Were his arguments mathematically sound?"

Suzuki took a sip from her teacup.

"Yes, sir, his arguments were basically very solid. Overall, I thought that he did a very good job of convincing Judge Noda that it's rather inconceivable that Mr. Hattori just happened by chance to be playing golf and staying in the exact same locations as the three robberies when they occurred. There's a perfect match between the times and the locations of Mr. Hattori's golf trips and the robberies, and Professor Shirane successfully demonstrated that it's very hard to believe that such a perfect match could have arisen purely by chance."

"Yes, I agree with you. I think that the professor's testimony must have made quite an impression on Judge Noda."

"I'm sure that it did, sir. If one had to, one could argue about the exact number that Professor Shirane came up with. For example, one might challenge the assumption that there were 77 golf courses that Mr. Hattori could choose from, because maybe he doesn't like some of the courses, or maybe he's not eligible to play at some of the courses, or maybe some of the courses are always fully booked up at the weekends a long time in advance. In that case, there may be less than 77 golf courses in Okayama prefecture and Kagawa prefecture from which Mr. Hattori could have selected his venue."

"Yes, I see what you mean."

"But on the other hand, I suppose that you might also argue that Mr. Hattori could have traveled to some of the other nearby prefectures besides Kagawa prefecture for his golf games, and that would mean that the calculations should include the golf courses in those other regions as well."

"Yes, that's a good point as well."

"So with that in mind, there is some leeway for Mr. Bando to dispute the exact odds of 225 million to 1 that Professor Shirane produced. But even so, no matter how you look at it, you still have to face the fact that it's very difficult to conceive of the exact match between the robberies of the cash machines and Mr. Hattori's golf games having arisen purely by luck. It's very difficult to believe that it was a purely random event."

"You're absolutely correct, Suzuki, and I'm sure that Mr. Genda can be quite confident that Judge Noda has taken that message on board."

"Yes, sir."

"But even so, there's still an interesting matter which needs to be considered, which is the extent to which the miniscule odds that Professor Shirane presented in the courtroom this morning imply that Mr. Hattori actually committed the robberies, or that he even knew anything about them."

Suzuki nodded.

"Ah…now that's a key point, sir, and that's ground that Mr. Genda didn't cover at all this morning. The truth is that we need to be very careful how we interpret the implications of Professor Shirane's testimony. What the court learned is that it's pretty much impossible for the perfect match between the golf games and the robberies to be attributable to a fluke chance. So in other words, Mr. Genda has established that there had to have been some kind of a connection or relationship between Mr. Hattori's golf games and the robberies."

"Yes, at least that's what he hopes he's managed to convince Judge Noda. But what kind of a connection might there be?"

"Well, the obvious answer is that Mr. Hattori used his golf trips as an opportunity to conduct some nefarious activities with a crowbar in the middle of the night on the local cash machines, and that Mr. Hattori is guilty as charged. That's the conclusion that Mr. Genda hopes that Judge Noda will come to."

"So in other words, the simplest explanation for why Mr. Hattori's golf trips matched the robberies is that he carried out the robberies during his trips."

"Precisely, sir. However, there are some other possible explanations that we ought to consider. For example, perhaps Mr. Hattori had some golf partners, and perhaps the robberies were conducted by one of his companions? Maybe the robberies were committed by one of Mr. Hattori's friends who accompanied him on the three golf trips to Shingo, Takebe, and Kotohira?"

"That's entirely possible, Suzuki. But then why would the crowbar and the bank notes have turned up in Mr. Hattori's kitchen?"

"Well, sir, as we deduced before, if Mr. Hattori is innocent then the informant Mr. Tokuda must be in cahoots with some other people who are trying to frame him. It's possible that Mr. Tokuda has teamed up with one of Mr. Hattori's golf partners who is actually the real figure behind the robberies."

"Yes, Suzuki, that's certainly a plausible explanation for what might have happened."

"Furthermore, sir, we should also consider the possibility that there's another set of events which has generated the link between the golf games and the robberies. For example, just for the sake of argument, let's suppose that each of the towns holds its annual festival on one weekend a year. Well, it may be the case that Mr. Hattori planned his golf games for those weekends so that he'd be able to enjoy some of the festivities during his visit. And maybe, completely independently, the robber decided that those weekends would be a good time to break into the cash machines because he expected that there'd be large crowds that he could blend in with, and because he hoped that the police might be preoccupied with all of the other activities that were going on. So as you can see, the match between Mr. Hattori's golf games and the robberies is then easily explained by the fact that they were both independently coordinated with this additional set of events."

"Ah, that's very clever, Suzuki. So what you're saying here is that there could be a very reasonable explanation for why Mr. Hattori's visits to the three towns coincided exactly with the robber's visits to the three towns. Both Mr. Hattori and the robber might have coordinated the timing of their visits with some other set of events, like the town festivals, for example."

"Yes, that's the general idea, sir. The important point is that if that's the case, then Professor Shirane's calculation becomes invalid because Mr. Hattori wasn't really selecting the venues of his golf games at random."

"Yes, I see what you're saying. So have you checked to see whether anything special was going on in Shingo, Takebe, and Kotohira on the days when Mr. Hattori played golf there?"

"I've had a quick look, but I haven't been able to come up with anything yet. There don't appear to have been any special events going on that coincided with the dates that we're interested in."

"Hmmm...well nevertheless, the idea that the golf games and the robberies might both be connected to a third set of events is an interesting explanation. Perhaps we should drop a hint along those lines to Mr. Bando? He might appreciate the tip. I've a feeling that he must be finding it rather difficult to come up with some good material for his cross-examination of Professor Shirane."

Suzuki smiled.

"That may very well be true, sir."

"Maybe you should drop by his office and lend him a hand? I'm pretty sure that there aren't any courses in probability theory in the law school curriculum, so he may find the topic more than a little perplexing. Anyway, are there any other explanations for this suspicious linkage between Mr. Hattori's golf games and the robberies that have occurred to you?"

"Well, we also ought to consider the possibility that the robberies were carried out by somebody who was not involved with Mr. Hattori's golf games, but who knew where the golf games were taking place."

"Yes, I see. So now you're raising the idea that the real criminal monitored where Mr. Hattori played golf, and then chose the locations of his robberies accordingly. And in that case, surely the real culprit must have been intending to frame Mr. Hattori for the crimes all along."

"Exactly, sir—it would certainly appear so. It could have worked like this. Let's suppose that the real robber decided that he or she wanted to break into some cash machines, and that they also knew about Mr. Hattori, and that for some reason they wanted to be able to make it look as though Mr. Hattori were the real criminal. So the real robber could have learned where Mr. Hattori was planning to go on his golf trips, and where he'd be staying overnight in the hot spring hotels. And then, whenever Mr. Hattori visited what the robber considered to be a suitable location, which is presumably a small town out in the countryside, the real robber could have gone there and carried out the robbery while Mr. Hattori was soundly asleep in one of the nearby hotels."

"That's a very interesting possibility, Suzuki."

"And then the real robber could have broken into Mr. Hattori's apartment and left the incriminating crowbar and the bank notes. And as you can see, even though Mr. Hattori is completely innocent, the robber's nasty scheme has enabled Mr. Genda to put together quite a convincing case against him."

"Yes, it has indeed. But if what you're saying is true, then what does it imply about the relationship between Mr. Tokuda and the real robber?"

"Well, I think that it implies that either Mr. Tokuda is the real robber, or that he must at least know the real robber, because he appears to be part of the plan to frame Mr. Hattori."

"Yes, I agree. But according to this theory, the real robber must be somebody who knew Mr. Hattori and who decided to frame him for the crimes. Why do you think that anybody would want to frame Mr. Hattori?"

"That's a very good question, sir. Perhaps we ought to have another chat with Mr. Hattori so that we can ask him whether he has any enemies who might be responsible for all of this?"

"Yes, that sounds like a sensible idea, Suzuki."

Morimoto stared out of the window at the afternoon sunshine for a while.

"You know, Suzuki," he said eventually, "if Mr. Hattori is guilty of these crimes, then it wasn't very clever of him to commit the robberies in these little towns on the exact same nights that he was staying there. That would appear to have been rather imprudent, wouldn't it?"

"That's a very good point, sir. I suppose that it's possible that Mr. Hattori might have thought that nobody would ever cross-check the hotels records of the three towns, and that nobody would ever discover his presence in the vicinity of all three of the crime scenes."

"That's not impossible."

"After all, let's not forget that nobody discovered the match until Mr. Hattori had been identified by Mr. Tokuda and the crowbar and bank notes had been discovered in his kitchen."

"That's very true, Suzuki."

"Anyway, who knows? Perhaps the fact that Mr. Hattori's actions seem so unwise will be part of Mr. Bando's defense? Perhaps Mr. Bando will simply turn to the judge and say 'Come on, your honor, surely you don't think the defendant is so stupid that he committed the robberies while he was checked into hotels in these three towns?' I wonder what Judge Noda's reaction would be to that?"

"Hmmm...well for Mr. Hattori's sake, I hope that Mr. Bando's got more up his sleeve than just that argument when the time comes for him to present his defense."

Chapter 20

▼

A short while after Inspector Morimoto and Police Officer Suzuki had concluded their assessment of the implications of Professor Shirane's testimony, Morimoto was gazing out of the window deep in thought when there was a tap on the door and Ms. Tsuda stepped into the office.

"Err...excuse me...are you Inspector Morimoto and Officer Suzuki?" she asked.

Morimoto swung his legs down from his desk.

"Yes, that's right, Ms. Tsuda. Good afternoon. How can we help you?"

"Good afternoon to you both. Actually, I was hoping that I might be able to arrange an interview with you sometime as part of the review that we're conducting of the Police Department."

"Oh, yes! Great! Wonderful! Please do come in and sit down, Ms. Tsuda, and make yourself comfortable. We've been looking forward to our chat with Tsuda Business Solutions, haven't we, Officer Suzuki?"

"We certainly have, sir."

Ms. Tsuda sat down at one of the desks in the middle of the office, next to Suzuki's desk.

"I had one of my junior staff members penciled in to conduct your interview next week," she said, "but I was just talking with the Chief a moment ago, and he asked me to take care of your interview personally."

"Oh, did he really?" Morimoto said quietly. "How very thoughtful of him. I wonder why he came up with that idea?"

Ms. Tsuda smiled.

"Well, I do recall him saying something about you being one of the most valuable detectives in the whole Police Department."

"Ah, did he really say that? Well, that was very kind of him. But on the other hand, I rather fear that he's singled us out for your personal services, Ms. Tsuda, because he probably has a strong suspicion that we need much more help getting ourselves properly organized than everybody else around here."

Ms. Tsuda laughed at this remark.

"Well, I'll be glad to give you any suggestions and advice that I can, Inspector."

"That's very good of you, Ms. Tsuda."

"Well then…err…when would be a good time for us all to sit down and have a talk?"

"Well, why not right now, Ms. Tsuda? We'll be glad to rearrange our schedule to accommodate you, because as I said, we've been looking forward to getting some input from you. Can we fit Ms. Tsuda in for half an hour now, Officer Suzuki, and push everything else back a little bit?"

Since Suzuki was well aware that they did not have anything else scheduled that afternoon, it did not strike her that this would be much of a problem.

"Err…let me check, sir."

Suzuki typed away at her computer for a moment.

"From what I can see, sir, the rearrangement of our schedule shouldn't be too much of a problem. We should be able to manage half an hour without too much difficulty."

Morimoto clapped his hands together.

"Perfect! Is that all right with you then, Ms. Tsuda?"

"Oh, yes, that's just fine. Would it be all right if I…err…perhaps just moved this tray to one side so that I could put my briefcase up on the desk?"

"Oh, the teapot? Yes, sorry about that…just move it out of your way. Incidentally, can we offer you a cup of tea and a chocolate biscuit, Ms. Tsuda?"

"No, thank you. Since we've got a lot of ground to cover in only half an hour, we don't want to waste any time."

"Ah, that's very wise, Ms. Tsuda. Officer Suzuki and myself are of exactly the same mind when it comes to wasting time—we hate wasting even a second, don't we, Officer Suzuki?"

"Oh, there's nothing worse, sir."

"I'm glad to hear that," Ms. Tsuda said, opening up her notebook. "And perhaps it would be a good idea then if we start off by going over your…"

"By the way, Ms. Tsuda, has anybody brought up the issue of the Judo Team's need for a new minibus with you? Sergeant Yamada has mentioned the issue to us on several occasions. Next time you're talking to the Chief, perhaps you could recommend to him that it would be a great way to improve morale?"

Ms. Tsuda looked surprised.

"A new minibus for the Judo Team? That's not something that I'm particularly concerned about."

"Oh, I see."

"Now, as I was saying…"

"So how long have you been in the business of management consultancy, Ms. Tsuda?"

Now Ms. Tsuda looked annoyed.

"Oh, for well over twenty years, in one way or another. I started my own company about ten years ago. Anyway, I wanted to ask you about…"

"That's a very valuable area to be working in. It should be clear to anyone who considers the matter properly that getting our businesses organized and operating efficiently can only benefit everybody in the long run. Isn't that right, Officer Suzuki?"

"Definitely, sir. After all, better management means better service and lower prices for the consumer in the long run."

"It does indeed. By the way, Ms. Tsuda, do you ever come across much opposition from management when you conduct your reviews of their operations? What sort of reactions do you generally find they have to the advice that you offer them?"

Ms. Tsuda stared firmly into Morimoto's face.

"There are a lot of interesting topics that I'd be glad to discuss with you, Inspector, when we have more time. But right now I'd like to discuss your time management procedures. Is that all right with you?"

"Yes, of course," Morimoto replied quietly.

"Thank you. Well then, do you use a rigid system of time management, whereby you stick firmly to your schedule in all circumstances, and if your business turns out to be unfinished within the allotted time frame you address that problem by scheduling an additional session in the future? Or do you perhaps prefer a more flexible system, whereby you allow your work to extend beyond the allocated periods, and you then make suitable adjustments to your schedule to compensate as a consequence?"

Morimoto's eyebrows shot up.

"Ah...yes, Ms. Tsuda...I'm glad that you've raised that point about our philosophies of time management. I've...err...been hoping to have the opportunity to discuss them with you, as I've told you. Err...let's see now. To tell you the truth, Officer Suzuki and I have had several fascinating debates about what really is the optimal method of time management...err...since as you are only too well aware, Ms. Tsuda, it is such a vital issue in today's busy world, with all of the hustle and bustle of modern life. In this office we fully appreciate the importance of establishing a proper set of time management principles. As a matter of fact, we've experimented with several different options, and...err...at the end of the day...err...that is after careful consideration...err...what we decided is this. Actually, would you like to describe our time management policies to Ms. Tsuda, Officer Suzuki?"

This time Suzuki's eyebrows shot up.

"Oh, I'd be delighted to, sir."

Ms. Tsuda turned around to look at Suzuki.

"When it comes to time management," Suzuki said calmly, "in this office we're convinced that the best option for us is a multi-task search algorithm."

Ms. Tsuda looked very pleased, and she started scribbling energetically in her notebook.

"Oh, I say...how interesting! A multi-task search algorithm. Well done! I'd better take some careful notes on this strategy. It sounds very impressive. So let me see. You're multi-tasking—that's carrying out several different tasks simultaneously—and you're also carrying out some kind of a search routine among the different tasks in order to optimize your efficiency amongst them, are you?"

"Well...err...no, not exactly," Suzuki replied. "Actually, what we do is we search for multiple people who we can give our tasks to."

Chapter 21

Early the next morning, Saturday, Inspector Morimoto and Police Officer Suzuki were sitting again in the Spartan meeting room of the City Jail accompanied by Mr. Bando, who was showing them the copy of the Okayama Tribune that he had brought with him. There was another full column on the front page with a report on Mr. Hattori's trial under the headline *'Odds Heavily Stacked Against Defendant in Robbery Trial'*.

"The professor's testimony yesterday seems to have made quite an impression on the reporters," Mr. Bando remarked as he folded up the newspaper and placed it in his briefcase. "That's why I have to admit that I was rather glad when you got in touch with me and asked to have another chat with my client. I hope that you'll be able to find out something significant about his golf games that will portray all of these probability calculations in a different light."

At that moment the door opened and Mr. Hattori was brought into the room by one of the guards. He sat down next to Mr. Bando with a truly glum expression on his face.

"Good morning, Mr. Hattori," Mr. Bando said cheerfully after the guard had left the room and closed the door. "How are you today? Inspector Morimoto and Officer Suzuki wanted to come back and ask you some more questions. We need to get to the bottom of this business concerning your golf games, and they're the perfect people to help us."

Mr. Hattori shook his head.

"Well, I don't mind telling you whatever you like about my golf games, but I don't think that it's going to do me any good. The odds of me being acquitted in this case seem to have grown quite remote, haven't they? I'm sure that the judge must have been influenced by that professor's testimony yesterday. We might as well all just give up."

"Now, that's completely the wrong attitude to take, Mr. Hattori," Mr. Bando replied, and he gave his client a reassuring pat on the back. "It's very important that we all remain positive. Don't forget that I still have my cross-examination of Professor Shirane when the trial resumes on Monday morning. We've still got a very good chance of putting some substantial dents in his testimony."

Mr. Hattori shrugged.

"All I can say is that the people who have set me up have done a very good job of it. I have to admit that. I've been racking my brains trying to think of who could be behind all of this, but I really have no idea at all who it is. As far as I know, I don't have any enemies. I can't think of anybody who'd want to do this to me."

"Well, the important thing is to convince Judge Noda that you've been set up, Mr. Hattori. And in order to do that we need to conduct our own analysis of your golf games, and Inspector Morimoto and Officer Suzuki are going to help us. What would you like to ask Mr. Hattori about his golf trips, Inspector?"

Morimoto leaned back in his chair and looked across the table at Mr. Hattori.

"Well, perhaps you could just start off by giving us some general information about your golf games. Was Mr. Genda's basic information about your golf trips accurate or not?"

"Oh, what Mr. Genda told the judge yesterday about my golf trips was absolutely correct," Mr. Hattori said in despair. "I can't deny any of it. There's a group of us from my factory who like to play golf, and as Mr. Genda pointed out, our arrangement is that we play once a month. And we also like to play at a different course each time so that we have some variety."

"I see. So how many of you typically go on these golf trips, Mr. Hattori?"

"Oh, it varies. Some months there are only two or three of us, but I remember that one month ten of us went together. But that was a bit unusual. Most of the time there are maybe about six of us who will make the trip."

"And you said that there's a golf trip every month?"

"Yes, that's right—there's one trip organized each month. In the winter we have to be careful about the weather—we have to find a place where there isn't any snow, of course. But so far we've always been able to find somewhere to play."

"Have you ever missed a trip yourself, Mr. Hattori?"

"Not recently. Not for about two years, in fact. I'm one of the regulars. I enjoy the trips and I've been on every one of them for the past two years."

Morimoto nodded.

"I see. Well, how do you all decide where you're going to play each month?"

"Oh, we take it in turns to organize and arrange the trips. Each month one of us is responsible for finding out how many people want to play, for choosing a course, and for making the booking. And the person in charge is supposed to coordinate the travel arrangements as well."

Morimoto rubbed his chin slowly.

"Have you ever been in charge of making the arrangements yourself, Mr. Hattori?"

"Oh, yes, I'm often in charge. Since I'm one of the regulars, I've been in charge several times. I organized the trip in March of this year, and I was the organizer twice last year as well."

"Did you arrange any of the trips to Shingo, Takebe, and Kotohira where the robberies took place?"

"No, I didn't—and I hope that the judge understands that point. I didn't select any of those locations. They were selected by one of the other players. That's important, isn't it?"

"Yes, it may be," Morimoto agreed, although he really was not at all sure that it would help Mr. Hattori very much in the eyes of Judge Noda.

Mr. Bando nodded encouragingly.

"We'll certainly make sure that Judge Noda is made well aware of that point," he said.

"Anyway," Morimoto continued, "what guidelines did the organizer have when it came to choosing a location for a particular month's golf game?"

Mr. Hattori shrugged.

"Well, it was pretty much up to whoever was in charge. Obviously, we didn't want to travel too far, so the venue had to be somewhere that we could all get to and come back from within a day, because some players made a day trip of it. But on the other hand, some of us liked to stay overnight, so it was also nice to find a course in an interesting place, like a resort town."

"So you've played all over Okayama prefecture have you?"

"Yes, pretty much all over—and we've often played in Kagawa prefecture as well, as that professor pointed out in court yesterday."

"I see. So how did you all travel to the golf games?"

"We either went by car or by train, depending on the location."

"Did you all travel together?"

"Not always, no. Sometimes we've gone in separate cars, or sometimes some people have driven while others have taken the train."

"Incidentally, when you played in Shingo, was there anything special going on in the town at that time? A festival perhaps? Or something else like that? Was there any particular reason why you decided to play golf in Shingo at that time?"

Mr. Hattori looked surprised.

"No...not as far as I know. At least, I can't remember there being any special reason why we went there. I doubt that there was a festival going on. I'm sure that we'd have noticed if there had been one. Why? Is that important?"

"Oh, it's nothing really. It's just an idea that we were working on. And I don't suppose that there was anything special going on in Takebe and Kotohira when you visited those two places either, was there?"

Mr. Hattori shrugged.

"No, I don't think so. At least, I don't know of anything."

"I see. And on those three trips—to Shingo, Takebe, and Kotohira—you did stay overnight in the towns after your golf games, didn't you, Mr. Hattori?"

"Yes, I did. But I usually stayed overnight on the trips. It wasn't just in those towns that I stayed for the night. Whenever we played on Saturday, I liked to take the whole weekend away—I enjoyed the break. And sometimes when we played on Sunday, I'd still stay in a hotel on Sunday evening if it wouldn't make me too late getting back to the factory on Monday morning. I really enjoy the hot springs hotels, you see. Whenever we played on a course close to some hot springs, I always stayed the night if I possibly could. It's wonderful soaking in the hot water after a day out on the golf course, and that's the main reason why I spent the night in Shingo, Takebe, and Kotohira—they all have excellent hot springs."

"Did any of the other players in your group like to stay overnight as well after the golf games, Mr. Hattori?"

"Some of them did, yes. Others liked to get home to Okayama as soon as they could, but there were often two or three of us who'd stay for the night—sometimes more."

"Well, what about when you stayed in Shingo, Takebe, and Kotohira? Did you stay by yourself, or did some of your golf friends stay with you?"

"Well, I've been thinking about that point while I've been sitting here in jail, and the answer to your question is that there were several of us who stayed together in Shingo and Takebe, but I stayed all by myself in Kotohira."

"I see. Can you remember how many other people there were who stayed with you in Shingo and Takebe?"

"Yes, I can. There were four of us who stayed in Shingo, including myself that is, and three of us who stayed in Takebe."

"And you all stayed at the same hotel, did you?"

"Yes, we did—a spa hotel."

"Did you share rooms or did you each have your own room?"

"We always had our own rooms, but we ate together and we sat around drinking together at night."

Suzuki was watching Mr. Hattori intently as he responded to Morimoto's questioning.

"How late at night did you stay up? Do you remember?"

"Well, on occasions we might have stayed up quite late, but I'd always have been in bed before midnight. And I suppose that's a problem, isn't it? I mean, I don't see how I can prove that I was in my hotel room for the whole night. I suppose that Mr. Genda's going to tell the court that I slipped out of the hotel in the early hours of the morning and sneaked off to demolish the cash machine with a crowbar that I'd brought along with me in my overnight bag."

"Hmmm...well he may not find it quite so easy to convince the judge of that," Mr. Bando said. "There are many issues that we're going to want to raise with regards to that suggestion, Mr. Hattori. We'll raise a strong objection to the idea that it would have been possible for you to get out of the hotel, and back inside, in the middle of the night without anybody having seen or noticed you."

Chapter 22

Inspector Morimoto and Police Officer Suzuki could see that in spite of Mr. Bando's repeated attempts to encourage him, Mr. Hattori did not appear to be at all reassured, and he continued to sit lethargically with a disconsolate look on his face.

"I'm wondering whether the two friends of yours who stayed with you in the hotel in Takebe also stayed overnight in Shingo as well?" Morimoto asked.

Mr. Hattori thought for a moment.

"One of them did," he replied. "There was one other person who stayed overnight both in Shingo and in Takebe, besides myself. He's a nice fellow, though—I'm sure that he's not responsible for the robberies, if that's what you're thinking."

"I see. And after all, he didn't spend the night in Kotohira as well, did he?"

"No, he didn't go on the Kotohira trip in February. Actually, there were only three of us on that trip."

"And you said that you stayed by yourself in Kotohira, so the other two players must have returned home after the game was over, did they?"

"Well, no, I don't think they did."

"Oh?"

"As far as I can remember, they were going to stay somewhere, I think, but I'm not sure exactly what they did."

"But I thought that you told us that you usually all stayed together at the same hotel?"

"Yes, that's right—we usually did. But on that trip to Kotohira things turned out differently because I hadn't been intending to spend the night there. You see, what happened was that on that particular Saturday, the day when the three of us went to Kotohira to play golf, one of my old school friends had a birthday party arranged in the evening. The party was supposed to be in a restaurant in Kurashiki, and I wanted to attend it, so I told my golf partners that I wouldn't be able to stay with them in Kotohira. So after we'd finished our round of golf, I said goodbye to them and got in a taxi to go back to the station. We'd all taken the train to Kotohira that morning, you see."

Suzuki was watching Mr. Hattori very carefully.

"As I said," Mr. Hattori continued, "I remember that the other two chaps were planning to spend the night somewhere around Kotohira in one of the hot spring hotels, but I'm not sure exactly what their plans were because I'd been expecting to return for the birthday party. But the thing is, just as my taxi reached the railway station in the center of Kotohira, I had a call on my phone telling me that the party had been cancelled at the last moment because my friend had got the flu, or something like that, and he wasn't feeling at all well."

Mr. Hattori shrugged.

"So there I was at the station in Kotohira wondering what to do, and since there was no longer any reason for me to have to return to Okayama straightaway, and since I enjoy the hot springs so much, I decided on the spur of the moment to spend the night in Kotohira. So I simply stayed in the taxi and asked the driver to take me to a hotel."

Morimoto stroked his chin slowly.

"That's very interesting, Mr. Hattori. So in the end, you spent the night all by yourself at a hotel in Kotohira, did you?"

"Yes, that's right. And that's rather unlucky, don't you think, because that's the night when the cash machine was robbed there! If it hadn't been for the fact that my friend became ill and needed to cancel his birthday party, I'd have been back in Kurashiki and Okayama that evening. And then nobody would have been able to accuse me of robbing the cash machine because I'd have had a cast-iron alibi."

"Yes, I see…I see."

Morimoto thought for a few moments.

"Do you know how many people had been planning to attend your friend's birthday party?"

Mr. Hattori looked a bit surprised and tugged on his beard.

"Well, maybe ten or twelve of us, I expect—somewhere around that number."

"And after spending Saturday night in Kotohira by yourself, you returned to Okayama by train the next day, did you? You returned to Okayama on Sunday, did you?"

"Yes, I did."

"And on Saturday evening, how many people knew that you'd changed your mind about returning to Okayama? How many people knew that you'd be spending the night in Kotohira instead?"

This time Mr. Hattori scratched his head.

"Well…err…nobody really. Not as far as I can remember. I don't think that anybody knew that I'd be staying in Kotohira after all. I can't remember telling anybody about it."

"Well, who called you and told you that the party had been cancelled?"

"Oh, that was my friend's sister."

"And she called you on your personal phone, did she?"

"Yes, I had it with me on my trip. As I said, her call came through when I was in the taxi, just as we reached the station."

"Didn't you tell her that since there wasn't going to be a party, you might as well stay the night in Kotohira?"

Mr. Hattori thought for a moment.

"No, I'm sure that I didn't tell her that. It was only after I'd finished talking to her and when we'd reached the station that it occurred to me that I might as well spend the night in Kotohira."

"I see. Well, what about after you'd reached your hotel? Did you call anybody from your room to tell them your change of plan?"

Mr. Hattori thought again and then shook his head.

"No, I don't think so."

"Did you call anybody at all at any time during that evening?"

"No, I can't remember calling anybody from Kotohira."

"So what you're saying, Mr. Hattori, is that on the Saturday night when the cash machine was robbed in Kotohira, there's nobody who knew that you were staying in a hotel in Kotohira?"

Mr. Hattori shrugged again.

"I've never thought of that before, but yes, I guess that you're right. Except for the receptionists at the hotel where I was staying—they knew that I was there. Mr. Genda showed my hotel registration card to the court yesterday, and it had my name on it, of course. But as far as I can remember, nobody else would have known that I was staying in Kotohira because I changed my plans at the very last moment. Even the two people that I'd played golf with that day didn't know that

I was still in Kotohira. Anyway, why are you so interested in that point? Do you think that it's important?"

Morimoto sat deep in thought, oblivious to Mr. Hattori's question.

"Well," he said eventually, "before we go perhaps you could let us have some details about your school friend, Mr. Hattori, and his birthday party in Kurashiki that you'd been planning to attend?"

CHAPTER 23

▼

Later that morning, Inspector Morimoto and Police Officer Suzuki stepped off a tram outside Okayama station, and they walked past the flower beds that surrounded Momotaro's statue on their way into the station building. The metallic green of the statue gleamed in the bright sunshine, and the long tailed pheasant that the sculptor had fashioned on Momotaro's right shoulder was not entirely dissimilar in shape and size to the gray pigeons that had landed on top of his head and on the fingers of his raised left hand. Another group of pigeons had congregated around the statue's marble base, mingling with the dog and the monkey, who as every child knew were Momotaro's faithful companions.

The digital clock high up on the outside of the building showed 10:32 as Morimoto and Suzuki entered the station and approached the ticket machines, and so they had plenty of time to purchase their tickets and choose their seats on the Nanpu Southern Wind express train, operated by the Shikoku section of the Japan Railway Company, before it pulled out of the station at exactly 10:49, and passed by the tall white building that was the Grandview Hotel as it headed towards the south and the west.

The Nanpu Southern Wind express train was comprised of three silver carriages, each of which had two light blue lines painted along its side, one above the large windows and one below them. As it left the station and trundled slowly along the rails, it traveled parallel to the elevated bullet train tracks that were high up on its left, but it suddenly veered sharply leftwards and passed directly underneath them. Then it quickly gathered speed and soon left the station and the bullet train tracks far behind it.

Morimoto and Suzuki were occupying two of the dark blue seats in the front carriage, which had newly cleaned bright white cloths draped over the headrests. By pressing the small black buttons in their armrests, they were able to recline their seats into more comfortable positions, and as they settled back for the journey they both noticed the alleyway pass by their window where an unfortunate businessman had been found with his throat cut in a case that they had worked on during the rainy season the previous year.

However, there was no need for anybody to be carrying an umbrella around with them that summer morning, and Morimoto was in an excellent mood, which was not surprising considering his general delight whenever he had the opportunity to take a train ride. But in addition to the pleasure that he derived from the rhythmic jolting of the carriage and the ever-changing view through the window, he was also looking forward to being able to discuss with Suzuki the implications of what they had just learned from their meeting with Mr. Hattori earlier that morning.

"Well, Suzuki," Morimoto said as he kept an eye on the outskirts of Okayama, "what do you make of the new information that we were able to gather from Mr. Hattori this morning?"

Suzuki folded her arms and took a deep breath.

"Well, sir, we certainly managed to obtain quite a lot of interesting new information, although I have to say that nothing that we learned appeared particularly favorable from Mr. Hattori's perspective."

"You may well be right."

"But anyway, we can use the new information to update the ideas that we discussed yesterday. We've got to figure out what implications the additional information may have to the different explanations that we proposed for why Mr. Hattori's golf games produced an exact match with the cash machine robberies. The first explanation that we considered yesterday was that Mr. Hattori really did carry out the robberies himself, and it has to be said that we didn't learn anything definite this morning which would imply that Mr. Hattori couldn't be guilty."

"No, we didn't, except that we've discovered that he must be an exceptionally smooth liar if he really is guilty. He obviously comes across as being extremely angry, but he also gave me the impression of being quite perplexed by the whole business as well, and he seems to have resigned himself to the fact that he's been well and truly framed."

"Yes, I agree, sir. So if he is innocent, we have to address the question of who it is that's framing him. And from what he said, he's also been giving that question a great deal of thought himself, although he told us that he doesn't know of any enemies he has who he could conceive of wanting to do a thing like this to him."

"Yes, that's what he said."

"Another idea we discussed yesterday was that somebody else in his golf group might be responsible for the robberies. However, we learned this morning that there isn't any other member of the group who stayed overnight in the three towns where the robberies occurred—at least nobody who played in the group's game and who joined the other players in the hotels."

"That's a good point. As far as we know, and as far as Mr. Hattori knows, none of his other golf friends stayed overnight in each of the three locations where the robberies took place. Mr. Hattori appears to be unique in that respect."

"Yes, he does, sir, which has turned out to be rather unfortunate for him."

"Hmmm...well, what other ideas did we come up with yesterday?"

"We considered the possibility that there might have been something else going on in Shingo, Takebe, and Kotohira which could have provided an explanation for why the golf games and the robberies happened in those places simultaneously. For instance, we mentioned the possibility that there might have been some town festivals, or something else of that nature. But Mr. Hattori didn't mention anything like that to us this morning—he couldn't give us any special reason why those three locations had been chosen at those times, although he was eager to point out that he himself wasn't responsible for selecting those particular golf courses. We can do some more research into this matter, but at the moment this particular line of inquiry doesn't appear to offer Mr. Hattori much hope."

"I agree."

The Nanpu Southern Wind express train was now heading directly southwards along the Seto Ohashi Line that led towards the Seto Inland Sea, on the other side of which lay the island of Shikoku and Kagawa prefecture. Much of the flat land that stretched out on either side of the railway tracks had been reclaimed from the sea in earlier times, and it had been turned into vast stretches of nutrient rich rice fields that were separated from each other by narrow canals and roads. Morimoto's keen eye picked out the pale blue and yellow chrysanthemum flowers in some of the gardens that they passed by, and in a schoolyard he noticed a team of young baseball players whose bright white uniforms shone in the sunlight as they went through the drills of their Saturday morning practice session.

Suzuki continued with her analysis of the relationship between Mr. Hattori's golf games and the robberies.

"So if we eliminate those possibilities, sir, and if we assume that Mr. Hattori is innocent, then that only leaves us with one other possibility for what happened, which is that the real robber knew in advance where Mr. Hattori would be going on his golf trips, and where he'd be staying overnight. The real villain could then have planned the robberies so that suspicion would fall on Mr. Hattori. The robber might have been associated with Mr. Hattori's group of golf players in some way, or he might have been connected to Mr. Hattori in a completely different way. And as we said before, we can also deduce that if that's what did happen, then it's very likely that the informant Mr. Tokuda must have been in cahoots with the real robber in some manner."

"Yes, that's right, Suzuki."

"However, the essential point of such a theory is that the robber must have known in advance where Mr. Hattori would be visiting and staying. The robber would have needed that information in order to coordinate the robberies with Mr. Hattori's trips so that they could frame him. But that raises a big problem, based on what Mr. Hattori told us this morning. I have to admit that yesterday I felt that this particular theory offered Mr. Hattori his best lifeline, but unfortunately for him, he seems to have dashed the possibility that this theory is correct when he told us this morning about the circumstances surrounding his overnight stay in Kotohira."

"You're exactly right, Suzuki. Mr. Hattori was quite adamant that on the evening that he stayed in Kotohira, there was absolutely nobody else who knew that he was spending the night there. And that fact clearly seems to render this particular theory kaputt!"

"It does indeed, sir, which as I said, is rather unfortunate for Mr. Hattori."

"Yes, it is. Sergeant Yamada's going to do a little checking into the birthday party that Mr. Hattori claims that he was planning to attend, but regardless of the exact details of what happened with the party, the important point is that everybody seems to have been expecting Mr. Hattori to leave Kotohira after his golf game. And that's what Mr. Hattori expected as well. So if somebody had wanted to frame Mr. Hattori for the robberies, as far as we can tell that person wouldn't have been planning to commit a robbery in Kotohira that night."

"Precisely, sir. And even if such a person had managed to find out somehow that the birthday party had been cancelled, they still wouldn't have known that Mr. Hattori had changed his mind and had decided to stay in Kotohira for the night."

"Not if Mr. Hattori is correct when he told us that he didn't tell anybody that he'd changed his plans and had decided to spend the night in Kotohira."

"Exactly, sir. Which means that all things considered, I'm afraid that the situation doesn't look particularly good for Mr. Hattori after all. In fact, it looks rather bleak. Yesterday we were able to come up with several reasonable scenarios that would have each provided an explanation for the match between Mr. Hattori's golf games and the robberies while maintaining his innocence, but today they all seem to have hit the rocks. And I have to say that those odds of 225 million to 1 that Professor Shirane presented in court yesterday morning are beginning to look more and more menacing for Mr. Hattori. I wonder how Mr. Bando's going to try to wriggle out from underneath them? I wonder what strategy he'll decide to adopt in his cross-examination on Monday?"

"Hmmm...I really don't know, Suzuki, but I imagine that he's having quite an anxious weekend wrestling with the problem."

Chapter 24

As Inspector Morimoto and Police Officer Suzuki analyzed the implications of what they had learned from their meeting with Mr. Hattori that morning, the Nanpu Southern Wind express train passed through a series of long tunnels, and they were rocked from side to side in the middle of one of the tunnels when another train raced by them on their right-hand side traveling in the opposite direction.

When they stopped at Kojima station, Morimoto and Suzuki caught their first glimpse of the sea away to their left, and the roller coaster and giant wheel at the amusement park on the hill in front of them stood out against the bright blue sky. After leaving Kojima station they passed through another tunnel beneath the amusement park, and when they exited the tunnel a fleet of fishing boats could be seen floating in the harbor down to their right as they started out across the spectacular Seto Ohashi Bridge. This engineering marvel was actually composed of several bridges, each with a different design, which connected several small islands together in order to span the 12 kilometer stretch of sea between Okayama prefecture and Shikoku island.

"You know, Suzuki, there was one other thing that occurred to me during our talk with Mr. Hattori this morning. He told us that he played golf with two other people in Kotohira, and that he knew that those two people were planning to spend the night in one of the hot spring hotels there. And he said that he left them at the clubhouse and took a taxi back to the railway station by himself because he was planning to take a train back to Okayama. But according to what he told us, when he reached the station he realized that he could spend the night in Kotohira as well after all. What concerns me is this—why didn't he call his two friends from the station and find out where they were staying? Why did he go to a hotel all by himself? After all, he told us that after the golf games the group of players usually all stayed together at the same hotel."

"Hmmm...yes, I see what you mean, sir. That is a rather interesting point. I suppose that one explanation might be that neither of his two friends had phones with them, or alternatively, perhaps he didn't know their numbers."

"Possibly."

"On the other hand, perhaps he just felt like being by himself?"

"That could also be true."

"Or perhaps he saw a good opportunity to rob the cash machine in Kotohira, so perhaps he thought that it would be better if he stayed all by himself. After all, it may not have escaped the notice of some of his golf companions that the robberies in Shingo and Takebe had both coincided with their golf trips. It's possible that they'd even joked about it. So maybe Mr. Hattori didn't want his friends to know that he was staying in Kotohira if he was planning to do another robbery there."

"Yes, I see your point, Suzuki. But Mr. Hattori comes across as being a reasonably bright fellow, so why wouldn't he have simply arranged the robberies so that they had absolutely no connections with his golf trips?"

"Hmmm...that is very puzzling, sir."

The first component of the Seto Ohashi Bridge was a majestic suspension bridge that had two white pylons reaching up into the sky at each end. The railway track was on the lower part of the bridge, underneath the roadway, and Morimoto and Suzuki were able to peer out of the window at the green water below them, which they knew was renowned for its treacherously fast flowing currents. They were also able to spot the buoys and nets that floated in neat square shapes in the water close by the coastline, marking the spots where various nutritious varieties of seaweed were being cultivated.

A small island separated the initial suspension bridge from the next section of the bridge, where four gracefully shaped towers supported the roadway and the railway track directly from cables. A large oil tanker was making its ponderous way through this part of the sea, and it was given a wide berth by the numerous fishing boats which each looked miniscule in comparison. The view that Morimoto and Suzuki had to their right across the Seto Inland Sea, filled with a multitude of small islands, bore the distinction of having been designated as providing one of the hundred best sunsets in the whole of Japan, but at this time the sun was shining brightly high above as the Nanpu Southern Wind express train crossed over two additional suspension bridges before finally making landfall in Kagawa prefecture.

Morimoto continued to contemplate the mysterious relationship between Mr. Hattori's golf games and the cash machine robberies, and the more that he reflected on the conundrum, the clearer it became to him that the intriguing match was the central issue behind the ultimate question of whether the otherwise apparently ordinary car factory worker was guilty or was innocent.

"Incidentally, Suzuki, if Mr. Hattori really is guilty, then we can deduce that he must have had a very heavy overnight bag with him on his trips to Shingo and Takebe, because he must have taken his blue crowbar with him. And I suppose that he must have had his mask with him as well, if that's what he wore while he carried out those two robberies, just like he did in Kotohira. And he'd have had to be very careful that none of his friends ever picked up his bag. They'd have given him quite a ribbing, I expect, if they'd found out how heavy it was. 'Hey, what have you got in here? Planning to stay for a whole week, are you?' I wonder how he'd have explained that away?"

"Hmmm…that's an interesting point, sir."

"And what about his trip to Kotohira? If Mr. Hattori is telling us the truth about the birthday party, then he wouldn't have even taken an overnight bag to Kotohira with him at all. All he'd have had with him would have been his golf clubs. So how would he have got hold of his crowbar and his mask? We know that the robber was wearing a mask in Kotohira because he was seen by Mr. Yosano, the sushi chef."

Suzuki thought for a moment.

"Yes, that's another good question, sir. I suppose that it's possible that the crowbar and the mask were hidden among Mr. Hattori's golf clubs. It must be possible to conceal a crowbar in a set of golf clubs somehow."

"I imagine it is, but again, the additional weight would surely have been noticeable to anybody who picked up the clubs. And the question then arises as to why Mr. Hattori would have bothered to take the crowbar and mask with him to Kotohira at all that day if he expected to be returning to Okayama that night?"

"Perhaps he knew in advance that the birthday party was going to be cancelled, sir?"

"Hmmm…well, Sergeant Yamada's inquiries might reveal something about that."

When they stopped at Utazu station, they had to wait while several additional carriages were attached to their train. During the pause in their journey, Morimoto watched the golf balls flying through the air inside the tall green nets of the golf range that was adjacent to the station, and he craned his neck to watch a purple train that suddenly sped through the station heading in the direction from which they had just come.

One of the station officials was standing on the platform in the bright sunshine, keeping an eye on his watch, and occasionally lifting up his cap so that he could wipe the perspiration from his forehead. After the train had been stationary for exactly seven minutes, he blew his whistle energetically and waved his white-gloved hand, and the Nanpu Southern Wind express train pulled away from the station and continued on its way.

Quite a few passengers had entered the train at Utazu station, and the level of noise in Morimoto and Suzuki's carriage increased as the new occupants engaged in happy chatter and took out oranges and cans of beer from their bags. And as the train continued along the tracks close to the sea, Morimoto and Suzuki were able to watch the many tall sturdy cranes that were busy at work in the harbors along the coastline, and which were conspicuously painted in alternate patches of bright red and white.

At Tadotsu station they broke off from the Yosan Line that continued along by the coast, and they headed south on the Dosan Line. As the train gathered speed and headed inland towards the hills, it passed houses where many of the housewives already had their Saturday morning clothes washing hanging out in the sun to dry, and the gardens that bordered the railway tracks were resplendent with tidy rows of light green lettuces, dark green and purple cabbages, and the ubiquitous onions and radishes.

Suzuki raised another point that had suddenly occurred to her.

"Come to think of it, sir, it's not impossible that Mr. Hattori checked into his hotel in Kotohira, and then went back to the railway station, hopped on a train to Okayama, retrieved the crowbar and mask from his apartment, and then took another train back to Kotohira again. I can check the train timetable just to be certain, but I'm pretty sure that he'd have been able to do that if he'd wanted to."

"Yes, I see what you mean. And in addition, that would explain why he hadn't wanted to join his two friends at their hotel."

"It would indeed, sir. And something else has occurred to me about the robberies in Shingo and Takebe. Perhaps Mr. Hattori hadn't needed to take the crowbar and his mask with him on his golf trip because perhaps he'd already deposited them in those towns prior to the robberies. What I mean is, perhaps Mr. Hattori secretly visited the towns by himself in advance of the golf trips, just to do some reconnaissance of the cash machines and the suitability of the locations for a robbery. Then, after he'd decided to go ahead with the robbery, he could have simply left the crowbar and his mask somewhere in the town at that time. In that case, he wouldn't have needed to worry about his bags being so heavy when he went on his golf trips, because he wouldn't have needed to have carried the crowbar with him at those times."

"Oh...that's a very intriguing possibility, Suzuki. In fact, perhaps Mr. Hattori scouted out the locations of all of his golf trips in advance, and perhaps Shingo and Takebe were the locations that appealed to him as suitable robbery sites. He could have left his crowbar and mask in a station coin locker, say, a day or two before his golf trip so that they'd be available when he was ready to carry out the robberies. Then he could have put them back in a locker afterwards, and returned a day or two later by himself to collect them."

"It's not impossible, sir. But that scenario raises the puzzle of why he didn't carry out the robberies during his initial secret visits by himself to Shingo and Takebe? Why did he specifically want to carry out the robberies during his golf trips?"

Morimoto stared out of the window for a while deep in thought.

"You know, Suzuki," he said eventually, "maybe we're looking at these incidents the wrong way around. We've been considering the idea that somebody has tried to frame Mr. Hattori for the crimes, put perhaps it's really the other way around? Maybe Mr. Hattori had been intending to frame one of his golf partners for the robberies?"

"Hmmm...what an extraordinary idea, sir! So you're saying that Mr. Hattori might have intentionally carried out the robberies during his golf trips so that he'd later be able to frame one of his partners."

"Yes, that's right. And he did tell us that there was one other player who had stayed in both Shingo and Takebe, although he mentioned that he's a particularly nice fellow."

"Perhaps Mr. Hattori is trying to deceive us, sir? And of course, if he had been planning to frame somebody else, then something obviously must have gone terribly wrong with his scheme because he got caught with the crowbar and the mask himself."

"Yes, that's true, and it's not clear who he'd have been trying to frame by carrying out the Kotohira robbery."

"No, it's not, sir."

"Anyway, Suzuki, all things considered, the Kotohira robbery seems to be particularly interesting by virtue of Mr. Hattori's sudden decision to spend the night there, and the existence of a witness to the robbery. I wonder what else we'll be able to learn about it today?"

"Yes, I wonder, sir."

Chapter 25

The Nanpu Southern Wind express train pulled into the small station at Kotohira at exactly 11:53, and when the train had come to a complete stop, a solitary persimmon tree in a garden next to the station was visible through the train windows with an abundance of vermilion colored fruit that would gradually ripen throughout the summer months. Inspector Morimoto and Police Officer Suzuki were glad to fill their lungs with the fresh country air as they stepped out onto the platform, and as they looked around, Sergeant Adachi of the Kotohira Police Force hurried over to greet them.

Sergeant Adachi's smart police uniform managed to add some sense of authority to his youthful looks, although Suzuki felt that he still appeared to be a little nervous about his assignment that day. After they had all introduced themselves, Sergeant Adachi led them out through the small white station building with its red roof, and they stood for a moment in the plaza outside the station where two statues of lion-like animals were set on plinths at the end of two rows of stone lanterns.

Morimoto looked out across the town at Mt. Zozu, which rose up in front of them. The Kompira shrine was located halfway up its side, and the shape of the mountain was said to resemble that of an elephant's head, although Morimoto could actually see little resemblance himself as he stared at it.

"If you go down here to the left along by the railway tracks," Sergeant Adachi explained, "you'll come to the cash machine where the robbery took place. There's a new machine there now, if you want to go and take a look at it."

Morimoto shook his head.

"No, I don't think so, thank you. Let's go to the hotel straightaway."

"All right, then. We need to go down this street directly in front of us."

Sergeant Adachi led Morimoto and Suzuki between the rows of stone lanterns and along the street towards Mt. Zozu. Just before they crossed over the river, he pointed out the ancient lookout tower to them on their right-hand side and told them a few facts about its history, which he had conscientiously memorized that morning. A little further down the street they passed by a pastry shop where a crowd of tourists were peering through the large window at the baker who was preparing a new set of small square-shaped sweet cakes.

At the end of the street they turned right, and after walking for a further two minutes they stepped through the automatic glass doors of one of Kotohira's largest hotels. Sergeant Adachi hurried over to the receptionist to inform him of their arrival, and a moment later the hotel manager himself came out into the lobby to greet them. After a further series of bows and introductions, the manager led them through the restaurant and showed them into the busy kitchen, where the apron-clad Mr. Yosano was busily preparing several plates of sushi.

"Ah hello, Sergeant Adachi," Mr. Yosano said cheerfully.

"Hello, Mr. Yosano. How are you today? Two detectives have come from Okayama and they'd like to have a word with you, if that's all right?"

"We're very sorry to catch you at such a busy part of the day," Morimoto said.

Mr. Yosano laughed.

"Oh, don't worry about that, Inspector. I'll be happy to talk to you while I get on with my work. In fact, I'm quite used to it. Before I moved to this restaurant I used to work behind a sushi bar where I always chatted away with the customers while I was working. To tell you the truth, I rather miss that side of the job."

Mr. Yosano was a short man with a very slender build. His bald head was covered with a blue and white cap that matched the jacket that he was wearing underneath his apron, and he had a well tanned face with a hint of a rosy luster that suggested that he was no stranger to a bottle of rice wine.

Suzuki noticed how beautifully clean and smooth his hands were, thanks to the fish oil that they became covered with on a daily basis, and it was also clear to her that his fingers were very nimble as he reached for a fillet of dark red raw tuna and rapidly angled his long sharp knife through it, slicing it into bite size pieces. To become the head sushi chef at a restaurant like the one at this hotel required years of apprentice work, and neither Morimoto nor Suzuki were deceived by how easy Mr. Yosano made his work look.

"Your phone message was waiting for me when I got here this morning, Sergeant," Mr. Yosano continued. "They told me that you'd be coming in around lunchtime, so I've been expecting you. It's about that fellow who robbed the cash machines, isn't it? He gave me quite a fright, I can tell you. I've been reading the papers to keep track of what's been going on in his trial. What was it that they said in the paper this morning? Something about the odds being heavily stacked against him?"

Mr. Yosano held a slice of the raw tuna in his left hand, and used one of the fingers of his right hand to dab a spot of bright green wasabi horseradish into the middle of it.

"Yes, that's what we'd like to talk to you about," Morimoto replied.

"I guessed that's what your visit would be about. It was last February when I bumped into him. I told the police all about it right away."

"Yes, I've read the statement that you made for the police—that was very helpful. But if you don't mind going through it all one more time with us, I'd be very grateful."

"Oh, I don't mind at all. I love talking about what happened. My wife thinks that I'm quite a hero!"

Mr. Yosano laughed again as he wet his hand in a cup of water and reached over to a wooden bowl where he scooped up some sushi rice that he had cooked earlier, and which had been prepared with a dressing of vinegar, sugar, and salt. Elsewhere in the kitchen the other chefs were busily bent over their pots, frying pans, and chopping boards, and the waiters and waitresses formed a constant stream of traffic back and forth through the doors that led into the restaurant.

"Well, Inspector, it all happened on a Saturday evening after we'd had a particularly large crowd in the restaurant. It was around about midnight by the time that I'd got everything cleaned up in the kitchen and was ready for the next day, and after I left I went down the road to one of the bars for a drink. I often do that after I've finished working on a Saturday night. My wife is quite used to the fact that I might be a little late getting home!"

Mr. Yosano deftly shaped the rice into a ball with his right hand, and then placed it firmly onto the tuna that he was holding in his left hand. With a few deft squeezes that he had fine-tuned with years of practice, he quickly fashioned a beautifully proportioned piece of sushi that he gently placed onto the plate that he was preparing. Then he reached for the next slice of raw tuna and began to repeat the process all over again, maintaining an efficient rhythm to his work.

"And as I told the police," he continued, "I drank a few bottles of hot rice wine before heading home. It's only about a twenty minute walk from the bar to my apartment. I walked up the main road to the station, and then I turned right onto the road that goes along by the railway tracks. And that road took me straight by the cash machine. From what I can remember, it was a nice enough night—it wasn't raining or anything like that—and I've walked along those roads hundreds of times before on my way home. But that night was different…oh, yes it was! I'm never going to forget that night."

Mr. Yosano added a second piece of tuna sushi to the plate that already contained a colorful mix of sushi made from pink and white shrimp, some white sea bass, and several golden brown slices of eel. He added a final garnish of thinly sliced pink pickled ginger to the plate while he finished describing his encounter with the cash machine robber.

"So, what happened is that I turned around the corner to cross over the railway tracks, and there he was, stuffing handfuls of cash into his backpack. It gave me quite a shock, of course, and I realize now that he was probably just as startled as I was!"

Mr. Yosano gave Suzuki a wink.

"I'd like to be able to tell you that I challenged him and bravely chased him away like a real superman, but the truth is that it must have taken me a few moments to fully comprehend what I was seeing."

Mr. Yosano gave another cheerful laugh.

"And then he strapped his backpack onto his back, turned around, and just ran away. And that's pretty much the end of the story. When I came to my senses I called the police, and I waited there by the cash machine until they drove up in their squad car. Sergeant Adachi and one of his colleagues were the first ones to arrive."

Morimoto nodded as Mr. Yosano began working on a slab of bright white squid with his knife.

"I see, Mr. Yosano. Thank you very much. That's very interesting. And when the robber ran away, you called the police at once, did you?"

"Yes, as soon as I'd got a grip on my senses and realized what had just happened."

"So you were carrying a phone with you, were you?"

"Yes, I was. My wife gave it to me at the beginning of the year. I think she likes to keep track of where I am and what I'm up to!"

Mr. Yosano grinned.

"What time was that phone call logged in at the call center, Sergeant?" Morimoto asked.

Sergeant Adachi consulted his notebook.

"The Kagawa prefecture emergency call center recorded it at 1:11, sir."

"Thank you," Morimoto replied. "So what time do you think you must have left the bar that night, Mr. Yosano?"

"Well, just before one o'clock, I guess. It's only about a ten or fifteen minute walk from the bar to the cash machine. And I left here at about midnight, which would mean that I must have spent about an hour in the bar, and that sounds about right to me."

"Okay. Good. So I suppose that you had a fair amount to drink that evening, did you?"

Mr. Yosano grinned again.

"Yes, rather a lot—I have to admit it. But not enough to stop me from walking home by myself. And the more I've thought about it afterwards, the more it seems to me that in a way it was a good job that I had been drinking. That's because it dulled the shock of coming across that fellow at the cash machine. If I'd been completely sober, I have to tell you that I'd probably have been scared out of my wits!"

Sergeant Adachi chuckled at Mr. Yosano's admission, and Mr. Yosano grinned back at him.

"In your report," Morimoto continued, "you stated that the robber was wearing a mask, didn't you?"

"Oh, yes. His whole head and face were covered by a mask."

"You're certain of that are you?"

"Oh, yes—I'm quite certain. I couldn't see his face at all. One of the first things that Sergeant Adachi did was to me ask me what he looked like, and I told him about the mask. There were just two narrow slits for his eyes, and that's all."

"Could the robber have had a full beard?"

"Err…yes, he could have. The whole of his chin and upper neck were covered by the mask."

"I see. Well, what sort of build did this person have? Was he tall or short?"

"Well, he was bigger than me for sure—but most people are bigger than me! He was about average height, as I recall—not that I paid much attention to the matter at the time. Anyway, you've got the fellow on trial, haven't you? So can't you see how tall he is?"

Morimoto rubbed his chin.

"Well, we'd like to get as much independent information as we can from you, Mr. Yosano. We're still interested in any details that you can remember from your encounter with the robber that night. By the way, is it possible that the person who you saw at the cash machine could have been a woman?"

Mr. Yosano looked surprised.

"Ah…does this mean that you're not totally certain that you've got the right person? Wow…who'd have thought it?"

"It's just a question of being completely sure about the evidence," Sergeant Adachi said, trying to be helpful.

"Oh. Well, I don't think that anybody's ever asked me if it could have been a woman before. I doubt that it was a woman, but I guess that I couldn't really say for sure that it wasn't. But if it were a woman, then she must have been pretty handy with that crowbar!"

Mr. Yosano's hands were in constant motion while he talked, and after finishing with the squid he turned back to another fillet of raw tuna.

"Was there anything unusual about that crowbar?" Morimoto asked.

Mr. Yosano shook his head as he picked up his knife and sliced through the tuna with a rapid series of decisive cuts.

"Not really. It was blue, but I've seen some like that before. They have them in most of the hardware stores."

Morimoto nodded.

"I see. Well, that's been very helpful, Mr. Yosano. I'm sorry to have disturbed your work."

"Oh, don't worry. Is that all of the questions that you wanted to ask me? I'm glad to have been of some service again. And are you really not sure that you've got the right fellow on trial? Can I tell my wife about that? She's been keeping a very close eye on the trial—she's very interested in it considering my involvement in what happened. We both had the impression from the newspapers that the trial's been going very well for the prosecution."

"Yes, it has, but there's still a long way to go yet. Anyway, watching you prepare those lovely plates of sushi has made me rather hungry. Shall we find somewhere to have lunch, Sergeant?"

"Very well, sir," Sergeant Adachi replied. "And with due respect to Mr. Yosano's excellent sushi, perhaps I might recommend that you try some Sanuki noodles while you're here? They're a speciality of this region."

"Oh, yes, I'd second that suggestion!" Mr. Yosano added with a smile. "You really shouldn't pass up on that offer, Inspector."

"Well," Morimoto said, "some Sanuki noodles would be just wonderful. How about it, Officer Suzuki?"

"It sounds like an excellent idea, sir."

Chapter 26

A short while later, Sergeant Adachi, Inspector Morimoto, and Police Officer Suzuki were seated around a small table in a nearby restaurant, with three large bowls of steaming noodles set in front of them. They had each made their choice from the detailed menu which had allowed them to specify whether they wanted their noodles served in the same water that had been used to boil them, doused in cold water after boiling, or transferred to a new bowl of hot water after boiling. In addition, they had also made their selections from the array of seafood items and vegetables that were available to be included with their noodles.

"Umm...they're delicious," Suzuki said, holding up a noodle with her chopsticks and inspecting it. "They're a bit firmer than the noodles that we typically have in Okayama."

"Yes, that's the main characteristic of Sanuki noodles," Sergeant Adachi said. "They're quite a bit harder than the noodles made in other parts of the country. I think it's something to do with the flour that's used here in Kagawa prefecture, and the salt that they add to the dough, and it might also be related to how long they store the dough before rolling it out flat and cutting it up into the noodles."

"They're very tasty," Morimoto agreed. "In themselves, they're well worth the trip in fact, although I'm glad that we had the opportunity to have a chat with Mr. Yosano as well. He mentioned that you were the first person on the scene in answer to his phone call on that February night, Sergeant."

"Yes, that's right, sir—I was. It only took my colleague and me about five minutes to get there from the police station. When we drove up we saw Mr. Yosano standing right next to the cash machine, and we could see at once that he was quite inebriated. I don't know how much rice wine he'd had to drink in that bar that he visited after leaving the hotel where he works, but it must have been a fair amount. At first we thought that it might just be a prank—we thought that somebody might have filed a false report about a robbery just for a joke. But we soon saw how smashed up the cash machine was, and we noticed lots of debris lying on the ground. That's when we realized that we really were dealing with something serious."

"So at first sight, Mr. Yosano wasn't what you'd consider to be a particularly reliable witness then?"

"No, I'd have to say that he wasn't, sir. But on the other hand, I should point out that his story has been completely consistent throughout, so I can't see any reason why it shouldn't be taken at face value. As far as I can see, there's no reason for him to have made up any part of his story."

Morimoto nodded.

"Yes, I take your point, Sergeant. But you arrived too late be able to track down the culprit, did you?"

"Yes, unfortunately we did. We put out an alert immediately, of course, but nothing came of it. At the time we assumed that the robber must have driven away—we thought that he'd probably just run off to a car that he'd left somewhere nearby. But according to the recent newspaper reports, it seems that he was staying here at the Kotohira Hot Bath Inn all along. In that case he must have escaped on foot, and he probably just ran back to his hotel—or maybe he walked back so as not to attract any attention."

"Yes, maybe."

"In his statement, Mr. Yosano indicated that the culprit ran away down the street across the railway tracks. That wouldn't be the quickest way to get to the Kotohira Hot Bath Inn, but he could have cut back through some of the quiet residential streets. Anyway, in my opinion it would have been quite easy for him to get back to his hotel without being spotted by anybody at that time of the night. And I guess that once he was out of sight of Mr. Yosano, he must have taken off his mask so that he wouldn't have appeared at all suspicious to anybody who might have happened to see him."

"That sounds very reasonable, Sergeant."

They all munched on their noodles for a while.

"By the way, Sergeant, I noticed in the report that your investigation was able to obtain some useful information from a taxi driver," Morimoto said a moment later.

"Yes, that's right, sir. We publicized the fact that we were interested in talking to anybody who'd been in that area at that time of night, and a taxi driver came forward. He said that he'd picked up a pair of ladies from the corner next to the cash machine at about one o'clock."

"Which taxi company did he work for?"

"Oh, the local Kotohira company—we only have the one main company here."

"And he was sure of the time, was he?"

"Oh, yes—there's no doubt about that, sir. The ladies called the taxi company at 12:45 and said that they were waiting on the corner next to the cash machine, and when the taxi reached them and the driver started his meter, it was exactly 12:59. The meter recorded the precise time—we checked into that very carefully. And the taxi drove off with the two passengers along the road towards the railway station, and we deduced in our investigation that they probably must have passed Mr. Yosano as he was walking down the road in the opposite direction. There's very little time between when the taxi picked up the ladies at 12:59, and when Mr. Yosano called the emergency line from the same spot at 1:11."

"Yes, I see…you're quite right. And the taxi driver was certain that the cash machine wasn't damaged when he picked up the passengers, was he?"

"He was completely certain, sir. He said that he pulled right up to the curb next to the cash machine, which is where the two ladies were standing and waiting for him. When we talked to him he was adamant that he'd have noticed if the cash machine had been all smashed up. And don't forget that his two passengers had been waiting for about fifteen minutes on the corner next to the cash machine."

"Did you interview those two ladies?"

"Oh, yes—I talked with them both before they left Kotohira. It was easy to trace them because the taxi had taken them to a hotel. They were from Takamatsu, and they'd just come here for a weekend break for the hot springs. They told me that they'd been out late eating and drinking and enjoying themselves, but when they'd started to walk back to their hotel they'd got disoriented after taking a wrong turn. So they gave up and called for the taxi. Anyway, the point is that they also confirmed that there'd been nothing wrong with the cash machine, and they'd certainly have noticed if it had been damaged while they were waiting for their taxi."

"Yes, I see. How old were the two ladies, Sergeant?"

"Err…in their forties, I'd say. I have their contact information if we need to get in touch with them again."

"Is there any chance that they'd have been at all handy with a crowbar?"

Sergeant Adachi laughed.

"Strictly speaking, that's not impossible, sir. But if they did smash open the cash machine, then the taxi driver must be in cahoots with them, because don't forget that he reported that there was nothing wrong with the cash machine when he picked them up."

"You're absolutely right, Sergeant. Incidentally, isn't that a bit late for two ladies to be out walking the streets?"

"Well, that's not all that unusual for Kotohira, sir. When people come here they usually like to have some fun and to live it up a bit. They probably wanted to make the most of the weekend away from their families. We're a popular resort town and people from all over Shikoku come here for a weekend break. And it's very safe here—there's practically no crime at all. The cash machine robbery has been quite a sensation, in fact."

"Yes, I see. Well, what do you make of it all, Suzuki?"

Suzuki finished chewing on a mouthful of noodles.

"Well, sir, one important point is that we have some very accurate information on the time of the robbery here. Unlike the robberies at Shingo and Takebe, the facts that Sergeant Adachi and his team were able to uncover in their investigation allow us to pinpoint the time of the crime here in Kotohira very precisely. Specifically, based on the information from the taxi driver and the two ladies who he picked up, the crime must have occurred after 12:59. Moreover, the crime must have occurred before 1:11 when Mr. Yosano made his call to the police."

"That's exactly right, Suzuki. And moreover, from that information we can also deduce how long the robber must have taken to accomplish his task."

"That's a good point, sir. It can't have taken him any more than ten minutes. Of course, we can surmise that he must have known the best way to go about his job because it seems that he'd managed it twice before in Shingo and Takebe. And by the way, Dr. Jimbo's team managed to reconstruct the crime in their laboratory within a ten minute time frame, so there can't me much doubt that ten minutes was ample time for the robber to do what he needed to do."

"Ah, yes—that's when Dr. Jimbo let his assistants loose with a crowbar on a brand new cash machine, much to the Chief's chagrin. Did you hear about that, Sergeant?"

Sergeant Adachi smiled.

"Err...yes, we did hear some rumors about that."

"I thought that you might have."

"And...err...about the timing, sir," Sergeant Adachi added hesitantly. "I would imagine that the culprit must have been hiding somewhere in the vicinity of the cash machine, and that he must have been waiting for the taxi to collect those two ladies before he was able to get to it."

Morimoto nodded.

"Yes, that's a very good point, Sergeant. What do you think, Suzuki?"

"Yes, I agree with Sergeant Adachi. That seems to be the most likely explanation. Presumably, the culprit approached the scene on foot sometime between 12:45 and 12:59, say, when we know that the two ladies were waiting on the corner. Obviously, he couldn't carry out the robbery while the ladies were standing there, so he had to wait until they left. And as Sergeant Adachi said, it looks as though he must have hidden in the shadows somewhere. As soon as the taxi picked up the ladies, he was able to start his work, and he was just about finished when Mr. Yosano staggered around the corner on his way home from the bar with quite a lot of rice wine inside him."

"That's what I think happened," Sergeant Adachi said. "That seems much more likely than the other possibility, which is that the culprit just turned up by chance after the taxi had left, but with enough time to have pretty much finished the job by the time that Mr. Yosano appeared."

"That's a very good deduction, Sergeant," Morimoto agreed as he finished up the last of his noodles. "And there's one other thing that I wanted to ask you about. Your report said that there was some money left in the cash machine when you arrived on the scene."

"Yes, that's correct, sir. Presumably, Mr. Yosano's interruption of the robbery caused the robber to leave without having completely finished his work. There was only a small amount of cash left though, so the robber unfortunately managed to get away with the lion's share of the money."

"I see. Doesn't that mean that Mr. Yosano could have helped himself to some cash before you arrived?"

Sergeant Adachi frowned.

"Yes, in theory it does, sir. In the five minutes between when Mr. Yosano called the emergency number and when we reached him, he must have been standing all by himself next to the bank notes. I have to admit that we never searched him, so it's not impossible that he did slip a little cash into his pockets."

"Hmmm...in theory, it's possible that he could have concealed a few thick wads of bank notes in his coat pockets, isn't it?"

"Err...that's not impossible, sir."

"In fact, for all we know, if Mr. Yosano scared the robber away just when he'd got started, then he might have ended up with more cash for himself than the robber managed to take away with him."

"Yes, I guess so…if he'd had enough pockets to hide it all in, sir. But in that case, surely he could have simply taken all of the cash and walked away without calling us?"

"That's true, Sergeant."

"Nevertheless," Suzuki added, "the possibility that Mr. Yosano helped himself to some of the cash does have some implications to the case that Mr. Genda's putting together. I'm thinking about the bank notes that were found in Mr. Hattori's kitchen. Mr. Izumi from the Metropolitan Trust Bank testified that those bank notes came from the cash machine here in Kotohira. The point is that we can't rule out the possibility that those bank notes were taken from the cash machine by Mr. Yosano, and not by the actual robber."

Morimoto nodded slowly.

"Yes, that's a very interesting possibility, Suzuki."

The waitress cleared away their empty bowls, and they all sat back in their chairs comfortably digesting their meals.

"Well, it's been very good of you to take the time to meet us today, Sergeant," Morimoto said. "I'm glad that we made the trip. It's been very useful, but I don't think that we'll need to be troubling you any more this afternoon."

"Oh, I'm very glad to have been of some service, sir."

"I imagine that you'll be wanting to be getting back to Okayama, will you, Officer Suzuki?"

"Err…yes, sir…now that we've finished here. Yoshi and I have some plans for the rest of the weekend."

Mr. Yoshi Sasaki was a young insurance agent at the Calamity Assurance Company who Suzuki had met on one of their earlier cases.

"All right then," Morimoto said. "My wife's away for the weekend on one of her mountain climbing expeditions, so I'm not in much of a hurry to get back to Okayama myself. And since I'm here, I think that I ought to take the opportunity to do a little bit of sightseeing—and it would be a terrible shame to leave without having had a soak in the invigorating hot spring water, so I believe that I might stay for the night as well."

Chapter 27

▼

After bidding farewell to Sergeant Adachi outside the restaurant, Police Officer Suzuki and Inspector Morimoto went their separate ways. Suzuki headed back towards the railway station, while Morimoto wandered slowly down the street together with all of the other tourists and pilgrims who were heading towards the entrance to the Kompira shrine. It was a warm sunny afternoon, and Morimoto took off his light jacket and folded it over his arm as he strolled along the busy street. The shopkeepers were standing outside their shops trying to sell boxes of Sanuki noodles to the passers-by, and in the window of one of the restaurants, Morimoto watched a chef rolling out a large round piece of dough, which he then folded over and began to chop up into the long strips that formed the noodles.

When Morimoto finally reached the large gate at the bottom of Mt. Zozu that marked the entrance to the shrine, he passed by five ladies sitting under large white umbrellas who were selling souvenirs of the shrine, and who represented the five farming families that traditional laws dictated were the only people allowed to offer their merchandise for sale within the precincts of the shrine. Then another smaller gate led to a tree flanked avenue that had a multitude of small stone lanterns standing on either side, that were each similar in design to those that were located in the plaza outside the railway station. When he reached the end of the avenue, Morimoto began his leisurely climb up the 1,368 stone steps that led to the highest of the temple buildings, and as he climbed he marveled at the work that had been done in transporting the stones from the islands in the Seto Inland Sea where they had originally come from.

The crowds of people that labored up the steps along with Morimoto were in a jovial mood, as everybody was enjoying both the summer sunshine and the challenge presented by the long flights of stairs that stretched up in front of them. Many of the climbers stopped to recover their breath from time to time, and they wiped the sweat from their faces with the small flannel cloths that they carried with them, and then they leaned on their bamboo walking sticks that had the advantage of being both sturdy and light.

Morimoto was not in a hurry, and he took his time as he steadfastly rose from one step to the next. As he climbed, he reflected on the status of Mr. Hattori's trial. He still had an open mind about whether Mr. Hattori was guilty or not, but he was troubled by several aspects of the situation that still remained unclear to him. The incriminating crowbar and the bank notes that Sergeant Yamada had discovered in Mr. Hattori's kitchen made it apparent that Mr. Hattori was either guilty or was being framed, and Morimoto was particularly intrigued by Mr. Tokuda's account of his conversation with Mr. Hattori in the Pickled Cabbage bar. If Mr. Bando's suggestion that Mr. Tokuda had genuinely misheard what Mr. Hattori had said to him was disregarded, then there were only two other possibilities. One was that Mr. Hattori was lying about the incident, and the other was that Mr. Tokuda was lying about the incident.

But if Mr. Hattori had committed the robberies, would he really have been unwise enough to boast about his crimes to a virtual stranger who he had only known for an hour or two? And would he have robbed the three cash machines while he was staying at hotels in the three towns? And why had he kept the incriminating crowbar hidden away in his rice container? If Mr. Hattori had been intending to carry out some additional robberies, then where was his mask? Sergeant Yamada's careful search of Mr. Hattori's apartment had failed to turn up any masks. Surely it would have been natural for Mr. Hattori to have hidden his mask with the crowbar?

But on the other hand, if Mr. Tokuda was lying, then why was he trying to frame Mr. Hattori? If Mr. Tokuda had fabricated his account of what Mr. Hattori had said to him, then the inescapable implication had to be that Mr. Tokuda was involved in the attempt to frame Mr. Hattori, and that Mr. Tokuda was therefore somehow connected to the robberies.

After 785 steps, Morimoto reached the main shrine with its gracefully curved thatched roofs and intricate architectural design. More than a thousand years before, the shrine had been dedicated to the Hindu crocodile god of the River Ganges who had been imported to Japan from India, but a nearby room full of model ships bore testament to its current dedication to the deities who protected sailors. The panting pilgrims formed a line in front of the main temple building as they waited to make their offerings and say their prayers, and Morimoto watched them as he lingered at the top of the steps and caught his own breath. Then he headed over to the sightseeing area that offered a stunning view as some sort of a compensation for the effort of the climb.

The town of Kotohira lay spread out before him between the bottom of Mt. Zozu and the hills on the other side of the valley, and he could see the trains running along the railway tracks and into the station as though they were part of a miniature railway set. Off to the left stretched the broad Sanuki Plain that was filled with wheat fields and rice paddies, and in the far distance over to his right the sparkling blue water of the Seto Inland Sea that he had crossed over that morning could just be made out.

After savoring the view for fifteen minutes and enjoying the respite from the stairs, Morimoto headed back to the next section of stone steps and continued with his climb. There were many fewer people on this section of the stairs since most of the visitors did not climb to the very topmost point of the shrine, and those people on their way down who he passed by smiled and offered their encouragement. As he persevered up the seemingly endless steps, he contemplated once again the odds that Professor Shirane had derived in the courtroom the previous day—225 million to 1. How could Mr. Hattori explain away those odds? Surely it would have been very imprudent of him to rob cash machines in small towns while he was staying in one of the hotels? Surely it would have been better for him if he had driven to the towns, committed the robberies, and then left immediately afterwards?

But on the other hand, would Mr. Hattori have expected anybody to ever discover that he had been staying in each of the towns when the robberies had occurred? The truth was that the match had not been discovered until after Mr. Hattori had become the focus of attention due to the information that had been received from Mr. Tokuda. And what about Mr. Hattori's golf friends? Had some of Mr. Hattori's workmates noticed the match between the golf games and the robberies?

But if Mr. Hattori had not been responsible for the attacks on the cash machines, then what explanation could there be for why the robberies matched his visits to the three towns? Was it really just luck—or bad luck from his perspective? What strategy was Mr. Bando going to adopt to explain away the odds that appeared to be so damaging to his client? Was he simply planning to tell the judge that the match was a strange fluke? 'Well, your honor, these things can happen, you know. It's a remarkable coincidence to be sure, but just because Mr.

Hattori was always in the right place at the right time doesn't prove that he committed the robberies.' But if the match between the golf trips and the robberies was simply a remarkable coincidence, then what were the crowbar and the bank notes doing in Mr. Hattori's kitchen?

Morimoto reflected on the various scenarios that he had discussed with Suzuki, which had each offered an explanation for why Mr. Hattori's visits to the three towns had coincided with the robberies. He could easily believe that the true criminal might have engineered the robberies in that way in order to frame Mr. Hattori in a really convincing manner—that had seemed to be Mr. Hattori's best way out of the sticky situation that he found himself in—but the fact that nobody seems to have been aware of Mr. Hattori's overnight stay in Kotohira put a very serious snag in that escape route. If the true criminal had expected Mr. Hattori to be partying in Kurashiki that evening, then why had he carried out the robbery in Kotohira if he had been trying to frame Mr. Hattori?

Morimoto finally reached the top of the stairs, and as he recovered his breath once again, he stood for a while gazing at the small shrine that was picturesquely set among the tall pine trees. There were several groups of people taking photographs at the nearby viewpoint, and he walked over to join them. The town of Kotohira was even smaller than before, and it appeared very idyllic and peaceful as it straddled the narrow river whose water was flowing gently towards the Seto Inland Sea. Morimoto could well believe Sergeant Adachi's exhortation that it was a very safe town, unused to the levels of crime that occurred in larger cities, and the image of a masked man opening up a cash machine with a crowbar in the middle of the night seemed quite incongruous in such a serene setting.

Morimoto thought about how the robbery of the cash machine in Kotohira had been different from the previous two robberies. Firstly, there was the fact that the crime had been witnessed—albeit that the witness had been in a somewhat intoxicated state at the time. And secondly, Mr. Hattori's golf trip to Kotohira had not included plans for him to stay overnight. What clues did those two differences provide? The sushi chef had seemed very sure of his story when Morimoto had talked with him earlier that day, but was it possible that he was hiding something? Had he helped himself to a substantial portion of the missing cash? And what if the three cash machine robberies had not all been carried out by the same person? Is it possible that the Kotohira robbery had been a copycat crime carried out by somebody who had not been connected in any way with the first two robberies?

Morimoto took several deep breaths, and he let the clean mountain air fill his lungs as these questions floated through his head, one after another. And as he looked down at the town of Kotohira on that lovely summer afternoon, he felt sure that the unique circumstances associated with the robbery that had taken place there in February held the key to unraveling the mysteries behind all three of the cash machine robberies, and ultimately held the answer to Mr. Hattori's fate.

Chapter 28

Later that afternoon, the automatic glass doors of the Kotohira Hot Bath Inn slid smoothly open as Inspector Morimoto entered the lobby and walked up to the reception desk.

"Good afternoon, sir. How may I help you?" the receptionist decked out in a smart purple uniform asked.

"Ah, good afternoon. I'd like a room for tonight, please. On the ground floor, if possible, please."

"Certainly, sir."

After Morimoto had filled out his name, address, date of birth, and phone number on the hotel registration card, the receptionist handed him his room key together with a sheet of paper.

"Here's your key, sir," she said. "Your room's on the ground floor just as you requested. We hope that you enjoy your stay here, and we'd be very grateful if you took a moment to fill out this form and left it in the box over there before you leave."

Morimoto looked at the sheet of paper that he had been given. It was headed 'Kotohira Hot Bath Inn Customer Evaluation Sheet'.

"And if you hand in your evaluation," the receptionist added, "you'll be entered into the drawing that we have each month, and there's a chance that you could win a free night's stay for two."

"Oh, really? That would be very nice."

Morimoto remained standing at the reception desk, and he studied the sheet of paper carefully. He was particularly intrigued by the small note at the bottom of the page that indicated that the form had been prepared by Tsuda Business Solutions.

"Err...actually...I was wondering," he said. "How long have you been handing out these evaluation sheets?"

The receptionist looked surprised.

"Let me see...umm...it's been about three months, I think. Is there any problem, sir? It's completely voluntary. You don't need to fill out the form if it's too much of a nuisance for you."

Morimoto scratched his head for a moment, and then he drummed his fingers on the top of the reception desk as he leaned on it, lost in thought. The receptionist began to look quite concerned.

"Is anything the matter, sir? I can take the evaluation sheet back from you if it's causing you some kind of a problem."

"Err...no...there's no problem. Don't worry. It's quite all right. But, come to think of it...if it's not too much trouble...I wonder whether I might have a word with the hotel manager?"

"The manager? Err...yes, of course, sir. I'll go and tell him at once that you'd like to speak with him."

Morimoto's request generated an even more concerned expression on the receptionist's face as she took a look at the registration card that he had just filled out.

"It's Mr. Morimoto, is it, sir?"

"Yes, that's right—Inspector Morimoto of the Okayama Police Department."

The receptionist disappeared with a very worried look on her face.

A few minutes later, Morimoto was shown into the elderly manager's office.

"Good afternoon, Inspector," he said with a smile. "How can I help you? I hope that there hasn't been any trouble? Are you here on police business? Have we done anything wrong?"

"Oh, no, don't worry. I'm not really here on police business. It's a very lovely hotel that you have, and I simply thought that I'd treat myself to a night here and a soak in your hot spring baths. But there is one small point that cropped up while I was checking in at the reception desk, and I was hoping that you might possibly be able to assist me with it."

The manager looked confused.

"I'll be glad to help you in any way that I can, Inspector. Is there some kind of police investigation going on that I need to be aware of?"

"Well, again, not really—at least not of this hotel. The only reason that I asked to meet you is that when I checked in I was given this evaluation sheet."

Morimoto held up the Kotohira Hot Bath Inn Customer Evaluation Sheet that he had been given.

"Yes, Inspector, we give that evaluation sheet out to all of our guests. Is there anything wrong with that? We've not had any complaints before. Whether you choose to fill it out or not is completely up to you—it's completely voluntary."

"No, there's nothing wrong with it—nothing at all. It's just that I wondered whether I might be able to check a few details of the evaluation program with you."

The manager was clearly surprised.

"By all means, Inspector. Are you particularly interested in evaluation programs like this one? What is it about our evaluation program that you'd specifically like to know?"

"Well, I noticed that this form has been prepared by Tsuda Business Solutions. Do you deal with them directly?"

The manager picked up a copy of the evaluation sheet from one of the trays on his desk.

"Tsuda Business Solutions, did you say? Oh, I see what you mean—their name's written down here in the bottom corner. Actually, to tell you the truth, I hadn't really noticed that before. At this hotel we don't really deal with these forms at all. This evaluation drive was instigated by HoSHA."

"HoSHA?"

"Yes, the Hot Spring Hotel Association."

"Oh, I see. You're a member of that association, are you?"

"Yes, practically all of the hotels that qualify as providing genuine hot spring spa facilities are members of the association. They help us to get bookings from large groups, and they organize a lot of our advertising and promotional campaigns."

Morimoto nodded.

"Ah, yes...I understand."

"This evaluation business started three or four months ago, and it was HoSHA's idea. We just do what they tell us to do. So I'd imagine that it must have been HoSHA who contracted that company...err...Tsuda Business Solutions to prepare these evaluation forms for them. They were sent to us by HoSHA."

"I see."

"I remember that when this matter started, we had a letter from HoSHA explaining what it was all about. As well as collecting data from these evaluation forms which some of our guests fill out, they've also been collecting information about our guests directly from the registration cards. They said something in their letter about how they were intending to compile a data set of our clientele, or something like that."

"Oh, did they really? That's rather interesting."

The manager shrugged.

"Do you think so? It might be worthwhile, perhaps, but I'm not really convinced myself. But perhaps I'm just an old fuddy-duddy who's too set in his ways? I imagine that the general idea is that they hope that they'll be able to target their advertising campaigns more effectively—I think that's what they said in their letter. Anyhow, as I said, HoSHA is in charge of the whole business. We just hand out the blank evaluation sheets that they send us, and we return the ones that have been filled out back to them."

"I understand. Well, that's all that I wanted to know. Thank you very much for your time, and I'm sorry to have had to trouble you over this matter."

The manager stood up and smiled again.

"Oh, is that all you needed to know? Well, I'm happy to have been of service. I hope that you enjoy your stay with us, and I hope that we'll have the pleasure of welcoming you back again in the future."

"Yes, I hope so too."

As soon as he reached his room, Morimoto picked up the phone and called Police Officer Suzuki.

"Oh, hello, Suzuki. Did you make it back to Okayama all right?"

"Yes, I'm back at my apartment, sir."

"Good. I've just checked into the Kotohira Hot Bath Inn."

"Isn't that where Mr. Hattori stayed in February?"

"Yes, it is. Anyway, I'm sorry to mess up your plans for the weekend, but I was wondering whether you'd have time to carry out a little job tomorrow."

"No problem, sir. What's the job?"

"Well, I was wondering whether you could arrange to have a little chat with Ms. Tsuda."

"Ms. Tsuda?"

"Yes."

"On Sunday?"

"Err...yes."

"I wonder what her time management philosophies are for Sunday?"

"Yes, I was wondering about that myself. And I'm rather afraid that she may not have a very favorable opinion of us after our little meeting with her yesterday, so you might need to deal with her very delicately."

"Don't worry, sir, I'll give her a call right away and try to fix something up. We most probably ruffled a few of her feathers during our interview yesterday, but I'll see what I can do to smooth things out. What do you want me to ask her about?"

"Her work with HoSHA."

"With who?"

"HoSHA—the Hot Spring Hotel Association."

"Oh, I see."

Morimoto spent a few minutes telling Suzuki about his meeting with the hotel manager.

"I understand, sir. I'll see what I can find out from her."

"That will be very useful. And by the way, didn't you say that you had some plans with Mr. Sasaki for the weekend?"

"Yes, that's right."

"Well, why don't you take him along with you when you meet Ms. Tsuda? He always seems to enjoy a touch of police work now and then."

"Oh, he'll be absolutely delighted, sir—he'll be quite thrilled."

After he had finished speaking with Suzuki, Morimoto quickly changed into the light cotton yukata gown that had been laid out for him on his bed, and without further ado he headed off to the public baths in the hotel basement. Inside the locker room a sign on the wall displayed some photographs of several clear petri dishes which the hotel management offered to the guests as evidence that no particularly lethal bugs had been found in the spa water when it had been scientifically tested, and with that assurance, Morimoto eagerly went through to the bathing area.

As he sat and soaked his body in the outdoor hot spring bath that was in a fenced off enclosure at the back of the hotel, Morimoto watched the steam rise from the water and drift around the decorative rocks and plants that surrounded the bath. The water had risen from deep underground, where it had been naturally heated by the volcanic activities that had at one time been responsible for the formation of the island of Shikoku, and although it had been cooled down to a temperature that was just about bearable before being piped into the bath, it still carried a cocktail of dissolved minerals that were considered to be particularly healthy as the pores of the skin opened up and absorbed them.

Morimoto slowly dipped a small square flannel cloth into a bowl of water that was at the side of the bath, and he placed it on top of his head, letting the water drip onto his face and down the back of his neck. He breathed deeply and slowly as he let the hot water relax his body, and he gazed up at the clear blue sky through the clouds of rising steam. And as he reached a blissful state of tranquility and comfort, he went over what he knew about the robberies one more time in his head, and he reflected on how Mr. Hattori's penchant for staying at hot spring hotels had ended up landing him in such hot water.

Chapter 29

The next morning, Sunday, Police Officer Suzuki tightened the belt of her dressing gown as she stood next to the well-stocked wine rack in her kitchen and waited for the coffee maker to finish preparing her exotic blend of coffee. The toaster, the rice cooker, the bread maker, and all of the other appliances in her spotlessly clean kitchen looked as though they were all brand new, and the cupboards were full of neatly stacked plates and dishes made from the finest quality china.

Two slices of toast popped up from the toaster, and she placed them on a plate that had an exquisite floral pattern around the rim. After carefully covering both slices of toast with a thin layer of butter and a very generous layer of orange marmalade, she carried the plate together with her coffee mug to her living room where she set them down on the table. As she sat down and began eating, she watched her state of the art flat screen television that was showing the breakfast news program from the national NHK television channel.

Her tidy living room was filled with a white leather sofa, a desk where she kept her laptop computer, and plenty of wide bookshelves that were packed full of books and CD's. There was a hand woven Indian rug on the floor, and several prints of classical masterpieces from art museums in London and Paris hung on the walls. Two flower boxes full of geraniums were arranged on the small balcony that was connected to the living room by a large sliding glass door, and there was also a wooden wind chime hanging over the balcony that was perfectly still in the breezeless morning.

After finishing her breakfast and washing up the plate and mug, Suzuki settled into her sofa to watch a recording that she had made of the previous day's fifteen minute installment of the daily soap opera that was so popular throughout the country. When that had finished, she took her phone out of her handbag and pushed the buttons to select one of her stored numbers.

"Hello?" a sleepy voice answered.

"Good morning, Yoshi, are you awake yet?"

"Oh, hello, Atsuko. What time is it?"

"You're supposed to be picking me up in twenty-five minutes."

"Oh, really? Twenty-five minutes? I hadn't realized that it was so late."

"I know, Yoshi…that's why I'm calling you."

The suite of offices that belonged to Tsuda Business Solutions was located on the third floor of a modern looking building in the business district just across the Asahi River from the castle, and Suzuki and Mr. Sasaki were waiting outside the door when Ms. Tsuda arrived promptly at ten o'clock.

"Oh, good morning," Ms. Tsuda said. "Have I kept you waiting? We did say ten o'clock, didn't we?"

"Ah, good morning, Ms. Tsuda," Suzuki replied. "Yes, ten o'clock is what we said. And as I told you yesterday, I'm really sorry to have had to trouble you on a Sunday morning."

"Well, it's all right because I was able to rearrange the other plans that I had for today since you insisted that it was so important for us to meet."

"I'm afraid that police work can be like that, Ms. Tsuda. When you're in the middle of an important case things never seem to fit themselves into a nicely planned schedule."

"I'm sure that you're right," Ms. Tsuda replied curtly, and she unlocked the door and led them inside.

"By the way," Suzuki added, "this is my friend, Mr. Sasaki. He works for the Calamity Assurance Company, and he sometimes helps me out with my work."

"Good morning, Ms. Tsuda," Mr. Sasaki said cheerfully. "How very nice it is to meet you."

Ms. Tsuda looked at Mr. Sasaki a little doubtfully.

"Good morning," she replied, as she took them into her office and sank into the chair behind her large desk. "Now, Officer Suzuki, what is it that you need to discuss with me so urgently?"

Suzuki and Mr. Sasaki sat down in front of Ms. Tsuda's desk.

"Well, it's just a loose end that we're tidying up, actually. I wanted to ask you whether you've been doing any work for HoSHA—the Hot Spring Hotel Association?"

"HoSHA? Yes, they're one of our clients. Why?"

"Oh, it's nothing really, but perhaps you could tell me a little bit about the work that you've been doing for them? When did you start working with them?"

"We've had a contract with them since the beginning of this year. They're one of our newest clients."

The look on Ms. Tsuda's face made it abundantly clear that she did not consider a discussion about her work with HoSHA to be sufficiently important to warrant the disruption that it had caused to her Sunday morning schedule.

"I see," Suzuki persevered. "And what exactly is it that you're doing for them?"

"Oh, the usual kinds of thing. Our primary goal is to help them find ways to improve their relations with their customers—just like we're doing for you at the Police Department. We've been carrying out a very thorough analysis and breakdown of their clientele, and we've been looking for ways to improve their service. Our ultimate objective will be to broaden their market and to find ways to make the hot springs hotels appeal to a much larger sector of the population."

Mr. Sasaki nodded.

"Yes, I understand what you mean," he said. "It's surprising what you can learn if you collect some detailed information on a customer base. That sounds like a very useful study that you're doing for them. We do some similar things in the insurance industry."

Ms. Tsuda looked pleased.

"Yes, well, we're still in the early stages of our work for them, but the way that things have turned out so far, I think that we're going to be able to give HoSHA some very helpful advice that will make their industry much more competitive and much more modern in its outlook."

"That's great! I wish that some of the businesses that we provide insurance services to were just as forward-looking as HoSHA. It would make our job so much easier. Just between the three of us, some of the companies that I work with have very old-fashioned management practices—they're very set in their ways. They could do with some of your expertise, Ms. Tsuda. I'm sure that you'd be able to blow away some of the cobwebs and give them a very thorough overhaul!"

Ms. Tsuda began to view Mr. Sasaki more favorably.

"Oh, well I'm glad to hear that you see things that way," she said as she reached into her desk draw and withdrew a handful of her business cards. "Here…please take these, if you don't mind. If you have the chance to pass some on to your clients, I'd be very grateful."

"Oh, yes—I'll certainly do that, Ms. Tsuda—that will be no problem," Mr. Sasaki replied as he studied one of the cards.

"Err...I was wondering what sort of information you've been putting together about HoSHA," Suzuki said. "What kind of analysis are you conducting of the hot spring hotel industry? What kind of data have you collected so far?"

"Well, since March we've been handing out evaluation sheets to everybody who's stayed at one of HoSHA's hotels. We designed a customer evaluation sheet for them—rather like the Double-PS forms that you've been using at the Police Department—and we've distributed them to all of the association's hotels. We already have a couple of months of data from those sheets that we've started to analyze. And in addition, we've also been developing a database of HoSHA's clientele over the past two years from the registration records that each of the hotels has."

"Ah, yes...the registration records at the hotels. I think that's what we might be especially interested in. How exactly have you been compiling that database, and what kind of information do you have in it?"

"Oh, it's quite simple, really. We went to every hotel that's registered with HoSHA in this region, and we obtained copies of their registration cards stretching back to the year before last. You know what I mean, don't you? The registration cards that everybody has to fill in when they check into a hotel. They have information on the name and address of the guest, their date of birth, their telephone number, and the number of nights they stayed at the hotel—that kind of thing."

Suzuki and Mr. Sasaki both nodded.

"Well," Ms. Tsuda continued, "we went to each hotel and made photocopies of all of their old registration cards. We then brought all of the copies back here and sorted through them—they're in that room around the corner, actually. And our purpose was to create one big database with all of the information from those photocopies. We knew that when that had been done we'd be able to use it to compile some statistics on how many nights a year people stayed at the hot spring hotels, whether specific individuals returned to the same hotels, how many different hotels people visited, together with some basic socio-demographic information on the clientele of HoSHA's hotels."

"That's very clever," Mr. Sasaki said. "We do a very similar thing with our clients to keep track of their claims. It helps us to assess industry wide risk levels, and we also use the information to calibrate our premiums."

"Yes, that sounds very sensible," Ms. Tsuda said approvingly.

"Do you by any chance have a copy of this database that you've compiled, so that we could take a quick look at it?" Suzuki inquired.

Ms. Tsuda nodded as she reached over and opened up the laptop computer that was on the corner of her desk.

"Oh, yes, I'd be delighted to show it to you. It's so nice to come across somebody who's interested in that kind of thing."

Chapter 30

Inspector Morimoto and Police Officer Suzuki had both been rather worried that Suzuki's meeting with Ms. Tsuda on Sunday morning might turn out to be rather awkward, since they were both quite certain that Ms. Tsuda had not left their interview at the Police Headquarters with a very favorable impression of their organizational abilities. With that in mind, Suzuki was relieved to notice that Ms. Tsuda seemed to be warming up to the meeting, and that she appeared to be particularly flattered by Mr. Sasaki's interest in her database.

"I can show you the latest version of the database, at least," Ms. Tsuda said as her fingers flew over the keyboard. "It's not completely finished yet, because there's still some data from the hotel visits during the last month or so that haven't been entered yet. And for the latest guests, we're also adding the information from their evaluations sheets if they completed them, and not all of that data have been entered yet either."

"Oh, so you can cross-tabulate the evaluation scores against the information from the registration cards!" Mr. Sasaki exclaimed. "That'll be very interesting to look at!"

"Yes, that's what we're hoping to do. It should be fascinating, shouldn't it? Anyway, here's the database that we've managed to put together so far."

Ms. Tsuda proudly turned her computer around, and Suzuki and Mr. Sasaki leaned on the desk so that they could see the screen.

"Ah, that's exactly the same spreadsheet software that we use in our office," Mr. Sasaki said.

"Oh, really?" Ms. Tsuda replied. "I like it. It's very easy to use, don't you think?"

"Oh, yes—it doesn't take very long to get the hang of it. It's very user-friendly—at least for all of the basic functions. Did you update to version 5.3?"

"Yes, we did—I make sure that all of the computers in my company have regular software updates. There are some patches that you can download as well. Have you installed those in your office?"

"Yes, we've downloaded the patches as well, and I've found that the new version seems to have got rid of most of the bugs that we encountered in the previous versions. What do you think? The previous version that we used always had a nasty habit of freezing up whenever I tried to perform a cross-tabulation of two variables that happened to both have zeros in the same row."

"Oh, that happened to you too, did it? We had some terrible problems with that here—it used to be an awful nuisance."

"Yes, it was, wasn't it? But they seem to have fixed it in the latest version."

"Yes, I think so—we haven't had any problems like that with the new version yet."

Suzuki was content to sit back and listen to Mr. Sasaki and Ms. Tsuda share their mutual enthusiasm for the spreadsheet software and compare their experiences with it.

"So we decided to set up this first column here with some basic identification numbers," Ms. Tsuda explained, "so that we'd always have a convenient way to track the source of a given set of information."

"Yes, that's a good idea," Mr. Sasaki replied.

"And then we've put the surnames in this column, which is followed by several other columns that contain the other information that we collected from the guests' registration cards—do you see?"

"Yes, I see. That's very nice."

"And over here we've made a column which has the codes for the hotels."

"Hmmm...yes...that's wonderful. I can see that you've set it up very well. So there are lots of ways that you can play around with it, aren't there? If you highlight a name, for example, you could presumably search for all of the other entries in the database that are related to that person, couldn't you?"

"Oh, yes—that's quite simple. Let me show you. First of all you have to open this command box here—and as you suggested, let's search for repetitions of a name. So you just have to click on this options button and then check these boxes."

"Yes, that's right."

"Now, let's try it out. If I take this person here, and double-click, then we should get an output that shows us all of the hotels where she stayed over the past couple of years. Yes, here it is!"

"Wow! That's great!"

"We can see straightaway that this lady visits hot spring hotels on a regular basis, and we can see which of the hotels are her favorites."

"Yes...lucky lady," Mr. Sasaki said as he grinned at Suzuki.

"And there are lots of other ways that I can search through the database to find answers to all of the questions that I'm interested in. Let me show you something else. If I'm interested in a specific hotel, for example, then I can search through all of the information relating to that specific hotel, and collect those entries that match another criterion. So, for example, if I take this hotel here, then I might want to know how many of its customers are from Okayama city, say."

"Oh, you can set some delimiter values, can't you?"

Ms. Tsuda nodded.

"Yes, that's how I like to do it. I can specify Okayama city in this box here...and then I just have to click here...and there you are. All of the information pops up in this window over here."

"That's really fantastic, Ms. Tsuda. If you'd like to come over to my office some time, I'd be more than happy to show you some of the similar kinds of things that we do with our database of insurance claims. It's amazing what you can find out if you set it up to search for the right kinds of configurations."

"Oh, yes, it is, isn't it? I'd very much like to take you up on that offer some time, Mr. Sasaki. From what you've told me, I can tell that the Calamity Assurance Company is very forward-looking in its employment of databases. There's a wealth of information out there in databases that companies have access to that's just waiting to be tapped—information that's essential for constructing and fine-tuning optimal marketing and growth strategies. But some companies just don't seem to realize what they're missing."

The meeting was going much better than Suzuki had dared hope.

"Well," she said, "I can see just how tremendously useful this database must be for your work, Ms. Tsuda, and to tell you the truth, I can also see just how useful it could be to an investigation that we're in the middle of at the moment. Would you have any objections if I took a copy of this database back to the Police Headquarters with me?"

Ms. Tsuda looked surprised.

"Oh, really? You'd like a copy of it, would you? Hmmm...I need to think about that. What exactly do you want to use it for? If it's connected to your police work then that would be acceptable, I imagine. Technically, it's probably the property of HoSHA, I think. Can you give me an assurance that the database won't be leaked to any other organizations that might be able to benefit from it to HoSHA's disadvantage?"

"Oh, absolutely. You don't need to worry about that, Ms. Tsuda. We'll just put a copy of it on the computer in my office at the Police Headquarters, and nobody else will have access to it."

Ms. Tsuda shrugged.

"Well, all right then. I'll make a copy for you, but I'd better call HoSHA tomorrow and let them know that you've requested a copy."

"That will be fine."

As Ms. Tsuda inserted a CD into her computer and began to copy the database, a puzzled expression suddenly appeared on Suzuki's face.

"By the way, Ms. Tsuda, it must have been quite a lot of work transferring all of the information from the photocopies of the registration cards and from the evaluation sheets into the database. Did your company do all of that work?"

Ms. Tsuda shook her head vigorously.

"Oh, no—that would have been far too much work for us to handle all by ourselves. That was done by the computer company who we have a contract with. They've been handling all of that side of things for us. I've had a contract with them for a number of years now. They service all of our computers, and they send someone over to provide software training whenever we need it. I asked them whether they could handle all of the data entries for the database, and they were glad to oblige."

"I see."

"Every few weeks they send one of their men over here to update us to the latest version of the database that they've produced. He makes sure that we have everything installed properly and that the software is working properly. He's very good—he's been handling my company's computer affairs for a number of years now."

"I see."

"Yes, I'm very pleased with him."

"Good. What's his name?"

"His name? Err…Tokuda…Mr. Noritoshi Tokuda."

Chapter 31

▼

It was early afternoon when Inspector Morimoto walked into his office at the Police Headquarters to find Police Officer Suzuki and Mr. Sasaki hunched over the computer on Suzuki's desk. The table in the middle of the room was covered with empty boxes and wrappers from a rather extensive take-out lunch that Suzuki and Mr. Sasaki had obviously enjoyed just a short while before.

Mr. Sasaki stood up when he saw Morimoto.

"Oh, good afternoon, Mr. Sasaki. How are you today? It's nice to see you again."

"Good afternoon, sir. I'm doing very well, thank you. I've been helping Atsuko look through this database that Ms. Tsuda copied for us."

"Well, we're very glad for your help, Mr. Sasaki. Did your meeting go well, Suzuki?"

Morimoto sat down and lifted his feet up onto the corner of his desk.

"It went very well, sir. Yoshi and Ms. Tsuda really hit it off after they'd discovered a mutual fascination with software programs for database management. They had a great time playing around with the latest spreadsheet manipulations that they're both familiar with."

Morimoto smiled.

"I say...that is good news. Well done, Mr. Sasaki! You may have gone some way towards restoring our reputation with Ms. Tsuda. Did Suzuki tell you about our interview with her last week?"

Mr. Sasaki grinned.

"Oh, yes, I heard all about that, sir."

"Good. Well then, Suzuki, what exactly did you learn from Ms. Tsuda this morning?"

Suzuki went through the details of their meeting with Ms. Tsuda, and Morimoto nodded his head and rubbed his chin as he listened.

"And so," Suzuki finally said, "the hunch that you had when you spotted that Tsuda Business Solutions had prepared the evaluation sheets at the hotel turned out to be quite correct. Ms. Tsuda's company has indeed been organizing the compilation of a database of HoSHA's guests."

"That's very interesting."

"By the way, sir, how was the Kotohira Hot Bath Inn? Did you enjoy your stay?"

"Oh, it's a wonderful hotel. I had a very nice soak yesterday afternoon after I called you, and I had another one this morning before breakfast."

"That sounds lovely, sir. And did you get up in the middle of the night to see whether you were able to slip out of the hotel unnoticed?"

"Well, as a matter of fact, I did have a little wander around the hotel at thirty minutes after midnight this morning, and you'd be surprised how much activity there was. There were several groups of guests sitting around in the lobby chatting, and the reception desk was still staffed as well."

"Oh, I see. So if it had been like that when Mr. Hattori stayed in February, he wouldn't have been able to slip out through the lobby without being noticed."

"That's correct."

"If it had been me," Mr. Sasaki offered, "I'd have looked for a way out around the back of the hotel, or maybe out through a window."

"That's a good point, Mr. Sasaki. Actually, I specifically asked for a ground floor room, and I could easily have left by the window if I'd wanted to. It was quite dark outside, and I'm pretty certain that I could have slipped away unnoticed."

"Well in that case," Suzuki said, "it is plausible that Mr. Hattori could have managed to get out of the hotel at about that time without anybody knowing about it. And if he did, then he must have made his way to the cash machine in time to find those two ladies standing next to it while they were waiting for their taxi. And when the taxi had picked them up and driven away at 12:59, he must have started work on the cash machine with his crowbar, only to be interrupted by Mr. Yosano at 1:11, at which time he must have run away and made his way back to the hotel. He'd have been back in his room by about 1:30, I suppose."

"That sounds about right," Morimoto agreed.

"And in any case," Suzuki continued, "Mr. Hattori may not have been all that concerned about being spotted anyhow—at least not in the vicinity of his hotel. He'd obviously only have worn his mask while he was at the cash machine, and his crowbar could easily have been concealed underneath his jacket, say, or even in the backpack that he took with him to carry the cash."

"Yes, Suzuki, that sounds reasonable to me. Everything seems to indicate that Mr. Hattori could have managed to carry out the robbery if he'd wanted to. We haven't uncovered any evidence to suggest that it couldn't have been him. But the question still remains—was it really Mr. Hattori who did it?"

"Yes, that's the question, sir."

Morimoto thought for a moment.

"Incidentally, Mr. Sasaki, having you here today reminds me of that wonderful bottle of champagne that we drank with you when you visited us before—and we still have that other bottle over there that you brought for us."

Morimoto pointed towards the oversized bottle of champagne that was standing between the cactus plants in the middle of the low cupboard underneath the window to his right. It was the second of two bottles that Mr. Sasaki had given them when they had been working together at the end of the previous year.

"You know, Suzuki, we really should get around sometime to drinking that bottle of champagne."

"That sounds like an excellent idea, sir."

"Oh, and have you seen our lovely piece of Bizen pottery, Mr. Sasaki?" Morimoto asked, and this time he pointed to a small round teacup that was standing next to the champagne bottle. "That was made by a very important potter—somebody who we can expect to be hearing a great deal about in the future."

"Oh, yes, it's fantastic!" Mr. Sasaki exclaimed. "Atsuko showed it to me earlier on when we arrived—it's very pretty. And while we were having lunch she told me all about that dark red umbrella that you have over there in your umbrella stand as well."

"Ah, yes…the dark red umbrella. That'll come in very handy when the rainy season begins again in a month or two. Anyway, we'd better get down to work. What have you both been able to learn from that database so far?"

Later that afternoon, Mr. Sasaki dropped Suzuki off outside the tall building that was just down the road from Okayama station, on the other side of the Okayama Central Hospital. The top floors of the impressive building were occupied by Mr. Bando's law firm, and a minute later Suzuki was shown into Mr. Bando's office by his secretary.

Mr. Bando looked very relieved to see Suzuki as she walked across the plush golden yellow carpet and sank into one of the comfortably padded upholstered red leather armchairs in front of his large mahogany desk.

"Ah, Officer Suzuki, you don't know how glad I was when I received your phone call. I must confess that this probability business has been quite a challenge for me. And to tell you the truth, I don't think that I've really been able to make much progress with it at all. It's had me at sixes and sevens all weekend."

Suzuki looked at the piles of books on Mr. Bando's desk with titles like *'Teach Yourself Probability'*, *'Probability Theory in Three Easy Steps'*, and *'Probability Without Tears'*.

"I've done a fair amount of research on the topic, as you can see," Mr. Bando added, "but no matter which way I look at it, those odds of 225 million to 1 that Professor Shirane calculated in the courtroom last Friday morning look fiendishly difficult to discredit."

The secretary returned and placed a solid silver coffee set on the table next to Suzuki's chair.

"Ah, well don't worry because we've been busy this weekend as well," Suzuki said cheerfully, "and I believe that we may have come up with something that you'll find rather useful for your cross-examination of Professor Shirane tomorrow morning."

Chapter 32

Early the next morning, Monday, Inspector Morimoto and Police Officer Suzuki were having a cup of tea in their office at the Police Headquarters with Sergeant Yamada.

"There doesn't seem to be anything at all peculiar about the birthday party that Mr. Hattori was planning to attend in February, sir," Sergeant Yamada explained.

"I see," Morimoto replied. "Who did you manage to talk to about it?"

"Well, I went over to Kurashiki to interview Mr. Hattori's friend. He's quite upset that Mr. Hattori's on trial, by the way, and he can't believe that Mr. Hattori has been involved in anything like the cash machine robberies. But anyway, he confirmed that his birthday party had been arranged for the night when the Kotohira robbery occurred, and he explained that he'd cancelled it at the very last moment because of a sudden illness."

"And what about the phone call to Mr. Hattori that day?"

"The account that Mr. Hattori gave you seems to be quite correct, sir. His friend's sister called Mr. Hattori in the middle of the afternoon to tell him that the party had been cancelled—I spoke with her as well. She also said that she didn't know that Mr. Hattori had decided to spend the night in Kotohira after he'd received her call. In the end, they rearranged the party for two weeks later."

A short while after Sergeant Yamada had left, the Chief banged energetically on the door with the knuckles of his large hand and bounded into the room. The wide grin on his face showed that he was starting off his week in an excellent mood.

"Ah, good morning, Morimoto! Hello, Officer Suzuki! It's another fine morning, isn't it?"

"Very nice, sir," Morimoto replied, glancing at the cloudless blue sky out of the window.

"Have you noticed that the cash machine robbery trial's on the front page of the newspaper again this morning?"

The Chief pointed to the morning issue of the Okayama Tribune that was lying on the table in the middle of the room. There was a column on the far right of the page that discussed the status of the trial under the headline *'Very Small Probability That Defendant Will Make Headway in Cross-Examination'*.

"Yes, we've read through the report, sir."

"Mr. Bando's going to have a terribly tough job on his hands this morning, that's for sure. I bet he'll make a good try of it, though…he's very professional. But I'm sure that in his heart of hearts he must already have accepted the fact that he's not going to win this case."

The Chief's grin widened even more.

"Anyway, Morimoto, will you and Officer Suzuki be going over to the courthouse this morning?"

"Yes, we'd been planning to go, sir."

"That's good, but unfortunately I won't be able to make it myself. I have several other things to take care of, and I have to get ready for a rather special lunch that we're having here today. It was Ms. Tsuda's suggestion, actually. We're hosting a lunch for those members of the general public who have been particularly noteworthy in helping us out during the past year. It's meant to show our appreciation for how the general public helps us to fight crime. It's a jolly good idea, don't you think?"

"It should be very enjoyable for you, sir."

"Oh, yes, I'm certainly going to enjoy myself…it should be tremendous fun! I'm really looking forward to it. Incidentally, that chap who came to see you is going to be the guest of honor. Do you know who I'm talking about? You know…what's his name? The fellow who we watched giving evidence in court the other day. He spilled the beans about how Mr. Hattori had boasted that he'd done the cash machine robberies."

"Do you mean Mr. Tokuda, sir?"

"Yes, Tokuda! That's right. What a fine fellow he is. As I say, he'll be the guest of honor at lunch today, and I'm going to give him the inaugural Double-PA!"

"Double-PA?"

"Yes, Double-PA. You know, PAPA."

"PAPA?"

"Yes, the Police Appreciation Plaque Award. Haven't you been reading the newsletters that I've been sending around, Morimoto?"

Morimoto thought that it would be better not to answer this question.

"Well anyway, Morimoto, we've come up with these Double-PA's to recognize those members of the general public who distinguish themselves by contributing to our work in one way or another. And we're going to give the first one to Mr....err..."

"Tokuda, sir."

"Yes, that's right. I'm going to present him with the award at lunch today. It's just a little plaque for him to put on his wall...it's nothing too grand. The budget's very tight and I couldn't spare that much money for the actual award, to be completely honest with you, but it's the thought that counts, isn't it? And after all, he'll be getting a free lunch as well, so he doesn't really have anything to complain about. Anyway, this luncheon should make the point that we do appreciate the little ways in which the general public contributes to our work, don't you think so?"

"Undoubtedly, sir."

The Chief looked over his shoulder to check that there was nobody outside the office, and he lowered his voice.

"Incidentally, between you and me, this luncheon and the award are about the only good ideas that Ms. Tsuda's been able to come up with. She's been working with us for over a month now, and to tell you the truth, she's not nearly as good as I thought she'd be."

"Oh, really, sir?"

"Yes...there's no doubt about it. And do you know what? I'll let you into a little secret. I've decided to terminate her contract prematurely."

"Oh, that is surprising!"

"Well, I'm afraid that I really have no other alternative. It's my responsibility as head of the department to make unsavory decisions like this from time to time, and there's nothing that I can do about it. You see, Morimoto, their analysis of how we go about doing things here in the Police Department just hasn't turned out quite how I'd hoped."

"No?"

"No, it hasn't. For instance, one thing that I can tell you is that Ms. Tsuda's company is not at all good at data collection."

"It isn't?"

"No, it isn't—there's no doubt about it. In fact, the truth is that there's no escaping the fact that they're really completely hopeless when it comes to data collection."

"Oh, I see. Why do you say that, sir?"

"Well, the point is that Ms. Tsuda has been showing me some of the summaries that she's made from the evaluation sheets that we've been handing out…you know, the Double-PS's. And in particular she was showing me how people have been evaluating the work that I do. And I could see at once that she'd got it all wrong. It should have been completely obvious to anybody! They'd made a complete muddle of it!"

Morimoto looked puzzled.

"Oh, I was surprised by it as well, Morimoto…I can tell you. It's unbelievable, isn't it? And I think that I've been able to put my finger on where they made their mistake…where they went wrong. You know how there's that part on the form where you can fill out your degree of satisfaction on a scale of 1 to 5. Well, that's where Ms. Tsuda messed things up, Morimoto…that's where they'd made a total hash of compiling my statistics. Do you know what they'd done? They'd got the 1's and the 5's completely mixed up!"

Chapter 33

▼

Later that morning, Inspector Morimoto and Police Officer Suzuki were occupying their usual seats in the back row of the visitors gallery when Judge Noda reopened the court proceedings.

"Mr. Bando," she said in her clear authoritative voice, "we're ready for your cross-examination of the witness now."

Mr. Bando rose from his desk and confidently strode out into the courtroom wearing another expensive pinstripe suit, and his solid gold watch chain glistened in the strong fluorescent lighting as he looked down at Professor Shirane, who was calmly sitting in the middle of the room.

"Good morning, Professor Shirane."

"Good morning."

"I'd like to examine the testimony that you presented to this court at the end of last week. In your testimony you mentioned some odds of 225 million to 1, didn't you?"

"Yes, I did."

"And could you please remind the court what, in your opinion, those odds represent?"

"Yes, certainly. In my testimony I showed that if the match between Mr. Hattori's golf games and the cash machine robberies had arisen purely by chance, then the probability of that having happened was only 1 out of 225 million. Or in other words, to put that the other way around, there's only an extremely small probability that the match could have occurred just by chance."

"Well let's concentrate on that probability of 1 out of 225 million. Would you be surprised to learn that an event with such a low probability had occurred?"

"Yes, I'd be extremely surprised. I think that we all would be. The analogy that I presented when I considered the chance of choosing a single correct word out of 3,750 volumes of a book should give us all an easily understandable conception of just how small that probability is."

"And you were asked by the prosecution team to calculate that probability, were you, professor?"

"The odds of 225 million to 1? Err…yes…basically, that's right. I was asked to perform an analysis of how unlikely the match between the golf games and the robberies would be if they were unconnected."

Suzuki noticed that despite his attempts to comb it, Mr. Genda's bushy hair appeared particularly unruly that morning as he sat behind his desk, monitoring the performance of his witness.

Mr. Bando continued to fire his questions in rapid succession.

"The calculation that you made was based on the defendant having spent the night in the town of Shingo last August on the same day that the cash machine robbery occurred there, wasn't it?"

"Yes, it was. That was one component of my calculation."

"How do you know that the defendant stayed in Shingo that night, professor?"

"Well, I was told that he did."

"You were told by the prosecution team, were you?"

"Yes, I was."

"Did you verify that information for yourself?"

Professor Shirane shrugged.

"No, I didn't…I didn't see any reason to. I was told that Mr. Hattori had stayed in Shingo on the night in question, and I was asked to incorporate that fact into my analysis."

"So you were given that piece of information, and you didn't feel that you needed to verify it?"

"Yes."

"How many hotels are there in Shingo, professor?"

Professor Shirane looked surprised.

"Err…I really don't know."

Now Mr. Bando affected a look of surprise himself.

"You don't know how many hotels there are in Shingo?"

"No."

"Well, do you know how many people spent the particular Saturday night in August of last year that we're talking about in a hotel in Shingo?"

Professor Shirane shook his head.

"Err...no, I don't know."

"You didn't bother to find that out, professor?"

Professor Shirane smiled.

"Well, I don't need that piece of information for my calculation, so I didn't need to find it out."

"So you don't need to know the number of people who were staying in a hotel in Shingo that night, in order to perform the calculation that the prosecution team asked you to undertake?"

"Yes, that's correct."

"Well, let's suppose that for the purpose of our discussion here this morning, I was to tell you that there were only 10 hotel guests in the whole of Shingo that evening. Would that sound reasonable to you, professor?"

Professor Shirane shrugged again.

"Well, I'd have expected there to be many more hotel guests than that. I'm led to understand that Shingo is a popular resort town, and since we're talking about a Saturday night in the middle of the summer, I'd have expected it to be rather crowded with visitors."

"All right then, shall we say that there were 2,000 hotel guests in Shingo that evening?"

"Okay, if you want."

"If you were told that the defendant was one of those guests, and if you assume that one of the hotel guests was responsible for the cash machine robbery, doesn't that imply, professor, that the chance that the defendant committed the crime is only 1 out of 2,000?"

Professor Shirane smiled again.

"Well, I'm afraid that you don't really understand the nature of my calculation. I was considering the matter from a different perspective."

"Please answer the question, professor. Wouldn't the chance that the defendant committed the crime be only 1 out of 2,000?"

"Well, it's possible that you might want to say that if you looked at that specific question. But you're asking the wrong kind of question—that's not a very helpful question to consider."

"Do you mean that it's not the question that you were told to analyze by the prosecution team?"

"Well, it's not a very important question. The key point here that we need to focus on is the match between Mr. Hattori and the robberies at all three locations. What I analyzed was the extraordinary coincidence that Mr. Hattori was in

Shingo when the robbery occurred, and that he was also in the other two locations when the robberies occurred in those places. You have to look at those three events together. You don't need to be concerned with who else or how many other people were also staying at those locations. That's the way that the probability theory works."

"That's the way that the probability theory works for the way in which you were asked to consider the problem, is it?"

"Well…yes."

"So you're saying that you don't need to be concerned with how many other people were also staying in Shingo, Takebe, and Kotohira for the analysis that you were told to pursue by the prosecution team?"

"That's correct."

"And you didn't collect that additional information?"

"No. As I've said, that information is not needed for the calculation that I performed."

Mr. Bando walked up and down in front of his desk for a few moments, and he surreptitiously glanced up at the judge, whose immutable expression was as usual betraying none of her feelings.

"Well, Professor Shirane, you mentioned that your calculation involved all three of the cash machine robberies. You just told the court that we should look at all three events together, didn't you?"

"Yes, that's right."

"Well, let's do that now—let's look at all three of the events together. You were told by the prosecution team, were you not, that the defendant stayed in Shingo on the night of the robbery, that he stayed in Takebe on the night of the robbery, and that he stayed in Kotohira on the night of the robbery?"

"Yes, I was. That was the basis for my calculation."

"How many other people were also present in those three towns at those times?"

Professor Shirane looked unsure.

"Are you asking me whether there were any other people who were also in each of those three places on the specific days of the robberies?"

"That's exactly what I'm asking you, professor."

"Well, again…I've really no idea."

Mr. Bando took a step backwards in apparent shock, and he put a hand down on his desk to steady himself as he paused to let the courtroom digest Professor Shirane's answer.

"I'm sorry, professor," he said in a stunned voice, "did you say that you don't know?"

"Yes…I don't know. It's not information that I need for my calculation."

"Now, just a minute, professor. Have you not told this courtroom that your calculation is based on the fact that you've been told that the defendant was at the scene of each of the robberies on the exact days when they occurred?"

"Yes, that's true."

"And you have told the court that it's extremely unlikely for that to have occurred, haven't you?"

"Yes, I have—I've said that it's extremely unlikely to have occurred just by chance."

"And now you're telling the court that you don't know how many other people also fit that description?"

Professor Shirane shifted around in his chair and scratched his head.

"Well, it's not that important, really—not in terms of my calculation, I mean. It's really not. That information is not pertinent to my calculation."

"So you're saying, are you, that whether or not there were any other people who also stayed in the three towns at the times of the robberies, is not important information for the calculation that you were asked to perform?"

"Yes, that's right."

"And so you didn't bother to find out that information?"

"Well…no…because I didn't need to. As I keep telling you, that information is irrelevant to my calculation and to the point that I'm making."

Mr. Bando waited for a moment, allowing there to be a carefully measured period of silence in the courtroom before he continued.

"Let's suppose, professor, for the purpose of our discussion, that there were five people who stayed in hotels in each of the three towns on the nights in question. And let's suppose that the defendant was one of those five people. And let's suppose as well, that you were told that one of those five people committed the robberies. Would you expect that the defendant was guilty of committing the robberies?"

Professor Shirane thought for a while.

"Well, it all depends on what you mean by expect, doesn't it? Since the crowbar and the bank notes were found in Mr. Hattori's kitchen, I guess that I would expect that he was the criminal."

"Excuse me? Did you mention the crowbar and the bank notes, professor? Could you please clarify whether or not you used that information when you derived your odds of 225 million to 1?"

"Err...no, I didn't."

"I don't believe that you referred to the crowbar nor to the bank notes at all in your testimony last week, did you?"

"No, I didn't."

"And please remind the court again what it was that the prosecution asked you to do for them?"

Professor Shirane was starting to look annoyed.

"As I told you before, I was asked to analyze how unlikely it would be that the match between Mr. Hattori's golf games and the robberies had arisen purely by chance."

"And does that task have anything to do with the contention that the crowbar and the bank notes were found in the defendant's kitchen?"

"No."

"Well then, let's put that point aside, and let's go back to my original question. If there were five people who stayed in hotels in each of the three towns on the nights in question, and if the defendant was one of those five people, and if you were told that one of those five people had committed the robberies, would you expect that the defendant was guilty of having committed the robberies?"

Professor Shirane hesitated before answering.

"No, I guess not...not if you put the question like that."

"Why not, professor?"

"Well, according to the scenario that you've just described, there'd only be 1 chance in 5 that Mr. Hattori was responsible for the robberies."

"And that means that the defendant would be four times more likely to be innocent than to be guilty, doesn't it?"

"Well, yes...in that context. But I must protest! You're missing the whole point of my calculation. You don't seem to have understood my argument at all. What we should be focusing on here is the fact that Mr. Hattori was staying in those towns as compared with being somewhere else. It doesn't matter to me who else was staying in those towns. It doesn't matter to me how many other people stayed in those towns on those days."

Professor Shirane jabbed the air with his finger as he made his points.

"And it doesn't matter to me who those other people might be, or what they were doing there, or where else they'd stayed. That's all completely irrelevant to me. I'm just concentrating on one issue, which is that Mr. Hattori was in those towns on those days, and I've shown that it's extremely unlikely for that to have happened by chance. I derived the odds as being 225 million to 1, and I stand by my calculation and its implications."

Chapter 34

Along with everybody else in the courtroom, Inspector Morimoto and Police Officer Suzuki were completely absorbed by the intellectual tussle that was taking place between Mr. Bando and the witness, which had all of the hallmarks of a championship boxing match between two heavyweight contenders. Mr. Genda sat monitoring the battle on his side of the ring, trying to offer moral support to his witness with a show of unperturbed confidence, although his bushy hair had become even more ruffled than it had been at the start of the proceedings. On the other side of the ring, the defendant, Mr. Hattori, sat sandwiched between the two policemen who were his constant companions in the courthouse, and he made his contribution to the battle by staring disdainfully at the witness whenever Professor Shirane suggested that he was responsible for the robberies.

Each person in the courtroom had their own personal feelings about which one of the two contestants had managed to land the stronger blows, but everyone was also well aware that the only scorer who really counted was Judge Noda, and as usual she was giving nothing away about her interpretation of the contest up to that point.

With his eyes fixed on the witness, Mr. Bando began his next round of questions.

"Professor Shirane, I'm interested in the meaning of these odds of 225 million to 1 that you keep quoting. You said earlier this morning that you'd be extremely surprised to learn that an event with such a low probability had occurred, didn't you?"

"Yes, I think that anybody would be surprised by that."

"Well, it's you that I'm particularly interested in, professor, because you're professing a level of expertise in this field of probability theory. You yourself would be extremely surprised, would you?"

"Yes, I would. The example that I gave about being able to guess the one correct word out of 3,750 volumes of a book should make it clear to everybody how extremely surprised I'd be."

"Thank you. And by implication, you're suggesting to the court that you'd be extremely surprised if the match between the defendant's golf games and the robberies was just a chance event, are you?"

"Yes, I am."

"I understand. By the way, do you ever play in the National Lottery, professor?"

Professor Shirane smiled.

"Well, I must admit that I do have a little flutter occasionally, but I've never been lucky enough to win."

"Would you be surprised if you won the jackpot, professor?"

"Yes, I would be—pleasantly surprised, though!"

Professor Shirane let out a short chuckle, and he looked up at the judge who returned his gaze with her usual deadpan expression.

"Would you be extremely surprised, professor?"

"Yes, I think that it's fair to say that I would be."

"And why would you be so extremely surprised, professor?"

"Well, obviously the chance of winning the jackpot is very small."

"The odds of winning the jackpot are very small, aren't they?"

"Yes."

"And the odds of 225 million to 1 that you've quoted are very small, aren't they?"

"Yes," Professor Shirane replied patiently, "they're very small as well."

Mr. Bando walked over to his desk and picked up a newspaper.

"This is a copy of the Osaka Times from two weeks ago. You live and work in Osaka, don't you, professor?"

"Yes, I do."

Mr. Bando opened up the newspaper.

"There's an article here about the National Lottery, and I'd like to read you the first few sentences, professor. This is what it says. 'The drawing for the early summer jackpot was made yesterday afternoon at the National Lottery Headquarters, and the winner was seventy-three year old Mrs. Toyoshima from Tokyo. She was reported to have been overwhelmed by the news, and she said that she'd never won anything else in her life before.' Did you read that article, professor?"

"Err...I don't really remember. I don't recall having read it."

"Would you have been surprised if you'd read it?"

"Surprised? No."

"You wouldn't have been at all surprised to open up the newspaper and find that article?"

Professor Shirane shrugged.

"No."

"So you certainly wouldn't describe yourself as being, shall we say, extremely surprised if you'd read that article?"

"No, not at all."

"Do you think that Mrs. Toyoshima had a good chance of winning the jackpot?"

"Well, no. She must have had about the same chance as everybody else who played...although it's possible that she might have bought a lot of tickets, I guess. I don't know."

"But the odds of Mrs. Toyoshima winning the lottery must have been very small, mustn't they?"

"Yes, they undoubtedly were."

"And Mrs. Toyoshima won the lottery just by chance, didn't she?"

"Yes, I presume so."

"Well, professor, could you please explain to the court why you wouldn't have been at all surprised to discover that Mrs. Toyoshima won the lottery purely by chance, while at the same time you claim that you'd be extremely surprised to discover that Mr. Hattori happened to have played golf at the three crime scenes purely by chance."

Professor Shirane fidgeted with his necktie while he thought about Mr. Bando's tricky question.

"Err...well...umm...they're different. They're two completely different things...they're not the same thing. You're confusing the issue. I mean...I don't know Mrs. Toyoshima."

"Do you know the defendant?" Mr. Bando shot back quickly.

Everybody noticed that Professor Shirane turned just a little pink.

"Well, no...I don't...I don't know the defendant."

"Well then, professor, why is it that you claim to be not at all surprised by one of these unlikely events, but extremely surprised by the other one?"

Professor Shirane shifted around in his chair again and gazed up at the ceiling for a while.

"Well...err...you see...it's a question of how you look at the two events. I mean, as I said, if it had been me who'd won the lottery, then I'd have been extremely surprised by that."

"So, are you telling the court, professor, that you'd have been surprised if you'd won the jackpot, but that you wouldn't have been surprised if you'd learned that Mrs. Toyoshima had won the jackpot?"

Professor Shirane scratched his head and began to look more and more perplexed.

"Well, as I said, you're confusing the issue here. Of course I'd have been surprised if I'd won the jackpot. Anybody would be surprised if they won the jackpot, wouldn't they? But I'm not surprised that somebody else won it. And that's the point, you see—as far as I'm concerned, Mrs. Toyoshima is just somebody else. She's just one of the people out there that I don't know. I mean...what I'm trying to say is...if I'd known Mrs. Toyoshima, and if she were a friend of mine, say, then I'd have been very surprised that she'd won the jackpot. So in that sense, winning the jackpot and the perfect match between the golf games and the robberies are two extremely unlikely events, and I'd be very surprised to learn that either of them had occurred."

It was clear to those members of the courtroom who had a clear view of Professor Shirane's face, including Judge Noda, Mr. Genda, and Mr. Bando, that Professor Shirane did not appear to be completely convinced by his own answer.

Mr. Bando felt that he was gaining the advantage, and he eagerly continued with his determined and relentless assault.

"So, is the courtroom to understand, professor, that if the jackpot is won by somebody who you know, then you'd register extreme surprise at that event, but on the other hand, if the jackpot is won by somebody who you don't know, then you wouldn't be in the least bit surprised?"

"Well...yes...you could say that. And I think that most people would feel exactly the same way. We'd all be pleasantly surprised if somebody we knew won, but we wouldn't be surprised if somebody else won. I mean, after all, somebody's got to win the jackpot, haven't they?"

"Well then, professor, is it not also true to say that you'd be surprised if something unlikely happened to somebody that you knew, but that you wouldn't be surprised if that unlikely event happened to somebody somewhere who you had no connection with?"

There was a long moment of silence while Professor Shirane thought about Mr. Bando's subtle generalization of the National Lottery.

"Well...yes...there is some truth to what you said."

"Is what I said true or not true, professor?"

"It's true, I guess."

"A moment ago you said that you didn't know the defendant—am I right?"

"Yes."

"And you've never had any previous connection with the defendant, have you, professor?"

"Err...no...not as far as I know. Not before I was asked to undertake the work for these legal proceedings."

"Well then, professor, since the defendant is somebody that you have no connection with, just like you have no connection with Mrs. Toyoshima, doesn't it follow from what you've told the court this morning that you shouldn't be at all surprised that an unlikely random event, such as the match between the golf games and the robberies, happened to the defendant, just in the same way that you're not at all surprised that Mrs. Toyoshima won the lottery?"

There was silence again in the courtroom. Professor Shirane was not at all sure whether he had slowly dug himself into the hole in which he found himself, or whether he had been pushed into it headfirst, but he was quite certain that he had not been expecting such an exhausting and difficult morning.

"I am extremely surprised at the perfect match between Mr. Hattori's golf games and the three robberies because I calculated the odds of that match to be 225 million to 1," he said, having decided to retreat to his own testimony.

"But you do agree, do you not, professor, that it's not surprising that unlikely events will happen to some people at some times?"

"It depends on exactly what you mean."

"Well, winning the jackpot is an unlikely event, isn't it?"

"Yes."

"And as you said, it's not surprising that somebody somewhere wins the jackpot, is it?"

"No, of course not, because somebody's got to win it."

"So it's not surprising that the unlikely event of winning the jackpot happens to somebody, is it?"

"No—that's what I just said."

"Well, why are you telling the court that it would be surprising if this supposedly unlikely thing happened to the defendant?"

Professor Shirane decided that he had better launch an attack of his own.

"Well, I understand more clearly now the mistake that you're making here. You see, the prosecution team contacted me, and they asked me to evaluate the likelihood that Mr. Hattori had stayed in the same places as the three robberies, and at the exact same times, just by chance. They asked me to calculate that probability for Mr. Hattori—for that specific person—and I came up with a value of 225 million to 1. And that's a very unlikely event. So what I've shown is that it's very unlikely that Mr. Hattori—the person of interest in this trial—could have done that purely by chance. Consequently, it would be extremely surprising if the match between the golf games and the robberies happened to Mr. Hattori. That's a fact, and there's no way around it!"

Professor Shirane began to jab his finger in the air again as he spoke to emphasize his points.

"And the mistake that you're making," he continued, "is that you're confusing my analysis for Mr. Hattori with some theoretical question about whether there's somebody else out there—somebody who none of us know about—who also might have stayed in the same places as the three robberies at the exact same times. But as I explained before, whether there were any other people who also did what Mr. Hattori did is irrelevant to my calculation."

Mr. Bando did not flinch at all, and he calmly asked his next question without any hesitation.

"Would you be surprised if there were some other people?"

Professor Shirane shrugged.

"No, it wouldn't necessarily surprise me. It doesn't matter to me. I don't care about that."

"So you wouldn't be surprised if there happened to be somebody else besides Mr. Hattori who stayed in Shingo, Takebe, and Kotohira on the nights of the cash machine robberies?"

"No."

"So if the prosecution team had asked you whether it would be surprising for there to be somebody who had stayed in Shingo, Takebe, and Kotohira on the nights of the cash machine robberies, what would you have advised them?"

Professor Shirane shifted around in his chair some more.

"Well…you have to be very careful how you state that question. If you present a specific person to me and ask me whether I'd be surprised to learn that they'd done that, then I'd say that I'd be extremely surprised. But on the other hand, if you ask me in general terms whether there's somebody out there who did that, then I might not be surprised to find out that there was somebody."

"Well, professor, could you please clarify for the court exactly what the difference is that you're alluding to here? Suppose that I searched through all of the hotel registration records to find somebody who had stayed in these three places on the specific days in question, and suppose that I was able to find such a person, and suppose that I brought them to you and told you where they'd been staying at the times of the robberies. And suppose that the person was the defendant. Would you then be extremely surprised at what the defendant had done?"

"Oh, no—that's quite different. My probability calculation doesn't apply if you'd specifically gone and searched for somebody who'd been staying at the three crime scenes."

Mr. Bando contemplated with deep satisfaction his hopeful expectation regarding the effect that this last sentence uttered by Professor Shirane would have on the judge.

"Your probability calculation would be invalid in that case, wouldn't it, professor?"

"Yes, because those are different circumstances than I considered."

Mr. Bando walked away from the witness triumphantly.

"I have no further questions, your honor," he said to Judge Noda, and then he went and sat down behind his desk, and shot a glance over at Suzuki in the visitors gallery that was laden with gratitude.

Chapter 35

Inspector Morimoto and Police Officer Suzuki were sitting in their office at the Police Headquarters that afternoon when there was a polite knock on the door.

"Ah, Mr. Izumi!" Morimoto exclaimed. "How are you? Come on in and sit down."

"Good afternoon, Inspector—good afternoon, Officer Suzuki. How have you been?"

"Oh, we've been keeping pretty busy," Morimoto replied. "What brings you over to the Police Headquarters?"

"Well, I've just had lunch with the Chief of Police, as a matter of fact. I was invited to attend the special luncheon that he held to mark his appreciation for the contribution that ordinary members of the general public make to police work."

"Ah, yes—the Chief was telling us all about that this morning."

"He gave an award to the fellow who broke open the investigation into the robberies of our cash machines."

"Yes, we heard about that as well. By the way, before I forget—congratulations on your promotion!"

Mr. Izumi smiled.

"Well, thank you very much."

"How long is it since they moved you over to the main office?"

"Oh, it was only a little over a month ago. It's a step up the ladder, I guess, but I'm already missing the life I had at the Takashima Branch. Things were much less hectic there."

"Really? What kind of work are you doing now at the main office?"

"Oh, they've got me involved in all kinds of different projects. And one of the things that I'm in charge of is the coordination of our activities with regards to the cash machine robberies."

"Yes, we saw you give evidence in court last week when you identified the bank notes that were found in Mr. Hattori's kitchen as having been stolen from your cash machine in Kotohira."

Mr. Izumi nodded.

"I noticed you both sitting at the back of the visitors gallery with the Chief. The Public Prosecutor got in touch with me about those bank notes a couple of weeks ago and I've been assisting him with the matter."

"Yes, so I understand."

"Anyway, since I was in the building I thought that I'd drop by to say hello to you both."

"We're very glad that you did, aren't we, Suzuki?"

"Yes, it's very nice to see you again, Mr. Izumi. Your leg seems to have healed very well."

"Oh, thank you! It's as good as new, actually—I've not had any problems with it. Anyway, to tell you the truth, since I'm over here I was also hoping to bring up the matter of the reward with you—the reward that we've offered for information on the cash machine robberies. In fact, that's the reason why I was invited to lunch today, I expect—to meet Mr. Tokuda. The Chief introduced me to him after he'd received his award."

"Oh, did he?"

"Yes. Anyway, we've been monitoring Mr. Hattori's trial over at the bank, and we're anticipating that he's going to be convicted. From what we can see, the odds are very much tilted in that direction. And consequently, we're beginning to put together the arrangements for paying out the reward money."

Morimoto nodded slowly and rubbed his chin.

"As I recall, it's a very substantial sum of money that the Metropolitan Trust Bank has offered as a reward, isn't it, Mr. Izumi?"

"Yes, I think it's fair to say that it is very substantial. We haven't made public the exact amounts of money that were stolen from each of our cash machines, but between you and me, the truth is that the reward money is a considerably greater sum than Mr. Hattori obtained from his heists. That decision was made very high up in the bank. I believe that the idea is to demonstrate just how seriously we're treating this matter, and just how important we feel that it is to create a safe and secure environment for our customers."

"I see. And what rules have been specified concerning the distribution of the reward money?"

"Well, it's quite simple really. Anybody who provides any information that is consequential in obtaining a conviction for any of the robberies is eligible to share in the reward. And if Mr. Hattori is convicted, then the only person who meets that criterion is Mr. Tokuda."

"So how much of the reward money will Mr. Tokuda receive?"

"Well, he's on track to receive the whole sum himself. And as you might imagine, he was more than a little eager to bring the matter up with me when I met him at lunch just now."

"Yes, I can quite imagine that he was. Lucky Mr. Tokuda!"

"Yes, indeed! It's turned out to be quite fortunate for him that he happened to bump into Mr. Hattori in that bar."

"So it would seem. When are you planning to give the reward money to him?"

"Oh, it'll be as soon as the judge makes a decision in the trial. We won't waste any time over it. There will inevitably be a lot of publicity, I expect—perhaps another lunch and another award as well. Who knows? Anyhow, we'll want to make sure that the ceremony gets on television and into all of the newspapers. That's the point of it really—to act as a deterrent to anybody else who might be in the process of hatching some nasty plans to rob us."

"Yes, I understand. Well, that's very interesting, Mr. Izumi—and as I said, it's very nice to see you again."

"Yes, likewise. When we have the ceremony at the bank and present the reward to Mr. Tokuda, we'll be inviting you both, of course."

"That's very kind of you, Mr. Izumi. But if I might give you a little tip—just between the two of us—we were in court this morning, and Mr. Bando made a very good job of his cross-examination of Mr. Genda's probability expert. And incidentally, I'm very proud of the fact that Mr. Bando's clever angle of attack was arrived at after he'd had some very intense coaching from Officer Suzuki in the area of probability theory."

Mr. Izumi raised his eyebrows.

"Oh, is that true? I hadn't realized that you were working for the defense."

"Well, we're not really...we're only trying to solve some of the intriguing puzzles that the case has raised so that we can get to the bottom of what's really been going on. But anyway, I thought that I ought to let you know that in this office, at least, there's a growing suspicion that there's still a lot more to unfold in that courtroom before the trial is over."

Mr. Izumi looked even more surprised.

"Oh, really?"

"Yes, so you might want to bear that in mind as you begin to make your arrangements for disbursing the reward money. Who knows? Perhaps in the end the Metropolitan Trust Bank may decide that the most appropriate use of the reward money would be as a donation to the Police Inspector's Retirement Fund?"

Chapter 36

▼

After Mr. Izumi had left, Inspector Morimoto leaned back in his chair and lifted his legs up onto the corner of his desk as Police Officer Suzuki brought a cup of green tea and a chocolate biscuit over to his desk.

"Thank you, Suzuki. We've got some serious thinking to do now, and we've got to be quick about it."

"Indeed we have, sir."

"Let's go back to that database that you and Mr. Sasaki obtained from Ms. Tsuda. Precisely what have we learned from it?"

Suzuki sat down at her desk, crossed her legs, and folded her arms.

"Well, sir, the situation is this. The most important point from our perspective is that HoSHA's database contains information from all of the hot spring hotels in Okayama prefecture and Kagawa prefecture. And that information includes details of the guests who have stayed at the hotels within a time span that stretches back to the beginning of last year. And in particular, the three hot spring hotels in Shingo, Takebe, and Kotohira where Mr. Hattori stayed on the nights of the robberies are part of the database."

"So the first thing that we can do with the database is to confirm that Mr. Hattori really was checked into those hotels on those days."

"Exactly, sir, and the database does confirm that fact. Moreover, we can also see that Mr. Hattori stayed in some other hot spring hotels during the time period in question as well."

"Yes, and there's nothing particularly surprising about that because he told us that he often stayed overnight when he went on his golf trips, so we'd have expected to find the records of the other hotels where he stayed."

"That's right, sir."

"And it's also worth noting that several of the other hotels where Mr. Hattori stayed were also in small towns that had cash machines, although those cash machines weren't robbed."

"That's true, sir. So if Mr. Hattori is the robber, then that does suggest that he was somewhat selective when it came to deciding where to carry out his criminal activities."

"Or it means that some of his robbery attempts were thwarted in some way. Perhaps he had difficulty getting out of his hotel in some of the towns without being too conspicuous, or maybe the area around the cash machine was too busy and he didn't want to risk being caught."

"That's always possible, sir."

"However, if we go back to the database again, and if we just concentrate on the hot spring hotels in Shingo, Takebe, and Kotohira where Mr. Hattori stayed, we can also extract some information about who else stayed in those hotels."

"We can indeed, sir. And we can also perform a search to find out if there were any other people besides Mr. Hattori who stayed at those three hotels on those three nights. Moreover, there's more than one hot spring hotel in each of those three towns, so more generally, we can expand the search to find out whether anybody else besides Mr. Hattori stayed in a hot spring hotel in each of the three towns in question on the exact nights of the three robberies."

"And that's one of the things that you did yesterday afternoon with Mr. Sasaki."

"That's correct, sir. And the answer is that there's nobody else besides Mr. Hattori in the database who stayed in Shingo, Takebe, and Kotohira on the nights of the robberies."

"So does that mean that we can conclude that Mr. Hattori really is the only person who stayed in the three towns on the nights of the robberies?"

"Up to a point, sir. However, we should remember that Shingo, Takebe, and Kotohira have many other hotels which don't have hot spring facilities and which consequently aren't affiliated with HoSHA. Those hotels aren't in the database, so we don't have any information about their guests. Consequently, we can't definitely rule out the possibility that somebody else besides Mr. Hattori stayed in each of the towns on the nights of the robberies."

"That's true, Suzuki, and Mr. Bando made quite sure this morning that Judge Noda was made well aware of that fact. During his cross-examination he suggested the possibility that Mr. Hattori might be just one of five such people."

"Yes, he did—but that was pure speculation, actually. I doubt that anybody really knows for sure whether Mr. Hattori really is unique or not in that respect, and Mr. Bando also made a point of establishing for Judge Noda the fact that Professor Shirane himself certainly doesn't know, nor did he even try to find out."

"Yes, that's right. But anyway, let's go back again to the HoSHA database that we have. We've found out that in the database, Mr. Hattori is unique in that he's the only person whose stays in the hot spring hotels coincided with the robberies. And that leads us to the important matter of how that coincidence can be explained. Professor Shirane's point of view in his testimony last Friday was that the coincidence is so unbelievable that it leads us to conclude that Mr. Hattori must have had something to do with the robberies."

"Exactly, sir, and Professor Shirane's testimony was quite accurate from the point of view of the way that he posed the problem. But we might ask ourselves whether he posed the right problem. I think that Mr. Bando did an excellent job of addressing that issue this morning."

"Thanks to the training that you gave him yesterday evening."

Morimoto took a bite out of his chocolate biscuit.

"So what exactly did you explain to Mr. Bando last night?"

"Well, sir, we started off from the obvious fact that if Mr. Hattori committed the robberies, then that's the explanation for the match between where he stayed and where the robberies occurred."

"But as we said before, it would have been rather incautious of him to have committed the robberies while he was staying in the towns, wouldn't it?"

"Possibly, although it's not at all inconceivable that he never imagined that anybody would ever crosscheck the hotel registrations in the three locations."

"That's true."

"But anyway, sir, Mr. Bando and I then explored the more interesting puzzle of how the match between Mr. Hattori's hotels and the robberies could have arisen if Mr. Hattori is innocent and wasn't connected to the robberies in any way. And as you might imagine, that was something that Mr. Bando was much more eager to discuss."

"Yes, I'm sure that he was."

"The essential claim of Professor Shirane's testimony is that it's impossible for the match to have arisen purely by chance—or at least that it's too unlikely to be believable. Professor Shirane's claim is that if Mr. Hattori is innocent, then the chance of the perfect match is only 1 out of 225 million. Consequently, since there is a perfect match between Mr. Hattori's hotels and the robberies, the implication of Professor Shirane's testimony is that Mr. Hattori cannot be innocent."

"Yes, and that's what Mr. Genda is hoping that Judge Noda will decide. In simple terms, the prosecution's argument is that if Mr. Hattori is innocent, then the chance of him having stayed in the same locations as the robberies at the exact same times is extremely unlikely. Therefore, since there was such a match, we have to conclude that Mr. Hattori cannot be innocent."

"Precisely, sir. But following our discussion yesterday evening, Mr. Bando was able to put a dent in that sequence of logical arguments by pointing out that while it may be extremely unlikely that Mr. Hattori stayed in the same locations as the robberies at the exact same times, it may not be unlikely that there's somebody who did that."

"Yes, and that's what Mr. Bando just about succeeded in getting Professor Shirane to admit in court this morning. The distinction is whether you myopically focus on one single individual, or whether you broaden your horizons and look at everybody."

"That's the key point, sir. For example, I have HoSHA's database loaded onto my computer right in front of me here, so we could conduct another search if we wanted to. Let's suppose that we picked three new hotels at random in three new locations, and that we randomly specified three new dates. Then one question would be whether or not the Chief, say, stayed in those hotels on those dates. The Chief makes no secret of the fact that he enjoys a good soak in a hot spring from time to time, so it's not at all an unreasonable question."

"I understand, Suzuki. And it would be very unlikely that the Chief happened to be staying in each of those three hotels that we randomly chose, on those three days that we randomly specified. We could perform some sort of a calculation similar to Professor Shirane's to get an idea of what the odds might be, but they'd certainly be very small."

"That's correct, sir. So if I searched through the database right now and found that the Chief's hotel stays really did match our three random scenarios, then we'd both be extremely surprised."

"We would indeed. And that's why Professor Shirane said that he'd be extremely surprised if Mr. Hattori's golf trips matched the three robberies purely by chance."

"Exactly, sir. But on the other hand, another question that we could pose is whether we'd be able to find anybody whose hotel visits matched our random scenario if we searched through the entire database."

"Yes, and it's a completely different matter if we just look for anybody. It might still be unlikely, but it wouldn't be particularly remarkable if we did happen to be able to find somebody who'd done that."

"It wouldn't, sir, especially if we picked weekend dates at times when the hot spring resorts were crowded."

"That's a very good point. So the distinction that we're making here is between the first question, where we ask whether somebody who we identified in advance has the match, and the second question, where we more generally ask whether there's anybody who has the match."

"Yes, sir, and while the first situation may be extremely unlikely to have occurred, the second situation may not be so unlikely."

"And Mr. Bando's analogy of playing the National Lottery is an excellent way of clarifying the distinction between the two situations. It will be very unlikely for the Chief to win the next jackpot drawing, but it won't be at all unlikely for somebody somewhere to win it. In fact, it's guaranteed that somebody's going to win it!"

"Precisely, sir. As one of my professors at Tokyo University used to tell us, unlikely events happen all the time to somebody somewhere—it's just that it would be strange if they happened to you or me."

Chapter 37

Inspector Morimoto carried the teapot over to Police Officer Suzuki's desk and filled up her teacup. After he had also replenished his own teacup, he sat down and assumed his favorite thinking position again.

"Well, Suzuki, if we proceed on the assumption that Mr. Hattori is being framed for these cash machine robberies, then I believe that we can make the obvious deduction that the person who's framing him must have been aware of his trips to Shingo, Takebe, and Kotohira."

"Absolutely, sir, although to be a little more precise, we can deduce that at the time when this unknown person decided to frame Mr. Hattori, the person must have been aware of the trips. That doesn't imply that the person knew about Mr. Hattori's trips at the times when he made them."

"Yes—that's a very subtle point, Suzuki, but a very critical one. And consequently, we are inevitably led towards the vital question—who knew about Mr. Hattori's trips?"

"That's definitely the key question, sir. At first we thought that it must be one of Mr. Hattori's golf friends, or perhaps somebody who had been monitoring his activities, but we were confounded by the fact that nobody appears to have known about Mr. Hattori's stay in Kotohira at that time. But now that we know about the database, we can see that it's possible for somebody to have discovered the remarkable coincidence between Mr. Hattori's trips and the robberies long after the trips had been made and the robberies had occurred."

"Anybody with access to the database would have been able to discover that."

"That's right, sir."

"And furthermore, I believe that it's now clear why Mr. Hattori is the person who's being framed. He's the ideal candidate because he was staying at each of the crime scenes at the times of the incidents, and anybody with the database would have been able to discover that."

"That's quite correct, sir. And who do we discover was involved in the compilation of the database? None other than Mr. Tokuda, who wandered over here one Monday morning to tell us what he'd heard Mr. Hattori boast about in a bar the previous evening. Mr. Tokuda had access to HoSHA's database through his work for Tsuda Business Solutions, and consequently, all of the indications are that Mr. Tokuda has tried to frame Mr. Hattori."

"Yes, Suzuki, I agree with you. And on top of that, our theory also implies that Mr. Tokuda is likely to be the real robber."

"It certainly looks that way, sir."

Morimoto rubbed his chin as he pondered the implications of their deduction.

"So, can you lay it all out for us, Suzuki? Let's go right back to the beginning and let's make sure that all of the pieces fit together properly."

"Very well, sir. So we'll start off by assuming that Mr. Tokuda robbed the three cash machines. He probably used basically the same plan each time—driving at night to a small town and wearing a mask while he carried out the robbery. The only time that he was interrupted was when the rather inebriated Mr. Yosano stumbled across him in Kotohira. Mr. Yosano described the masked robber as being a man of average height with a rather muscular build, and that description could easily fit Mr. Tokuda."

"Yes, it could."

"I expect that Mr. Tokuda must have driven back to Okayama immediately after each robbery. And the choices of the locations of the three robberies were probably made somewhat randomly, although I expect that he selected locations that appealed to him by virtue of the fact that he thought they'd be quiet and easy to get away from."

"I imagine that's true."

"And the locations and the timings of the robberies had nothing to do with Mr. Hattori's golf games."

"No, they didn't—they were absolutely unconnected to Mr. Hattori in any way. When Mr. Tokuda carried out the robberies, he wouldn't have known anything about Mr. Hattori."

"Exactly, sir. And if Mr. Tokuda had left things just like that, then he'd most probably have been just fine because we really didn't have any leads on him—the investigation into the robberies wasn't really going anywhere. But it looks like the key event that seems to have changed things was when the Metropolitan Trust Bank decided to offer a very large reward for any information that resulted in the arrest and conviction of the robber."

"Yes, coupled with the fact that Mr. Tokuda suddenly found that he had access to HoSHA's database."

"That's right, sir. Some time this year, after he had completed the February robbery in Kotohira, Mr. Tokuda began helping Tsuda Business Solutions compile and analyze HoSHA's database. And he'd have had plenty of opportunities to play around with it by himself, and to do the search which I did yesterday with Mr. Sasaki—namely to find out that there was a person called Mr. Hattori who just by chance happened to have stayed in Shingo, Takebe, and Kotohira on the exact nights when the robberies took place there."

"And when he realized what this Mr. Hattori had done, purely by chance, he must have started to hatch a rather cunning scheme that would allow him to frame Mr. Hattori for the robberies, and which would put himself in a position to collect the reward money."

"That's the way it looks, sir."

"So according to this theory, Mr. Tokuda carried out the three robberies himself, and then was so greedy that he thought that it might be nice to try to collect the reward money as well."

"Yes."

"That's a nice little scheme, isn't it? And as Mr. Izumi explained to us earlier this afternoon, the reward money is actually a substantially larger sum than the total amount of cash that Mr. Tokuda was able to extract from the three cash machines. So if he'd been willing to run the risk of committing the three robberies, then it's perhaps not too surprising that he was unable to resist the temptation of having a go at getting the reward money as well."

"So it would seem, sir."

"It's rather comical in a way. First you commit the crime, and then you blame it on somebody else so that you can collect the reward money yourself. Mind you, I don't think that the management of the Metropolitan Trust Bank would find that idea very funny."

Suzuki smiled.

"No, sir, I doubt that's what they had in mind when they decided to establish the reward."

"Quite definitely not, Suzuki. Anyhow, how do you think that Mr. Tokuda must have gone about setting up his scheme?"

"Well, the database has information on Mr. Hattori's address, so I suppose that Mr. Tokuda would have started out by finding out as much about Mr. Hattori as he could. He probably spent some time spying on him and looking into his affairs. And I imagine that Mr. Tokuda must have been highly delighted when he discovered that Mr. Hattori was about his own age and of a fairly similar build. That's because Mr. Tokuda would have remembered that he'd been seen by Mr. Yosano as he was finishing up the third robbery. Mr. Tokuda would have realized that if he wanted to successfully frame somebody, then it would ideally need to be someone who looked as though they could have been the person that Mr. Yosano had seen in Kotohira."

"Yes, that's a good point, Suzuki. Mr. Yosano's account of what he saw hasn't been made public knowledge—there's been nothing in the newspapers or on the television about it—so Mr. Tokuda can't have been completely sure whether Mr. Yosano contacted the police or not. But just in case he did, Mr. Tokuda must have been very pleased that Mr. Hattori would be able to fit any description that Mr. Yosano might have provided for the robber."

"That's true, sir. And we should remember that Mr. Tokuda presumably won't have known who Mr. Yosano was—to him Mr. Yosano was just some tipsy resident of Kotohira. But as he was making his plan, Mr. Tokuda must have been aware that the person who disturbed his work in Kotohira could conceivably have contacted the police and provided some kind of a bodily description, so as you said, he'd have been relieved when he discovered that Mr. Hattori would easily be able to match such a description."

"That's quite correct. From Mr. Tokuda's point of view, the most important thing was that he'd been wearing a mask when Mr. Yosano had seen him. And on top of that, he'd have certainly detected that Mr. Yosano was rather inebriated at the time of their encounter, so all things considered, he wouldn't have expected there to be any difficulties in passing Mr. Hattori off as the real criminal based on what the police might have learned from Mr. Yosano."

"I agree, sir. So Mr. Tokuda must have watched Mr. Hattori for a while, and got to know the kinds of things that he did and the kinds of places that he went. And with that information he'd have been able to fill in the details of his plan. He'd obviously have realized that Mr. Hattori's trips to Shingo, Takebe, and Kotohira in themselves would not be sufficient to convict him for the robberies, so he'd have known that he needed to concoct some additional incriminating evidence against him. And that's why he must have decided to plant the crowbar and the bank notes from the Kotohira robbery inside Mr. Hattori's apartment."

"Yes."

"And finally, Mr. Tokuda needed a way to bring Mr. Hattori under suspicion so that the crowbar and the bank notes would be discovered, along with the venues of his golf games. Moreover, he knew that if he was the one who alerted us to the possibility that Mr. Hattori had carried out the robberies, then he'd be in line to receive the reward money, which was the whole purpose of his rather nasty scheme. And therefore, he must have come up with the idea of pretending to hear Mr. Hattori boast about the crimes in a bar."

"Exactly, Suzuki."

"So I imagine that based upon the information that he'd gathered about Mr. Hattori's habits, Mr. Tokuda must have been expecting Mr. Hattori to go out drinking on the Sunday evening when they met. Therefore, he'd have put his plan into action by leaving the crowbar wrapped up in brown paper outside Mr. Hattori's apartment late that afternoon. And presumably, it really was the crowbar that he'd used for the three robberies, and he'd have made sure that there were no fingerprints on it when he wrapped it up. Furthermore, I expect that Mr. Tokuda must have found a hiding place somewhere so that he could watch what happened when Mr. Hattori opened his apartment door and found the package on his doormat."

"Yes, that's probably what happened. He must have found a vantage point nearby from where he could monitor the door of Mr. Hattori's apartment."

"And after he'd seen Mr. Hattori open the door and pick up the package, Mr. Tokuda would have remained in his hiding place while Mr. Hattori went back inside his apartment to open it up, which is when he put his fingerprints all over the crowbar. Then, when Mr. Hattori finally left his apartment, Mr. Tokuda would have followed him to see which bar he went to."

"Yes, and after Mr. Hattori had entered the Pickled Cabbage bar, Mr. Tokuda must have waited for a few minutes before going into the bar himself. Then he'd have purposely selected a seat at the counter next to Mr. Hattori so that he was able to strike up a conversation with him."

"While making sure that it seemed just like a chance encounter to Mr. Hattori."

"Exactly, Suzuki."

"And it didn't really matter to Mr. Tokuda what they talked about as long as they talked long enough and drank enough. And I doubt that they even mentioned the cash machine robberies at all."

"No, they probably didn't. Mr. Hattori said that they didn't talk about them."

"That's right, sir. Anyway, when Mr. Tokuda got up and left by himself after two and a half hours of drinking, he must have hurried straight back to Mr. Hattori's apartment and got inside somehow."

"He must have known how to pick the lock."

"I suppose so, sir. And that's when he'd have hidden the crowbar and the bank notes in Mr. Hattori's rice container."

"So he must have had the bank notes with him all evening."

"Yes, it would seem so. And when he left Mr. Hattori's apartment, he made sure that he took with him the brown paper that the crowbar had been wrapped up in."

"Yes, because it wasn't there when Mr. Hattori returned to his apartment later that night. He told us that when he returned home, both the crowbar and the wrapping paper were gone, and that he didn't remember anything about them until the next day."

"Yes, that's what he said, sir. And then all Mr. Tokuda needed to do to finish his plan was to come in here the next day, and to make up a story about what he'd heard Mr. Hattori tell him in the bar."

"Which he managed to do quite convincingly, apologizing profusely in case he was wasting our time."

"He carried it off very well, sir. And of course, his information led to Sergeant Yamada's search of Mr. Hattori's apartment, and to the discovery of the hidden crowbar and the bank notes. And after that, it was inevitable that the Public Prosecutor would find out about Mr. Hattori's whereabouts on the nights of the crimes."

"That's absolutely correct, Suzuki. And all Mr. Tokuda has had to do since then is to look innocent and to play the part of the citizen who is just trying to do his small part to fight crime. And he knows that the moment when the Metropolitan Trust Bank is going to issue him with the very substantial reward money is getting closer and closer every day."

"So it would seem, sir."

Morimoto rubbed his chin and thought for a while in silence.

"By the way, Suzuki, what would have happened if Mr. Hattori had remembered about the crowbar when he returned home from the Pickled Cabbage bar on Sunday evening?"

"Hmmm...well since it was missing, he'd have known that somebody had entered his apartment while he was out. He might have surmised that it was his landlord, perhaps? But on the other hand, he might have called the police, and we'd have sent somebody around. If that had happened, then Mr. Tokuda would have been forced to cancel his plan."

"You're right. So probably, Mr. Tokuda must have been watching Mr. Hattori's apartment after he got home to see whether any police cars drove up."

"Yes, that seems likely, sir."

Morimoto rubbed his chin again and contemplated the matter some more.

"Well, Suzuki, if we're right about our theory, then I have to admit that Mr. Tokuda came up with a rather cunning scheme—and it was all based on that rather unlucky coincidence that Mr. Hattori just happened to be playing golf in the wrong places at the wrong times."

"That's how it looks, sir."

"And there's also a rather bizarre implication of our theory that we haven't mentioned. If our theory is correct, then there's still one very mysterious matter that remains unclear. Our theory implies that the Chief has just presented a rather nice plaque, or a Double-PA as he'd call it, to one of Okayama's master criminals. The mystery that still needs to be resolved is how he's going to come up with a way of explaining that to the newspapers."

Chapter 38

Later that afternoon, Police Officer Suzuki was working away on her computer when Inspector Morimoto left their office and took the elevator up to the seventh floor. The door to the Chief's office was open, and Morimoto tapped on it with his fingers.

"Oh, there you are, Morimoto. Come on in and sit down, will you?"

The constant effort employed by the Chief's secretary towards the objective of maintaining some tidiness and orderliness in the Chief's office had achieved some degree of success, although as usual, the Chief's large desk was covered with stacks of precariously balanced files and reports. Five large flags hung down from poles that stood against the wall next to the door, and while the leftmost was the national flag and the rightmost displayed the cherry blossom flower that was the police insignia, the three middle flags were championship banners that Sergeant Yamada's judo team had won.

"Have you seen the new flags that our judo team were presented with after their triumphs in the recent national competitions, Morimoto? Impressive, aren't they! I always enjoy showing them off to my visitors."

"Sergeant Yamada's a very valuable member of the force, sir."

"Yes, he is indeed. Anyway, were you at the courtroom this morning, Morimoto? I heard that Mr. Bando put up quite a fight. He's a fine lawyer, that man. If I ever need a lawyer to represent me in court, then he'll be my first choice…oh, yes, he will! Still, as Chief of Police, let's hope that things never come to that!"

"Mr. Bando did a fine job this morning, sir. As a matter of fact, he received some rather extensive training on probability theory from Officer Suzuki yesterday evening while he was preparing for his cross-examination of Professor Shirane."

The Chief raised his eyebrows.

"Oh, did he, indeed? Well, I bet the Public Prosecutor fellow won't be too happy if he ever finds out about that. What's his name now?"

"Mr. Genda, sir."

"Ah, yes…Genda…that's right. Still, we're all in favor of a fair trial, and if the defense needs some advice from the police, that's fine with me."

"That's what we thought, sir."

"Anyway, I've had an absolutely terrific day today. The lunch that I hosted was particularly enjoyable. You know, the one that I was telling you about this morning. I made a presentation to that wonderful chap who broke open this cash machine robbery case for us…err…Mr.…err…"

"Mr. Tokuda, sir."

"Yes, that's him! What a fine fellow he is! I presented him with the Police Department's inaugural Double-PA, and I made sure that all of the media came to witness the event. There should be some extensive coverage of the event on tonight's television news bulletins."

"Oh, is that true, sir?"

"Yes, it is. We made quite a publicity splash of it. And do you know, I wouldn't be at all surprised if the newspapers put a picture of me handing the award to Mr. Tokuda on all of their front pages tomorrow morning. That would be nice, wouldn't it?"

"Err…well, sir…"

"Oh, it's a great public relations coup for the Police Department, Morimoto. And I had a nice chat with the young fellow over lunch…he's a fine character to be sure. You know, Morimoto, we need more people like him in this city…they're the backbone of the community! Don't you think so?"

"Well, sir, in this particular case…"

"The point is, Morimoto, this particular case turned out to be the perfect opportunity to launch our Double-PA's! And I'll be handing out some more of them whenever somebody else of Mr. Tokuda's caliber turns up. Anyway, Morimoto, I had a thoroughly enjoyable lunch, but afterwards I had a meeting with Ms. Tsuda. And that was a little bit tricky…I can tell you! But I was quite firm with her…I told her that I'd made a decision that we'd be bringing her work to a conclusion, and I stuck to my guns. I had to…what else could I do? In light of her performance, I'm afraid that's the only option that I had open to me, don't you agree, Morimoto?"

Morimoto slowly rubbed his chin as he tried to think of the best way to dodge the question.

"Incidentally, sir, you may be interested to know that Officer Suzuki had a meeting with Ms. Tsuda yesterday."

"What? On Sunday? If Ms. Tsuda is of the opinion that she'll be able to bill us extra by conducting her interviews on Sunday, then the nasty surprise that I gave her this afternoon was really well-deserved after all!"

"Actually, the meeting wasn't related to Ms. Tsuda's work with the Police Department, sir. It was about the cash machine robberies."

"The cash machine robberies? What's Ms. Tsuda got to do with them?"

"Well, surprisingly enough, sir, we've turned up some evidence that strongly indicates that she is connected with the robberies. Specifically, we've discovered that Mr. Tokuda has done some work for her company."

"Has he indeed? Well, there's nothing wrong with that, Morimoto. He's some kind of a genius when it comes to computer work, as far as I can gather. He was telling me all about it at lunch today, although I couldn't grasp all of the details. He seems to be especially knowledgeable about gigabytes and servers. Do you understand those kinds of things, Morimoto?"

"Err...I'm sure that Officer Suzuki knows a fair bit about them, sir."

"Well, Tsuda Business Solutions is very lucky to have somebody like Mr. Tokuda helping them out. Has Ms. Tsuda been having any problems with her computers lately? Is that why she needed Mr. Tokuda's help? You know, Morimoto...come to think of it...that might be why she got the 1's and the 5's mixed up on my survey results. Perhaps she's got some kind of a computer bug? Anyway, if she pays attention to Mr. Tokuda, I think that she could learn a lot from him."

"Hmmm...well, it's funny that you should say that, sir, because actually, Officer Suzuki and I have a suspicion that it may in fact be the other way round. We believe that Mr. Tokuda may have learned something from his work with Ms. Tsuda's company that's very pertinent to the cash machine robberies."

"What on earth do you mean, Morimoto?"

"Well, we have this theory, sir."

The Chief leaned back in his chair and chuckled.

"Another theory, Morimoto? Where would this Police Department be without your theories?"

Morimoto was quite sure that the Police Department would be in considerably worse shape if it had not been able to benefit from the theories that he had worked out with Suzuki.

"If our theory is correct, sir, then Mr. Genda is prosecuting the wrong person for the cash machine robberies."

The Chief began to look uneasy. In spite of his joking, the Chief himself was also well aware of the quality of Morimoto and Suzuki's theories, and he knew that based on their track record it would be wise to afford a great deal of respect to any new theory that they brought forward.

"Oh, really, Morimoto?" he said quietly. "And according to your theory, just who should Mr. Genda be prosecuting?"

"Mr. Tokuda, sir."

The Chief's wonderful day had suddenly taken a very nasty turn, and he looked completely numb as Morimoto filled him in on the details of the theory. And when it had fully sunk in that Mr. Tokuda was potentially the real person behind the cash machine robberies, and that he had endeavored to frame Mr. Hattori in order to obtain the reward money, the Chief became very glum indeed.

There was a long silence after Morimoto had finished his explanation.

"I don't suppose, Morimoto, that you might have considered explaining all of this to me this morning before I made my lunchtime award presentation?"

"Err...well, sir...the truth is that we only put the final pieces into place this afternoon."

"Hmmm...I see. That's unfortunate, because if your theory is correct, it's going to be awfully embarrassing for me at the next national meeting of Police Chiefs. None of the other chiefs will be able to keep a straight face! They'll never stop asking me whether I'm planning to give out any new awards!"

Morimoto maintained a diplomatic silence.

"Well anyhow, Morimoto, what do you intend to do next? How are you going to establish whether your theory is correct or not? A theory is one thing, but don't forget that you don't have any substantive evidence for it yet. How are you going to prove that Mr. Tokuda really is the criminal?"

Morimoto looked at his watch.

"Ah...yes, sir. Well in half an hour, Officer Suzuki and I have a meeting arranged with Judge Noda in her chambers. We've also invited Mr. Genda and Mr. Bando along to attend the meeting, and I was rather hoping that you'd be able to accompany us as well, sir. I'm quite sure that we're going to need all of the support that you can give us."

Chapter 39

It was just after eight thirty the following morning, Tuesday, when there was a bold knock on the office door as Inspector Morimoto and Police Officer Suzuki were looking through the morning papers. The report on Mr. Hattori's trail was featured on the front page of the Okayama Tribune more prominently than it had been in previous days, next to a large photo of the Chief presenting a plaque to Mr. Tokuda, and the headline read *'Improbable Fight-Back by Defendant Alters Odds in Cash Machine Trial'*.

Morimoto and Suzuki looked up as Mr. Tokuda walked into the office with a happy grin on his face.

"Good morning, Inspector! I received your message. I was told that you wanted to see me about processing the reward money."

"Oh, good morning, Mr. Tokuda. Yes, that's right—I did need to see you. Thank you for stopping by so soon. I'm sorry to have had to trouble you with it, but there's quite a bit of paperwork, I'm afraid. Do sit down, will you?"

Mr. Tokuda sat down at the desk in the middle of the office.

"Oh, it's no trouble at all, Inspector. It was quite easy for me to stop by on my way to work."

"I'm glad to hear that, Mr. Tokuda. Now, where did I put those papers, Officer Suzuki?"

"The papers about the reward money for the cash machine robberies, sir?"

"Yes, that's what we need."

"Hmmm...weren't you working on them yesterday afternoon, sir? I expect that they're probably still somewhere on your desk."

Morimoto searched through a pile of folders on his desk and extracted one from the middle.

"Ah, you're right, Officer Suzuki—here they are. Now let me see...err...what exactly is it that we need you to do, Mr. Tokuda? I think that we just need your signature in a couple of places."

Mr. Tokuda waited patiently as Morimoto slowly leafed through the papers in the folder.

"Ah...here it is, Mr. Tokuda. We just need your signature at the bottom of this page."

Morimoto walked over to Mr. Tokuda and handed him a sheet of paper.

"Oh...and wait a minute...we also need you to initial another sheet at a couple of places as well. Here it is...please put your initials at the places where we've indicated."

Morimoto handed Mr. Tokuda another sheet of paper and returned to his desk. Mr. Tokuda took a pen out of his jacket pocket and eagerly signed and initialed the forms.

"As I say, Mr. Tokuda, I'm sorry for the trouble. There seems to be more and more paperwork in the Police Department these days, doesn't there, Officer Suzuki?"

"Oh, there's no doubt about it, sir. It's not like it used to be. Sometimes I seem to spend half of my day just filling in forms."

Mr. Tokuda stood up and handed the sheets of paper back to Morimoto.

"Oh, really—please don't worry, Inspector. It's not been any trouble. And by the way, when...err...how long will it be before I can get the reward money?"

"Well, we'll try to get it to you as soon as possible, Mr. Tokuda. I'll turn in the forms today, of course, and then as soon as there's been a conviction in Mr. Hattori's trial, you should be in line to get the money right away, I'd think. Wouldn't you agree, Officer Suzuki?"

"Yes, I should think so, sir. I wouldn't expect there to be any kind of delay. The trial seems to be a foregone conclusion, so I doubt that the judge will take much time to make her mind up, and the Metropolitan Trust Bank is generally very prompt at these kinds of things."

Morimoto leaned back in his chair and studied Mr. Tokuda's contented face.

"You're going to receive a considerable sum of money, Mr. Tokuda. I'm very envious! Do you have any ideas about how you're going to spend the money?"

Mr. Tokuda smiled.

"Well, I'm thinking of going on a nice holiday—I'd like to take a break."

"Oh, you'll certainly have enough money for a very nice holiday, Mr. Tokuda. It's a very substantial sum of money that the Metropolitan Trust Bank has designated as the reward in this case, and since you'll be receiving half of it, you'll be able to make a very nice trip and still have plenty of money left over as well. Where are you thinking of going?"

A look of astonishment appeared on Mr. Tokuda's face, and he sat down again.

"Err…half of the money, did you say?"

"Oh, yes…don't worry. I'm pleased to be able to tell you that the Metropolitan Trust Bank has agreed to give you half of the reward money, so you don't need to be concerned about that."

Mr. Tokuda was clearly bewildered.

"Umm…well, thank you. But…err…why am I only getting half of the reward? Shouldn't I be receiving all of it?"

Morimoto frowned.

"Well, no, Mr. Tokuda…you won't be getting all of the reward money. There's the other witness, you see, so you'll have to share it with him. Somebody else came forward and made a visual identification of Mr. Hattori at the crime scene, and so they'll be receiving the other half of the reward money."

A look of anger momentarily flashed across Mr. Tokuda's face.

"A visual identification of Mr. Hattori? At the crime scene? I didn't know anything about that!"

"Well, this person didn't contact us until rather late in the investigation, Mr. Tokuda. And we've been keeping it as quiet as possible in order to protect his privacy. And it's not been in the newspapers because I don't think that he's even given his evidence in court yet, has he, Officer Suzuki?"

Suzuki clicked the mouse attached to her computer and peered at the screen.

"I don't believe so, sir. Let me just check…I had a message about it from the Public Prosecutor the other day. Where did I put it? Ah…here it is. Let's see…oh, the new witness is scheduled in court first thing this morning, sir."

"Oh, is he really? Well, maybe we should go over to the courthouse and watch how it goes. You see, Mr. Tokuda, I probably ought to let you know that since this witness has been able to provide a visual identification of Mr. Hattori while he was performing the criminal act, and whereas your information about Mr. Hattori's boasting in the bar is considerably less substantial from a legal perspective, there was some discussion that the lion's share of the reward money might be due to this other person. But as I said, the Metropolitan Trust Bank came up with the decision to allocate the money equally between the two of you, and I myself think that's probably the fairest decision. After all, we're especially grateful to you, Mr. Tokuda, for coming in here in the first place and reporting what you heard Mr. Hattori tell you. That's really what broke the case open for us, wasn't it, Officer Suzuki?"

"Yes, it undoubtedly was, sir. You did us a great service, Mr. Tokuda."

"Yes, you did, Mr. Tokuda. And by the way, congratulations on receiving that award from the Chief yesterday! I know that he was very pleased to be able to give it to you personally. Did you enjoy the lunch yesterday?"

Mr. Tokuda's erstwhile buoyant mood had by now become completely deflated.

"Oh, yes, it was very nice," he mumbled.

"And we saw your picture on the front page of the Okayama Tribune this morning, Mr. Tokuda. That's a great shot of the Chief giving you your award. You'll be quite a celebrity now!"

"Yes, maybe."

"Well then, I'll be in touch with you again when the Metropolitan Trust Bank has informed us that they're ready to disburse the reward money, and I sincerely hope that you really enjoy spending your half of it!"

Chapter 40

Later that morning, Inspector Morimoto and Police Officer Suzuki were occupying their usual seats in the back row of the visitors gallery in Courtroom 3, when Mr. Tokuda slipped in through the side door and chose a front row seat next to the newspaper reporters. Immediately afterwards, Mr. Hattori was led into the courtroom by his police escort, and he took his designated seat just in front of the visitors gallery with his back to Mr. Tokuda.

At exactly ten o'clock, the door at the back of the judge's dais opened, and Judge Noda and her two advisors entered the courtroom and sat down. Judge Noda's expressionless face appeared just the same as it had done on every other day of the trial as she peered down in the direction of the Public Prosecutor.

"Mr. Genda, I believe that you have another witness for us this morning?"

"Yes, your honor."

"Very well—please proceed."

The witness was led into the courtroom, and he timidly took his seat facing the judge. The court assistant handed him the sheet of paper that he was required to read for his swearing in, and he mumbled his way through it in a wavering voice that was barely audible at the back of the courtroom where Morimoto and Suzuki were sitting.

After the court assistant had retrieved the sheet of paper, Mr. Genda walked out from behind his desk and offered the witness a reassuring look.

"Good morning. Could you please tell us your name?"

"Akio Yosano."

"Err…perhaps you could speak up just a little more, please."

Mr. Yosano cleared his throat.

"Yes…sorry…I'm Akio Yosano."
"Thank you. And where do you live and work, Mr. Yosano?"
"In Kotohira in Kagawa prefecture."
"And what kind of work do you do, Mr. Yosano?"
"I'm a sushi chef at a hotel."

The tight lines on Mr. Yosano's face revealed that he was very tired and under a great deal of strain.

"Thank you very much, Mr. Yosano. Now I want to take you back to the Saturday evening in February when the cash machine robbery occurred in Kotohira where you live and work. You know the day to which I'm referring, don't you, Mr. Yosano?"
"Yes, I do."
"Were you working at the hotel that evening?"
"Yes, I was."
"And what time did you leave the hotel?"
"At about midnight."
"Do you usually work that late, Mr. Yosano?"
"I often do, yes…especially at weekends when the hotel is very busy."
"And what did you do after you'd finished work at around midnight?"
"I walked home."
"And again, you usually walk home after finishing your work, don't you?"
"Yes, I do."
"And as you walked from the hotel to your home, your route took you by the cash machine belonging to the Metropolitan Trust Bank, didn't it?"

Mr. Yosano took a neatly pressed handkerchief out of his pocket and rubbed his forehead and the top of his bald head.

"Yes, it did."
"And can you please tell the court what you saw as you approached the cash machine on that particular night?"
"I saw a man taking handfuls of cash out of the machine and putting them into a backpack."
"Was the cash machine damaged in any way?"
"Yes, it was all smashed up."
"And was the man holding anything else besides the backpack?"
"Yes, he was holding a blue crowbar."
"And were you able to see the man's face?"
"Yes, I was."
"You had a clear look at his face, did you?"

"Yes, I did."

"Is the man who you saw robbing the cash machine in this courtroom today, Mr. Yosano?"

"Yes, he is."

"Could you identify him, please?"

Mr. Yosano slid around in his chair and looked in the direction of Mr. Hattori and Mr. Tokuda. He slowly raised his hand and pointed towards Mr. Hattori.

"That's him."

There was an audible gasp from the row of newspaper reporters sitting next to Mr. Tokuda.

"For the court records, you're pointing at the defendant, aren't you?" Mr. Genda asked.

"Yes, I am."

"And you're quite certain that the defendant is the person who you saw robbing the cash machine, are you, Mr. Yosano?"

"Yes, I'm quite certain."

"When you saw him, did he have a full beard just like he has now?"

"Yes, his beard was just the same."

Mr. Genda walked back towards his desk and looked up at the judge.

"That's all of the questions that I have for this witness, your honor."

Judge Noda nodded slowly, and as usual she conferred briefly with her two advisors before looking down in the direction of Mr. Bando.

"Does the defense wish to question this witness?"

Mr. Bando stood up and walked out into the courtroom.

"Yes, I do have some questions, your honor."

"Very well, then—go ahead."

Mr. Bando approached Mr. Yosano, and as he straightened up to his full height, he towered over the small frame of the witness.

"Good morning, Mr. Yosano."

Mr. Yosano peered up at Mr. Bando.

"Good morning," he replied timidly.

"You've told this courtroom that on the night in question you walked home from the hotel where you worked—is that correct?"

"Yes."

"I'm sorry, I can't hear you."

"I said yes."

Mr. Yosano had to make a significant effort to raise the level of his shaky voice, but in contrast, Mr. Bando's voice boomed across the courtroom.

"What time did you leave the hotel?"
"At about midnight."
"Was it a dark night?"
"Err...yes, it was."
"Was it very dark?"
Mr. Yosano wiped his forehead with his handkerchief again.
"Err...I'm not sure."
"You're not sure?"
"No."
"You can't remember?"
"No."
"Well, was there a full moon, perhaps?"
"Umm...I don't know."
"You can't remember whether the moon was shining?"
"No."
"But you can remember the defendant's face?"
"Yes."
"Even though it was a dark night?"
"There were some lights next to the cash machine. That's why I could see him so clearly."
"Were you surprised to come across somebody robbing the cash machine?"
"Yes, of course I was."
"So what did you do?"
"Well...err...what do you mean?"
"What did you do when you saw that somebody was robbing the cash machine?"
"I didn't do anything, really. I just stood there and watched. I was shocked."
"And what happened next? Did you just stand there while this man, who you say you saw, finished taking the money out of the cash machine and then went on his way?"
"Well, I didn't do anything because he threatened me."
"He threatened you?"
"Yes."
"What did he say to you, Mr. Yosano?"
"He told me to keep quiet. He's much bigger than I am. I was scared. He pushed me against the wall and he grabbed my wallet from my pocket. He took my driver's license out and looked at it."
"Are you claiming that this man stole your wallet?"

"No. After he'd found my name and address on my driver's license he dropped it on the ground together with my wallet."

"Did this man take any money out of your wallet?"

"No."

"So exactly how did this man threaten you, Mr. Yosano?"

"He told me that he knew where to find me if I made any trouble. He said that he'd memorized my name and address. And then he ran away."

"So you were left by yourself standing next to the vandalized cash machine, were you?"

"Yes."

"So what did you do then?"

"I waited for a while to make sure that the man had really gone, and then I walked home."

"You continued on your way home?"

"Yes."

"Did you have a phone with you, Mr. Yosano?"

"Err…yes, I had my phone in my pocket."

"So you didn't use the phone that you had with you to call the police?"

"No."

"Did you call the police when you reached home?"

"No. I was scared. I decided not to tell the police. The man knew who I was. I decided to keep quiet about what I'd seen. I didn't tell anybody about it. I thought that he'd come to my apartment looking for me if I told anybody about what I'd seen."

"In fact, isn't it the case, Mr. Yosano, that you only contacted the police about what you claim to have seen that night after this trial had already started?"

Mr. Yosano sat perfectly still.

"Yes."

Chapter 41

From their seats at the back of the visitors gallery, Inspector Morimoto and Police Officer Suzuki were maintaining a keen interest in the way that Mr. Yosano handled Mr. Bando's questioning, while out of the corners of their eyes they were also paying close attention to Mr. Tokuda's behavior. He was sitting only a few rows in front of them, and they could both see that he was glaring at the witness with ever increasing ferocity.

After pausing to allow the judge time to reflect on Mr. Yosano's admission that his information to the police had only been delivered a few days previously, Mr. Bando continued with his cross-examination.

"Now, Mr. Yosano, you've stated that you left the hotel where you work at about midnight on the night in question, haven't you?"

"Yes."

"And after leaving the hotel you walked straight home, did you?"

"Yes."

"How long would it have taken you to get from the hotel to the cash machine?"

"About ten or fifteen minutes."

"So that would imply, would it not, that if your evidence is to be believed, the cash machine robbery must have occurred at about 12:15?"

"Yes."

"Did you stop anywhere between your workplace and the cash machine?"

"No."

"Nowhere at all?"

"No."

"Did you perhaps stop for a drink somewhere?"
"No."
"Do you ever stop for a drink on your way home after work, Mr. Yosano?"
"Yes, sometimes."
"Where do you go for a drink?"
"Oh, there are plenty of bars that I pass by on the way home."
"I see. And would it be fair to say, Mr. Yosano, that you often go into one of those bars for a drink on your way home?"
"Well…yes, I suppose so."
"And on the night in question, you passed by several bars between the hotel where you work and the cash machine, didn't you, Mr. Yosano?"
"Yes."
"And are you telling this court that you didn't stop off in any of them for a drink on that night?"

Mr. Yosano shrugged.

"I didn't go into a bar that evening."

Mr. Bando glared down at the witness.

"Mr. Yosano, are you telling this courtroom that you hadn't had anything at all to drink by the time that you claim to have seen the defendant taking money out of the cash machine?"

Mr. Yosano shook his head and peered up at Mr. Bando with an almost pitiable look.

"I hadn't been drinking that night—I really hadn't! And that's the truth!"

With an expression of sheer disbelief fixed on his face, Mr. Bando slowly walked away from the witness and turned to the judge.

"I have no further questions for this witness, your honor."

After Mr. Yosano's testimony, Judge Noda called a short recess in the hearings, and Morimoto and Suzuki took advantage of the break to stroll around in the sunshine outside. As they were doing so, Mr. Tokuda suddenly appeared in the doorway of the courthouse, which was surrounded by a group of newspaper reporters who were excitedly phoning in the details of the morning's surprise developments to their offices. Mr. Tokuda looked around for Morimoto and Suzuki, and when he spotted them he hurried over to talk to them.

"Err…hello, Inspector. I wanted to ask you something. That person who just gave evidence—Mr. Yosano—is he the person who I'm sharing the reward money with?"

"Oh, hello, Mr. Tokuda. How are you? I noticed you in the courtroom. Are you taking the morning off work?"

Mr. Tokuda managed a smile.

"Well, I have to tell you that I was just a little bit curious about who was going to be giving evidence this morning, and I wanted to hear what he had to say."

"Oh, I see. Well, yes—you're quite right. As you heard, Mr. Yosano has provided a visual identification of Mr. Hattori, so he'll be splitting the reward money with you."

"That's what I thought. But...err...I mean...it's rather strange, isn't it? I mean, can we really believe him? I'm not an expert at police work, of course, but it seems to me that after the trial has started, anybody could just turn up at a police station and say that they'd witnessed the robbery. I mean, they could lie about it—they could just make up any story. What's to stop them? People can be very tricky, you know. Isn't it possible that Mr. Yosano made up his story just in the hope that he'd be able to get some of the reward money?"

Morimoto nodded slowly.

"Yes, I see what you're getting at, Mr. Tokuda. Mind you, that's quite a serious suggestion that you're raising concerning Mr. Yosano's actions. He'd be guilty of misleading the police for a start, and also of giving false evidence in a courtroom, which both carry very severe penalties, don't they, Officer Suzuki?"

Suzuki nodded.

"They do indeed, sir. They're both very serious offences. But I actually think that Mr. Tokuda has raised a good point. There's really only Mr. Yosano's word for what happened that night. For example, we don't even have any separate confirmation of the time of the robbery."

"Yes, that's quite true," Morimoto said. "Well, Mr. Tokuda, I suppose that it really all comes down to Judge Noda's interpretation of Mr. Yosano's testimony. She appears to have accepted that Mr. Yosano is a reliable witness, although we can't be too sure about how much weight she'll put on his testimony in her final analysis, bearing in mind the points that you've raised. But in my opinion, there seems to already be plenty of substantial evidence against Mr. Hattori anyway. However, as long as Mr. Yosano's testimony stands, he's going to be eligible for a share of the reward money according to the rules that have been established by the Metropolitan Trust Bank."

Mr. Tokuda looked very unhappy.

"Ah well, I guess that's the way it is then," he said bitterly, "but it seems a bit strange to me. Anyway, I'd better be getting back to work."

Morimoto and Suzuki watched Mr. Tokuda as he hurried off down the street.

"Well, Suzuki, that was an interesting morning's work, don't you think?"

"Hmmm…very interesting, sir."

"And I'm quite sure that we both deserve a good strong cup of coffee now. And come to think of it, I believe that I know just the place to go for that."

Chapter 42

The Okayama Orient Museum is situated close to the bank of the Asahi River as it bends around Okayama castle, and its architectural style with cream colored windowless tile façades and green roof gardens was purposefully designed to have an Arabian flavor. Upon entering the museum, Inspector Morimoto and Police Officer Suzuki admired the spacious central hall that admitted light from the open ceiling high above, and as they climbed the stairs to the second floor tearoom, they passed the museum's Chief Curator as he was leading a group of visiting foreign scholars on a guided tour through the collections of ancient treasures from Mesopotamia, Persia, and Syria, some of which dated back over five thousand years.

Morimoto and Suzuki were soon sitting at a table in the pleasant tearoom, although it was not tea that they had come for. Instead, the waitress set down two small cups of thick black coffee in front of them.

"This is the only place in Okayama where you can get a good strong cup of Turkish coffee," Morimoto remarked.

"Hmmm...and very nice it is too," Suzuki replied, taking a sip.

"It's just what we need after this morning's adventures."

"You're absolutely right, sir."

"And I dare say that it's just what Mr. Tokuda needs to buck him up after the shock that we engineered for him this morning."

"He did look very dispirited when he left the courthouse, didn't he?"

"Yes, Suzuki, which is exactly what we'd hoped for. So where exactly do we stand now?"

Suzuki replaced her cup in its small white saucer and reflected on the situation.

"Well, sir, the first point that occurs to me is that if our theory about Mr. Tokuda being the real criminal is incorrect, then we've landed ourselves in a considerable mess with Judge Noda."

"Yes, that's certainly true. She did take a rather substantial amount of persuading last night when we met her in her chambers, didn't she? And I still have my doubts that she's totally convinced that this is the best way to resolve the case one way or the other. What was it that she said last night? Something along the lines of having deep reservations about allowing the investigative branch to carry out its work in her judicial facilities? Wasn't that what she said?"

"That's exactly what she said, sir. In other words, she was trying to find a polite way of saying that in her opinion the police ought to find a better place to do their detective work than in her courtroom."

"Yes, that was certainly the message. Anyway, at least the Chief stuck up for us very valiantly during the meeting, and Mr. Bando was also particularly persuasive as he laid out the arguments for why he thought that our plan was worth a try. And actually, Mr. Genda didn't put up much opposition, did he?"

"No, he didn't, sir, and that's probably because if our plan fails and we end up making complete fools of ourselves, then he must feel that Judge Noda will have no other alternative that to proclaim Mr. Hattori guilty."

"I dare say that you're right, Suzuki. Anyway, everybody played their part very well this morning, don't you think? Mr. Genda and Mr. Bando both rose to the occasion."

"Oh, they were just like professional actors, sir. Come to think of it, perhaps that's what being a successful courtroom lawyer is all about? Perhaps it's just a matter of being a good actor?"

"That's a very good point, Suzuki."

"And throughout it all, Judge Noda managed to keep a very straight face."

"Ah, well judges are very good at that kind of thing."

"Yes, I suppose that you're right, sir."

"I think that it's part of their training."

"That may well be the case, sir."

Morimoto took another sip of his coffee.

"And Mr. Yosano remembered his lines very well, didn't he? Did you really stay up all night rehearsing them with him?"

"Yes, I did, sir—we were literally up all night working on his story. And I agree with you that he did an excellent job. The only thing that I was afraid of was that he might fall asleep right in the middle of his testimony!"

"Hmmm…well luckily he was able to stay awake long enough, although he did look particularly nervous. But the important point is the impression that the whole charade had on Mr. Tokuda, and as far as I can tell it seems that he found it all very convincing…and very annoying as well! Did you notice how he was glaring at Mr. Yosano in the courtroom?"

"Oh, there's no doubt at all that he was very unhappy with Mr. Yosano, sir."

"You're right. Anyway, as you said, if our theory is wrong then we've made complete fools of ourselves, and we've made a huge mess of the legal proceedings which we'd be wise to leave to the Chief to try and clear up. But, on the other hand, if our theory is correct, then where does that leave things?"

"That's a very interesting question, sir. According to our theory, Mr. Tokuda robbed three cash machines and was then greedy enough to try to claim the reward money for himself by framing Mr. Hattori for the crimes. And what he learned from his visit to our office this morning, is that while he'd been expecting all along to receive the entire sum of money that the Metropolitan Trust Bank has offered, he's in fact only in line to receive half of the money."

"A fact that's obviously irritated him a great deal."

"Understandably so, sir. And he did take the bait, just as we'd hoped he would, by turning up at court this morning."

"At least that part of our plan seems to have worked."

"Yes, sir. And now we have to try to figure out what's going through Mr. Tokuda's mind. If our theory is correct, then Mr. Tokuda knows that while he was robbing the cash machine in Kotohira in February, he was interrupted by a very inebriated Mr. Yosano."

"Whom he undoubtedly recognized as the witness this morning."

"That's certainly true, sir. But Mr. Tokuda knows that he carried out the robbery just after one o'clock, and he knows that he was wearing a mask so that Mr. Yosano never saw his face. And according to what we know from the statement that Mr. Yosano made for the Kotohira police at the time of the incident, when Mr. Tokuda's robbery was interrupted, he just ran off and left Mr. Yosano standing at the cash machine all by himself."

"Or swaying, to be more exact."

"Very true, sir. So if Mr. Tokuda really is the robber, then he knows that Mr. Yosano's testimony this morning was riddled with lies. He knows that the time that Mr. Yosano gave is incorrect, he knows that he was wearing a mask, he knows that he never threatened Mr. Yosano, and he knows that Mr. Yosano had been drinking heavily."

"That's absolutely right, Suzuki."

"But an important point is that Mr. Tokuda doesn't know what Mr. Yosano did after he ran off with his crowbar and his backpack stuffed full of money. Mr. Tokuda doesn't know that Mr. Yosano pulled out his phone and called the police straightaway."

"Because that information has never been released to the public. The Kotohira police released details of the robbery, but they never indicated the manner in which they'd learned about it."

"Exactly, sir. Which means that as far as Mr. Tokuda knows, Mr. Yosano might very well have staggered home in his drunken state and not told anybody about what he'd seen."

"And Mr. Tokuda may think that when Mr. Yosano woke up the next morning, he might not even have been too sure himself about what he'd seen the night before until he read all about the robbery in the papers."

"Precisely, sir. So I imagine that right now, Mr. Tokuda is trying to piece together the situation from Mr. Yosano's perspective, and he should come up with something along these lines. Mr. Tokuda will deduce that Mr. Yosano didn't contact the police on the night of the incident, or at any time afterwards when the robberies were receiving such attention from the media. But Mr. Tokuda will guess that once Mr. Hattori's trial had started, Mr. Yosano saw an opportunity to get some of the reward money. Mr. Tokuda will think that Mr. Yosano realized that he could pretend that the person he saw robbing the cash machine hadn't been wearing a mask. So Mr. Tokuda will conclude that's the reason why Mr. Yosano suddenly contacted the police and told them that he'd seen Mr. Hattori in the act of carrying out the crime."

"That makes sense, Suzuki. But Mr. Tokuda will also realize that Mr. Yosano must have faced two problems. The first problem would have been that he needed to come up with an explanation for why he hadn't contacted the police earlier, and the second problem would have been that his testimony might be doubted if it became known that he'd been drinking so heavily."

"Quite true, sir. And so Mr. Tokuda should come to the conclusion that Mr. Yosano solved the first of those two problems by inventing the story about having been threatened by the robber and having had his driver's license examined."

"Yes."

"And Mr. Tokuda will conclude that Mr. Yosano solved the second problem by altering the time of the robbery. In his testimony, Mr. Yosano claimed to have walked directly home from his work that night without stopping off anywhere for a drink."

"That's right, Suzuki. And so from Mr. Tokuda's perspective, what he heard Mr. Yosano say in court this morning, and what he'll conclude that Mr. Yosano must have done, will all make sense if he assumes that Mr. Yosano managed to come up with a clever little plan of his own to get his hands on some of the reward money."

"Yes, sir, and Mr. Tokuda must be seething with anger because he'll view Mr. Yosano as a diabolical liar who's managed to find a way of depriving him of half of the reward money."

"That's right, Suzuki, conveniently forgetting the fact that he's trying to put Mr. Hattori in prison for the crimes that he himself committed, just so that he can get the reward money for himself. But what we don't know is what Mr. Tokuda is going to do about the situation."

"No, we don't, sir."

"Nevertheless, I don't think that he'll come knocking on our door to point out that Mr. Yosano has to be lying because he knows that the robber was wearing a mask that evening!"

"Definitely not, sir."

"But will he try something else?"

"Hmmm...that's the question, sir."

At that moment the Museum Director walked into the tearoom.

"Ah, good morning, Inspector Morimoto. I'm glad to see that you've come to visit us again. Have you seen our new Assyrian relief?"

"Good morning, director. How are you? Actually, we just stopped by to enjoy one of your fortifying Turkish coffees, but since we're here it will be a shame not to take a look around at your wonderful collections. And we'll certainly have a good look at the new Assyrian relief."

"Oh, you really should. It's a gypsum panel from the northwest palace at Nimrud, just east of the Tigris River, showing an eagle-headed deity. You'll be amazed by the details on the head and the wings. We believe that the figure is carrying out some kind of an anointment using pollen from a fir cone that he's holding."

"That sounds very interesting—we'll certainly make a point of having a close look at it. And I always enjoy inspecting your cuneiform tablets, although they don't make any more sense to me than my own handwriting sometimes."

The director and Suzuki laughed.

"And to be completely honest with you," Morimoto continued, "I'm not in much of a hurry to get back to the Police Headquarters today. We're right in the middle of a rather tricky case at the moment, and the Chief's bound to be in a terribly nervous state. Roman glassware, Mesopotamian stamp seals, and Parthian silverware will suit me much better."

Chapter 43

It was Friday morning at the end of the week when Mr. Tokuda returned to visit Inspector Morimoto and Police Officer Suzuki in their office at the Police Headquarters. As he knocked on the door and walked confidently into the office, Morimoto put down his copy of the morning edition of the Okayama Tribune. The coverage of the trial had been moved to the inside pages under the headline *'Judge Noda Stalling in Robbery Trial Decision'*.

"Good morning, Inspector Morimoto. I heard that you wanted to meet me again. Has anything turned up?"

"Ah, Mr. Tokuda—I'm glad to see you again. Do sit down. Thank you for dropping by again."

"Oh, it's really no trouble at all. Why did you want to see me?"

"Well, I'm pleased that you've come over again because there have been some new developments regarding the reward money that I wanted to discuss with you."

Mr. Tokuda looked hopeful.

"Oh, really?"

"Yes. You'll remember Mr. Yosano, the witness who gave evidence in Mr. Hattori's trial on Tuesday morning, of course?"

"Yes, I remember him."

"Well, it turns out that he won't be receiving any of the reward money after all."

Mr. Tokuda's hope turned to undisguised joy.

"Oh, he won't? Why is that?"

"His testimony has been thrown out by the judge—it's been completely invalidated. It seems that he was lying the whole time."

"Oh, I say—that is shocking!"

"Yes, it's quite astounding, isn't it? Perhaps you'd be interested to hear the details of how we found out?"

"Yes, I am a little curious."

"Well, the precise point where we caught him was the timing that he gave—we discovered that he lied about the time of the robbery. We've been able to prove that the robbery in Kotohira couldn't have happened before one o'clock in the morning, whereas you'll probably remember that Mr. Yosano gave evidence in court that it occurred not long after midnight."

"Oh, how remarkable! That is interesting. How did you find out that the robbery couldn't have taken place before one o'clock?"

"Well, we've been in touch with the taxi company in Kotohira, and it turns out that one of their taxis picked up some passengers from right in front of the cash machine at just before one o'clock. And we found out that the passengers had been waiting there for about fifteen minutes. So you see, we can deduce from that information that the cash machine hadn't been vandalized before one o'clock. If it had been, the taxi driver and his passengers would certainly have known about it."

"I understand. That's very clever—very good police work. Well done!"

"In addition, we also suspect that Mr. Yosano had probably been drinking that night as well, but we haven't been able to put together all of the details regarding that yet. Anyway, the discrepancy concerning the time of the robbery was enough for Judge Noda to throw out Mr. Yosano's complete testimony, as I said."

"Well, goodness! What a surprise! I'm so glad that you've told me. Does that mean...err...will I now be able to...err...I guess that I ought to ask you whether I'll be able to receive the whole of the reward money now?"

"Perhaps you'd be interested to know how we learned about the taxi?"

"Oh...err...all right."

Morimoto picked up a folder from his desktop and opened it up.

"This letter was in an envelope addressed to the Chief of Police. As you can see, it's been made by cutting out words and letters from a newspaper. It says *'The Kotohira taxi company knows about the cash machine robbery—check their records'*. Can you see that?"

"Yes! What a strange letter! How extraordinary!"

"As you can imagine, after reading the letter it didn't take us long to find out about the taxi that had collected some passengers from right next to the cash machine at one o'clock that morning."

"That's fantastic! So will I be able to get all of the reward money now?"

"We are, of course, very interested in the person who sent this letter to the Chief. Whoever it was must obviously have been aware that the robbery had occurred after one o'clock, and it seems that the sole purpose of the letter was to contradict that part of Mr. Yosano's testimony where he indicated that the robbery had occurred at about 12:15. The letter was mailed in Kotohira."

"Was it really? Well perhaps it was sent by somebody from the taxi company—somebody who realized that Mr. Yosano had lied in his testimony? Perhaps the person was jealous that Mr. Yosano was going to get some of the reward money? Perhaps the taxi driver himself sent the letter?"

Morimoto and Suzuki were both staring hard at Mr. Tokuda.

"However," Mr. Tokuda continued, "I guess that does raise another question, Inspector. Why would the taxi driver, or anyone else from the taxi company for that matter, have sent such a strange letter? Why did they construct it from newspaper clippings? Do you think that it's simply because they wanted to keep their identity a secret? Do you think that they sent an anonymous letter because they didn't want anybody to know that they'd ratted on Mr. Yosano?"

Morimoto nodded slowly.

"Well, whoever sent the letter," he said, "must have been aware that a taxi stopped next to the cash machine at just before one o'clock on the night of the robbery. In fact, Officer Suzuki and I believe that the robber must have been hiding in the darkness somewhere in the vicinity of the cash machine when the taxi arrived. We think that the robber had to wait for the taxi to pick up the passengers before he could carry out the theft. In fact, we believe that it was the real robber who sent us this letter."

Mr. Tokuda looked startled, and he thought carefully for a moment.

"Ah, now just a moment, Inspector. Mr. Hattori is in jail, so he couldn't have sent the letter. But perhaps the letter was sent by a friend or an accomplice of Mr. Hattori? Is that what you mean? Have you done any forensic analysis of the letter? That might give you some clues about who sent it."

"Oh, we don't need to do any forensic analysis. We know exactly who sent this letter to the Chief."

Morimoto reached for another folder and took out a photo.

"We've been following you ever since you left the courthouse on Tuesday morning, Mr. Tokuda, and we know that you drove to Kotohira on Wednesday evening to mail this letter. In fact, here's a photograph of you putting the letter into the mailbox."

Time seemed to be frozen as Mr. Tokuda stared at the photo in disbelief. Then his chair tipped over and clattered to the floor as he jumped up and headed for the doorway. He was out of the room in three strides, and he managed two more strides along the corridor outside before running headlong into the substantial frame of Sergeant Yamada, who had positioned himself strategically for just such an eventuality, and who took only a few seconds to fasten the handcuffs around Mr. Tokuda's wrists.

Chapter 44

▼

Mr. Hattori was still unmistakably apprehensive when Mr. Bando led him into Judge Noda's chambers later that Friday morning. In addition to the judge, Inspector Morimoto and Police Officer Suzuki were also sitting in the room waiting for him.

"Is it really true?" Mr. Hattori asked anxiously. "Am I really free?"

Judge Noda's smile was in sharp contrast to the serious visage that had peered down at Mr. Hattori throughout the trial.

"You most definitely are, Mr. Hattori," she replied. "As of this moment, I'm quashing all of the charges against you. You are now free to do as you please."

"And you have Inspector Morimoto and Officer Suzuki to thank for it," Mr. Bando added, as he gave his client a hearty slap on the back that almost knocked him sideways.

Mr. Hattori looked gratefully at Morimoto and Suzuki.

"Oh, really? Plus the fact that I was innocent all along—like I kept telling everybody. Don't forget that. So was it Mr. Tokuda who carried out the robberies?"

"Yes, it was," Mr. Bando replied, "and he very nearly succeeded in framing you for them."

"That rat!" Mr. Hattori sneered. "I thought that he had to be behind it all. That's what I've been saying all along, haven't I? So how did you all finally figure out that he was the real criminal?"

"Well, Inspector Morimoto and Officer Suzuki were able to very cleverly deduce what had really been going on, and then it was simply a matter of finding a way to trap Mr. Tokuda. And we managed to convince Judge Noda to allow us to play out a little charade in her courtroom on Tuesday."

"On Tuesday? Are you referring to that sushi chef who identified me? His testimony was completely fishy! He was telling a blatant lie when he turned around and identified me! Surely you all know that now?"

"We know it now, and actually, we knew it then! We're the ones who asked him to lie."

"What? You purposely let him give false evidence against me?"

"It was for your own benefit, Mr. Hattori."

Mr. Hattori thought about this for a moment as he stroked his beard.

"Well, I wish that you'd told me what was going on. I didn't particularly enjoy having to sit there and listen to that fellow tell the judge that he'd seen me taking wads of cash out of the smashed up cash machine."

Judge Noda looked slightly shamefaced.

"I completely sympathize with your point of view," she admitted. "It was a very unusual circumstance, and to tell you the truth, I wasn't at all sure that I ought to agree to the scheme. But I'm glad now that I did go along with it. We've managed to avoid a very serious miscarriage of justice, so it's all turned out for the best in the end. I hope that you'll understand that there was some very serious evidence against you, Mr. Hattori."

"Oh, yes, I know that there was. Don't forget that I had to sit there in court and listen to it all. But I still don't completely understand what happened. How did Mr. Yosano's false testimony on Tuesday morning end up with Mr. Tokuda being trapped?"

Mr. Bando looked at Morimoto and Suzuki.

"Ah, well that's where the ingenuity of the plan that these two detectives concocted comes into play. I think that they'd be the best ones to explain the subtleties of their strategy to you."

Morimoto smiled at Mr. Hattori.

"It was all to do with greed, actually. We used Mr. Tokuda's greed to catch him. You see, not only did he rob the three cash machines, but he was also greedy enough to see the possibility of being able to claim the reward money as well. And you just happened to be the unfortunate person who he built his plan around, because one day he just stumbled across the fact that your golf trips coincided with his robberies."

"I'm going to be very careful where I play golf from now on," Mr. Hattori remarked.

"Well, it could have happened to anyone, really. You just happened by chance to be the person whose hotel stays matched the crimes, and when he discovered that, Mr. Tokuda saw that he had an opportunity to frame you for the crimes—and he was greedy enough to try to seize that opportunity. But we were able to turn his greed to our own advantage. Our hope was that Mr. Tokuda's uncontrollable avarice would lead him to give himself away, and that was exactly what happened, wasn't it, Officer Suzuki?"

"That's right, sir. You see, Mr. Hattori, we were able to convince Mr. Tokuda that Mr. Yosano was going to be given half of the reward money. And the reward money is a very substantial sum, so as you can imagine, that was not something that he was very happy about."

Mr. Hattori nodded.

"Ah, so that's what Mr. Yosano's testimony on Tuesday was all about."

"Yes," Suzuki said, "it was all for Mr. Tokuda's benefit. And on Tuesday morning he was sitting right behind you in the visitors gallery."

"Was he really? I didn't notice him. He'd come to gloat, had he?"

"Well, not exactly, Mr. Hattori. Actually, he wasn't enjoying himself at all as he had to sit and listen to Mr. Yosano identify you as the robber, because he thought that Mr. Yosano would be getting half of the reward money. We made sure that we explained to Mr. Tokuda that since Mr. Yosano's testimony appeared to be credible, the reward money was going to be shared between the two of them. And this was obviously a nasty shock for Mr. Tokuda, who'd been expecting to receive all of the reward money for himself. But anyway, the bottom line was that Mr. Tokuda realized that if he could invalidate Mr. Yosano's testimony in some way or other, then he'd be back in the position of being able to receive all of the reward money."

Mr. Hattori nodded.

"I think that I'm starting to understand what happened now. So Mr. Tokuda was greedy enough to fall for the trap, was he?"

"He was indeed," Suzuki said. "We knew that if Mr. Tokuda were the real robber, then he'd have known what a complete fabrication Mr. Yosano's testimony had been. For example, he'd have known that the robber had been wearing a mask and couldn't have been identified by Mr. Yosano."

"The robber wore a mask, did he? I never knew that. But Mr. Tokuda couldn't have told you that he'd been wearing a mask without giving himself away."

"That's very true, Mr. Hattori. So Mr. Tokuda needed to think of another way of discrediting Mr. Yosano without identifying himself as the real culprit.

And he realized that one way to do that was by focusing on the time of the robbery. Mr. Yosano gave evidence that the robbery had been at 12:15, but we knew that it had really occurred forty-five minutes later."

"How did you know that?"

"Because that's when Mr. Yosano had really seen the masked man carrying out the robbery."

Mr. Hattori began to scratch his head.

"This is starting to get a bit confusing."

Suzuki smiled.

"Well, to put it simply, Mr. Hattori, we knew that there was a taxi driver who could prove that the robbery hadn't occurred at 12:15 as Mr. Yosano had claimed, and we also guessed that if Mr. Tokuda were the real criminal, then he'd know about that taxi driver as well. And just as we'd hoped, Mr. Tokuda was clever enough to realize that if we were told about the taxi driver, then that would be sufficient information to discredit Mr. Yosano's evidence. Furthermore, if we were told anonymously, then it wouldn't give away the fact that Mr. Tokuda was the real criminal."

"So is that what Mr. Tokuda did?"

"Yes, that's exactly what he did. He sent the Chief an anonymous letter telling him about the taxi driver. And he didn't have the slightest suspicion that we were monitoring his activities—that he was being watched."

"Ah, that's fantastic!"

"The letter that Mr. Tokuda sent the Chief was sufficient to incriminate him for the crimes. Basically, Mr. Tokuda sealed his own fate by revealing that he knew what had been happening at the cash machine in Kotohira shortly before it had been robbed."

"And it serves him right!" Mr. Hattori exclaimed.

After leaving Judge Noda's chambers, Morimoto and Suzuki were spotted by the Public Prosecutor, Mr. Genda, as they were making their way out of the building.

"Good morning, Inspector Morimoto and Officer Suzuki. How are you today? I'm very glad that we've got this matter sorted out properly. Well done! If it hadn't been for your fine work, I rather fear that a very serious injustice might have been done to the defendant."

"It was an interesting case, wasn't it?" Morimoto replied. "And by the way, thank you for your cooperation with regards to Mr. Yosano's testimony. Your questioning of him in the courtroom was very realistic!"

"Oh, that was quite an experience! Rather unorthodox, I have to say, but something that will be talked about in the corridors of the Public Prosecutor's Office for a long time into the future, I expect. I have to admit that it's made me into something of a celebrity among my colleagues. We're accustomed to first accumulating the evidence and then presenting it in court, rather than using the court proceedings as a way to collect evidence! Anyway, I'm glad that all of the mysteries of this case have finally been resolved satisfactorily."

Morimoto rubbed his chin.

"Hmmm...well there is one final point that Officer Suzuki and I are still not quite sure about."

"Oh, really? What's that?"

"We're going to be very interested to find out what kind of spin the Chief puts on the awards luncheon that he presided over at the Police Headquarters on Monday. I'm sure that it won't take the press too long to find out that the perpetrator of the three cash machine robberies was the guest of honor at that luncheon, and that his picture was all over the front pages of the newspapers on Tuesday morning being presented with an award by the Chief."

Chapter 45

Inspector Morimoto and Police Officer Suzuki were enjoying another cup of Turkish coffee at the Okayama Orient Museum in celebration of the successful resolution of the case, when a young reporter from the Okayama Tribune newspaper was shown into the Chief's office at the Police Headquarters.

"Are you able to confirm the reports we've heard that a Mr. Tokuda has been arrested for the three cash machine robberies?" she asked. "And is it true that Mr. Hattori, who has been on trial for these robberies, has been released?"

The Chief beamed at her.

"I'm very happy to be able to confirm those reports. We've been involved in a very complex investigation, and I'm proud to be able to tell you that after some very fine police work we've been able to solve the case completely! We've tracked down and arrested the man responsible for the robberies, and the people of Okayama can be reassured that he'll now face the full force of the law."

The reporter scribbled in her notepad.

"And isn't it true that this Mr. Tokuda was the guest of honor at a luncheon that you hosted here on Monday? I attended that luncheon, and I wrote an article about it for our newspaper. I remember that you presented him with a plaque to express your gratitude for his exemplary help to the Police Department. You said that it was the inaugural award of its kind. You called it a Double-PA, didn't you?"

The Chief's grin was undiminished.

"I'm very glad that you've raised that point, and I'll be very happy to answer that question for you. What you have to understand is that in an investigation like the one that we've just been involved in, there are many different strands that all need to be woven together. A police investigation of this nature is an extraordinarily complicated affair. There are countless variables that we have to keep track of, and endless possibilities that we have to be aware of and that we have to be prepared for. This was a rather unique case for us, because the suspect—the man who we had our eye on all along—was giving evidence against somebody else who was on trial for the very crimes that our suspect himself had committed."

The reporter stopped taking notes and looked at the Chief blankly.

"Anyhow, after some very good investigative work, a team of my best detectives came up with a terribly ingenious scheme to trap the suspect. But it was a very delicate plan that was constructed around the objective of leading the suspect to give himself away and to provide us with the evidence that we needed to convict him. And the point is that it was paramount that we proceeded with extreme caution! Oh, yes...we had to be very careful indeed! One false step and the whole game could have been given away...it could all have been blown to smithereens!"

"So I asked myself how I could best assist in this operation. I wanted to know how I could best provide my detectives with the support that they needed to carry out their vital work. I wanted to know how I could help them maintain the superlative standards that have made this Police Department one of the very best in the whole country. And it was clear to me that a key element in our intricate scheme was the complacency of the suspect. Yes, complacency! I saw at once how important that aspect was. It was essential for the suspect to be quite relaxed and to be totally at ease...we needed to avoid giving him the slightest suspicion that we were watching him. Do you see what I mean?"

The reporter's blank expression remained unchanged.

"So that's when I came up with my idea for the luncheon. I decided to invite Mr. Tokuda along to a luncheon at the Police Headquarters, and I decided to make him the guest of honor. And on top of that, I decided to present him with an award! Can you see what a brilliant plan it was? The whole point of the luncheon on Monday was to lull Mr. Tokuda into a false sense of security. I'm afraid that I had to deceive you and the rest of the press corps about what was really going on, just to make it appear totally authentic, but what choice did I have?"

"It was an incredibly complex question that I had to grapple with, but it was clear to me that my first priority has to be the apprehension of criminals, and that it was my duty to do whatever I could to allay any worries that our suspect might have had concerning our attitude towards him. And I realized that the lunch was a perfect way to do that. After all, it makes sense, doesn't it? If the Chief of Police presents you with an award, then you're not likely to be too concerned about being at the top of a list of criminal suspects, are you? And as you can see, our plan couldn't have worked better!"

The reporter folded up her notebook and stared at the Chief.

"And I'd like to tell you that I consider this kind of thing to be a very important part of my responsibilities as the Chief of Police. I feel that it's important that I personally get involved in all of our investigations as much as I can...that I'm involved to the fullest extent possible...and that I endeavor to provide my detectives with that extra little bit of help that only I can give them."

The Chief offered the reporter a modest smile.

"But I can tell you...I certainly didn't enjoy hosting that luncheon! Oh, no, it was absolute torture! How do you think that I must have felt giving that inaugural award to somebody who we suspected was responsible for carrying out the worst series of bank robberies that we've had to deal with in a long time? I certainly had to grit my teeth, I can assure you of that. But I think that you'll find that I carried off the deception very convincingly. Don't you agree? If you go back and look at some of the photos that were taken at the luncheon on Monday, I'm sure you'll agree that I appeared to be having a wonderful time...all smiles and congratulations for everybody. I certainly wasn't going to give the game away, not me!"

The reporter nodded.

"Yes, that certainly was a very convincing performance," she remarked. "It was really quite unbelievable! In fact, I don't think that I've ever seen such acting before. Incidentally, are you planning to hold any similar events in the future? And how do you anticipate that the next recipient of the Police Appreciation Plaque Award will feel?"

"Ha, ha! You reporters always ask such wonderful questions! But anyway, in conclusion, I'd like to tell you how grateful I am for the fine detective work carried out by Inspector Morimoto and Officer Suzuki in this case. They've done some first rate police work, and the city of Okayama should be very proud of their efforts. It's outstanding work of this nature that goes such a long way towards ensuring that our community is safe and free from crime. And I'd also like to acknowledge the assistance of...err...one other person who provided invaluable assistance in helping us to carry out our plan. I'm talking, of course, about Mr....err...the splendid fellow who gave evidence in court on Tuesday morning. I'm trying to say that we should all be very grateful to Inspector Morimoto and the sushi chef!"

0-595-34950-1